Melting in Fear . . .

I pivoted toward the Jetta and caught a quick, shadowy movement out of the corner of my eye. My heart shot into my throat, and all my senses went to high alert. I could feel the hair on my arms, and suddenly the night sounds seemed amplified. Somewhere, buried deep beneath the soothing song of crickets and the whoosh of cars coming from the next street over, I heard the soft scuff of a foot on gravel.

Scarcely breathing, I tried to figure out whether I was closer to the Jetta or the door of Lorena's. Either way, I had to pass a row of darkened cars, any one of which could be hiding someone.

I took one step, then another, reminding myself that I'd grown up with a brother, and I'd taken countless self-defense courses while I lived in Sacramento. Not that I'd ever had to put any of the techniques into practice.

Another footstep caught my ear and the shadow loomed into my path. I held back a scream . . .

Candy Shop Mysteries by Sammi Carter

CANDY APPLE DEAD
CHOCOLATE DIPPED DEATH
PEPPERMINT TWISTED

A Candy Shop Mystery

Candy Apple Dead

Sammi Carter

BERKLEY PRIME CRIME, NEW YORK

THE BERKLEY PUBLISHING GROUP
Published by the Penguin Group
Penguin Group (USA) Inc.
375 Hudson Street, New York, New York 10014, USA
Penguin Group (Canada), 90 Eglinton Avenue East, Suite 700, Toronto, Ontario M4P 2Y3, Canada
(a division of Pearson Penguin Canada Inc.)
Penguin Books Ltd., 80 Strand, London WC2R 0RL, England
Penguin Group Ireland, 25 St. Stephen's Green, Dublin 2, Ireland (a division of Penguin Books Ltd.)
Penguin Group (Australia), 250 Camberwell Road, Camberwell, Victoria 3124, Australia
(a division of Pearson Australia Group Pty. Ltd.)
Penguin Books India Pvt. Ltd., 11 Community Centre, Panchsheel Park, New Delhi—110 017, India
Penguin Group (NZ), Cnr. Airborne and Rosedale Roads, Albany, Auckland 1310, New Zealand
(a division of Pearson New Zealand Ltd.)
Penguin Books (South Africa) (Pty.) Ltd., 24 Sturdee Avenue, Rosebank, Johannesburg 2196,
South Africa

Penguin Books Ltd., Registered Offices: 80 Strand, London WC2R 0RL, England

This is a work of fiction. Names, characters, places, and incidents either are the product of the author's imagination or are used fictitiously, and any resemblance to actual persons, living or dead, business establishments, events, or locales is entirely coincidental. The publisher does not have any control over and does not assume any responsibility for author or third-party websites or their content.

CANDY APPLE DEAD

A Berkley Prime Crime Book / published by arrangement with the author

PRINTING HISTORY
Berkley Prime Crime mass-market edition / September 2005

Copyright © 2005 by The Berkley Publishing Group.
Excerpt from *Chocolate Dipped Death* copyright © 2006 by The Berkley Publishing Group.
Cover art by Jeff Crosby.
Cover design by Steve Ferlauto.
Interior text design by Kristin del Rosario.

ISBN: 0-425-20532-0

BERKLEY® PRIME CRIME
Berkley Prime Crime Books are published by The Berkley Publishing Group,
a division of Penguin Group (USA) Inc.,
375 Hudson Street, New York, New York 10014.
The name BERKLEY PRIME CRIME and the BERKLEY PRIME CRIME design are trademarks belonging to Penguin Group (USA) Inc.

PRINTED IN THE UNITED STATES OF AMERICA

10   9   8   7   6   5

Chapter 1

"I swear, darlin'," Brandon Mills said in a sexy Texas drawl edged with sugar, "this fudge of yours is going to turn me into a butterball."

I looked up from the marble counter and took in the fine sight of him leaning against the glass counter. All around us glass jars filled with an endless variety of confections winked in the brilliant Colorado sunshine. I'd only been back for nine months and running my candy shop, Divinity, for six, and I still had to pinch myself sometimes to prove I was here at all.

This afternoon was one of those times.

Brandon looked deep into my eyes—I mean *deep*—and I, nearly forty and arguably intelligent, went weak in the knees. He's probably mid-forties, tall, dark, and incredibly handsome, and I defy any normal, red-blooded American woman to maintain her composure when he's around.

When he realized that he had my full attention, he tossed off a heart-stopping grin that almost made me believe he meant something by it. I knew better, of course. I hadn't known Brandon long, but it had only taken me a few minutes to peg him as a playboy. Since coming back to Paradise, I'd watched a handful of women flit through his life, and come to the regrettable conclusion that Brandon had about as much staying power in a relationship as cotton candy on a hot summer's day.

Too bad. He really was something to look at.

With a sigh, I tried to pull my mind back to business. We were alone in the store that afternoon since my part-time sales clerk, who also happens to be my cousin, was off taking care of real-life problems. It was mid-September, so tourist season had already tapered off, and there wasn't a single customer browsing Divinity for a tasty morsel to sweeten their day.

That made Brandon even more flirtatious than usual.

I didn't want him to guess how deeply that penetrating gaze of his affected me, so I did what I could to look irritated. "That fudge of mine is still a little too soft," I said, turning away from that full-on gaze. "I just can't figure out what I did wrong."

"Not a damn thing as far as I'm concerned." Slowly, and wearing a deliberately teasing grin, he licked chocolate from his fingertips and ran a slow glance along the length of me. He was standing in the spill of autumn sunlight, perfectly framed by a nine-pane window and sheer granite mountain peaks. "It's perfect, just like the woman who made it."

He could have gone all day without using that word. It makes me uneasy. Scowling slightly, I turned away to pull a new box of tissue paper from the supply cupboard. In the past year, I'd watched my "perfect" husband take up with another woman, my "perfect" marriage fall apart, and my "perfect" life unravel right in front of my eyes. Not my favorite word, no matter who says it.

"I'm not perfect," I protested. "Nobody is."

"Close enough." Stepping away from the counter, Brandon snagged one of the wrought-iron chairs from the seating area and straddled it. "You're working too hard, Abby love. Why don't you leave all this and come away with me?"

I had been working hard ever since Aunt Grace's death six months earlier. Actually, Grace was my mother's aunt, and I still hadn't been able to figure out why she left Divinity to me in her will. Sure, I'd worked with Grace when I was a kid, but so had most of the other cousins, and some of them seemed more obvious choices than me. But I was the one Aunt Grace chose, and so far nobody had done much more than mutter about her decision.

"So how about it?" Brandon asked.

I arched a skeptical eyebrow. "Away where?"

"Oh, I don't know. How about Rye-T On for a sandwich? I'll bet five dollars you haven't had lunch yet."

"You'd win that bet," I said with a reluctant smile, "but no thanks. You know, you're lucky I'm not some dewy-eyed young thing with romantic dreams. Another sort of woman might expect 'going away' to mean more than walking twenty feet down the sidewalk."

His expression sobered, and that lazy bedroom-look in his eyes made me think about things I probably shouldn't. "Well, now, for you, darlin', lunch would be just the beginning."

My thoughts were *definitely* moving into dangerous territory now. Anticipation tingled all through me, but I didn't want him to know that. "Really?" I asked, doing my best to sound bored. "What comes next? Dinner at McDonald's?"

"Not for you, Abby. You deserve better."

He sounded serious, so I stole another glance at him. He flashed a grin and reached for another piece of fudge. Oh yeah, he knew the effect he had on women, and he used it to his advantage. I just didn't understand why he was using it on me.

I didn't know why I was responding, either. Suddenly irritated with myself, I slapped his hand away. "I asked you to taste it," I snapped, "not eat the entire batch."

"Come and have lunch with me, and I'll stop eating."

"Tempting . . ." I said aloud this time. "But no. I have way too much to do."

"Do it later."

That's another problem with Brandon. No sense of responsibility. "I can't," I said. "I still have to put together those sample gift baskets before six. Come to think of it, I'm sure there are things *you* should be doing before the meeting, too."

He gave another lazy-shouldered shrug. "Nothing special. I left Chelsea in charge of the store for a while, and Lucas is there with her. It'll be fine."

"You hope." Chelsea isn't the sharpest tool in the shed. Unfortunately, I think Brandon's the only person on earth who doesn't realize that. He's protective of her for reasons I don't completely understand, and that means it's best to tread cautiously when talking about her. Steering away from that topic, I asked, "So you're all ready for the meeting then?"

For the first time that afternoon, Brandon's expression grew serious. For weeks he'd been wrangling with the city council and the Downtown Merchants Alliance over the changes he'd proposed to the city's annual Arts Festival. His motion included expanding the festival from two days to four and moving the whole thing to the center of town, but his ideas had stirred up a controversy that had split the town in two.

Thanks to Aunt Grace's dramatic sense of style, Divinity occupies a graceful old building that dates back to the earliest days of Paradise's history. Originally the territorial jail, the building is filled with enough cubbyholes, nooks, and crannies to stir anyone's imagination. The store and kitchen take up the entire first floor. Storage rooms and a large, airy meeting room—a courtroom during much of the nineteenth century—occupy the second level, and my apartment is on the third floor. I'd offered that second-floor meeting room for tonight's meeting, and I still wasn't ready for the crowd I was sure we'd have.

If we were lucky, we'd sway enough of the Alliance to make a difference at the next city council meeting. I had another reason for wanting the meeting here. In a couple of weeks, the council would be voting on whether to renew the long-standing contract between Divinity and the city that allowed me to provide gift baskets for visiting dignitaries.

The contract had been nothing special when I was a kid, but Paradise was garnering a fair share of overspill traffic from Vail and Aspen these days, and we needed the exposure. If Aunt Grace were still alive, contract renewal wouldn't even be a question. But she was gone, and I'd been out of the candy business too long. People considered me an unknown quantity. I guess I was.

Business had dropped off sharply right after Aunt Grace's heart attack, and I was desperate to build our clientele up again. Maybe people were skeptical about me. Maybe they thought I needed time to mourn—which I did—but I also needed an income.

In response to my question, Brandon shrugged. "I'm as ready as I'll ever be."

Considering how much he had at stake, his answer seemed oddly indifferent. "Yeah?" I replied. "Well, I'm not. I haven't had time to set up the chairs for the meeting. Even if I was ready to run away with you, I couldn't do it."

Brandon's scowl faded and a teasing light danced in eyes the color of Aunt Grace's blue Depression-glass candy dish. "Come on, Abby. Screw the city council. Divinity has always made VIP gift baskets, and anybody with a head knows that. Those shortsighted jerks have no business making you beg for the job."

I tossed him a modest smile and arranged a few toffee squares in a box. "First of all," I said, just to set the record straight, "I'm not begging. And *Aunt Grace* always made the gift baskets, but I've never done it before. If the council members want to make sure the quality of our candy hasn't slipped since I took over, I really can't object."

Brandon growled in protest. "Most of the city council members are idiots, and the ones who aren't stupid are dangerous." I would have argued with him, but he held up a hand to stop me. "Admit it. Kasie McGuire doesn't like anything, and Sherm Hitchcock won't breathe unless she tells him to."

I certainly couldn't argue with that. I couldn't figure out how Kasie, who probably wouldn't recognize the truth if she fell over it, had ended up in a position of authority. And Squirrelly Sherm? I was surprised the guy had guts enough to run for office.

"Yeah," I said grudgingly, "but they're not the only two who'll be voting."

"Don't tell *them* that. Kasie's convinced she's the queen of Paradise. If you don't believe me, just look into her eyes some time when you're talking to her."

I couldn't argue with that, either. "It's not Kasie I'm worried about," I told him. "It's Laura Applewood. She can be pretty persuasive when she puts her mind to it."

"Putting her mind to anything doesn't happen very often." Brandon rested both arms on the chair's back and tilted it onto two legs. "You'll keep the gift-basket contract, so try not to worry so much. The Arts Festival . . . ? That one I don't know about."

"Some of the council members think expanding the festival is a good idea," I said, trying to sound encouraging. "And half the Downtown Alliance agrees."

"That's because some of you have brains. I don't know what the rest of them think with, but I could take a guess. Old-fashioned thinking is going to kill this town, Abby. You know that as well as I do."

I happened to agree with him, but plenty of people didn't. My brother Wyatt is a prime example. If you ask Wyatt, expansion is going to kill the town. He avoids new, trendy restaurants and refuses to shop in any of the specialty stores that have sprung up in the past few years. He still gets his coffee at Sid's out on Highway 91, and he grumbles almost constantly about having newcomers underfoot.

Wyatt and Brandon have tussled a couple of times over their differences at town meetings, but I think Wyatt objects to Brandon more than he does his ideas. I'm not sure why he dislikes Brandon, and I haven't asked. Some subjects are better left alone.

"If the council members hear you talking about them like that," I said, turning away and pulling another stack of gift boxes from the cupboard, "you'll lose votes for sure."

Instead of looking worried, Brandon pitched another of his traffic-stopping grins. "What are you saying, Abby? You think I need to change my approach?"

That smile made me wonder—briefly—if I was really so smart for keeping him at arm's length. But flattering as the attention was, I wasn't stupid. My reign at the top of his list wouldn't last. I couldn't afford to forget that. "I don't think that changing your approach would hurt anything."

"You want me to play nice, is that it?"

"I just think that if expanding the festival is as important as you say, it's not exactly smart to antagonize the people who'll make the decision."

"So you want me to kiss ass."

"Actually, I was thinking of something sort of in between kissing up and in-your-face."

With a laugh, Brandon let the chair fall down on all four legs again. "Not in this lifetime, darlin'. In-your-face is the only thing some of the people in this town will listen to."

He was probably right. Paradise is an odd combination of old and new, and nobody ever seems to agree on exactly what we are or what we want to be. Half the folks in town share Wyatt's opinion about the changes taking place, even though most of those changes have been good for the town and the people in it.

We're an old mining community, but that industry died out a long time ago. New businesses springing up all over have helped stabilize our tax base, but unlike some of the more popular neighboring towns, we haven't reached the level where longtime residents can't afford to keep their homes.

In his own way, Brandon is a lot like Paradise. He's a successful businessman—at least by Paradise standards—and he usually dresses as if he's ready to hobnob with the rich and famous. On the other hand, he talks as if he has to scrape manure from the soles of his designer boots. Adding to his image is Max, the Doberman pinscher that's Brandon's best friend and the inventory retrieval specialist for the men's clothing store Brandon owns. Brandon likes to brag that he'll never need an expensive security system at Man About Town with Max around, and he's probably right.

At that moment, Max was laying on the sidewalk outside the front door of my shop, enjoying the late-September sunshine. Ever alert, he kept his head up, and his ears twitched as shoppers and local business people passed him by. Most of the locals were used to Max, but occasionally someone would cross the road to avoid him, and Brandon never ceased to find that amusing.

I slipped a small piece of almond toffee onto a scrap of tissue paper, nudged it in Brandon's direction, and began moving the remaining squares onto trays for that night's meeting. "If you play your cards right, everything will be decided tonight."

Grinning a thank-you, Brandon shifted the candy to his table. "Everything will be decided whether I play my cards right or not. People have been dragging their feet long enough. The festival is just six months away. If we're going to change, we need to decide *now*."

"For the record, I agree with you. I just think you'd be smart to back off a little. Don't hit people over the head with it all the time. *Inspire* them to see things your way. And maybe stop calling them idiots in public." I closed a box and slapped a gold-edged Divinity label on it as a seal. "You *might* even consider acting as if you're taking their opinions seriously."

The bell over the door tinkled, and the Gilbert sisters, two elderly ladies with nearly identical heads of silver hair came into the store, catching Brandon's attention momentarily. When he looked back at me, his face was expressionless. "You know what they say about opinions," he said. "They're like—"

The sisters are devout Christians who carry their Bibles everywhere they go. I was pretty sure they wouldn't appreciate the end of that thought, so I interrupted quickly. "I know what they're like. Everybody has one. All I'm saying is you'd probably have fewer problems if you exercised a little more tact."

Grinning as if the Arts Festival and its detractors didn't matter, Brandon stood and leaned across the counter, close enough that I could smell the faint hint of toothpaste and chocolate on his breath. Close enough to send a faint shiver of something I hadn't felt more than a handful of times in the past few years running up my spine.

"I'm not worried about it, darlin'," he whispered. "Nobody ever takes me seriously."

There was a hint of something I couldn't read in his eyes, but I wasn't sure I wanted to delve that deeply into his psyche. I might get caught there. "I hope not," I whispered back, "for your sake."

He pulled away and looked down at me from nearly a foot above. If I hadn't grown up with a brother, I might have felt a little intimidated. "My head's on straight, Abby. Don't you worry about that. I know what I want, and I know how to get it." He raked a long, slow gaze across my face and his expression grew serious. "Speaking of what I want, how 'bout you and me spend a little time together after the meeting?"

The invitation surprised me, but I can't say it didn't please me. I'm five-five and packing more on my hips and thighs than I'd like. Half the time my cocoa-brown hair looks like somebody ran over it with a lawnmower, and my wardrobe doesn't qualify as any kind of chic—but in that moment, I felt beautiful.

To give my heart a chance to slide back out of my throat, I swiped at the counter and tossed the cloth into the sink behind me. "Why Brandon Mills," I said when I trusted myself to speak, "if I didn't know better, I'd swear you were asking me on a date."

The grin on his face was deliciously wicked. "Yes, ma'am. I was thinking about dinner at Romano's. How does that sound to you?"

Was he kidding? Romano's is one of the best restaurants in town, and by far one of the most expensive. I could exist happily for weeks on their penne pasta with sun-dried tomatoes and pine nuts. Every excuse for keeping the relationship platonic flew right out of my head. I grinned right back while mentally diving through my closet for something to wear. "I think I could handle that."

"Then I'll see you at six-forty-five." He chucked me under the chin on his way out the door, and I stood there wearing a goofy grin until one of the silver-haired sisters drifted toward me with a question.

I'd had a couple of unsatisfactory relationships before my marriage, and a pretty rotten relationship *during* my marriage. I know from experience that a good chin-chuck delivered with meaning has it all over a dozen roses delivered out of resentment or duty.

When I realized that Miss Lily was looking at me strangely, I pulled my attention away from the fine sight of Brandon Mills leaving my store and struggled to remember everything Aunt Grace had taught me about fruit jellies.

I had three hours to wait until closing, four until the meeting, and one of the longest afternoons of my life stretching out in front of me. I just wish I'd known what was to come. If I had, maybe I'd have spent another thirty seconds of it watching Brandon and Max walk away.

Chapter 2

He didn't show.

I raced downstairs at quarter to seven, all dressed up and ready for a night out, and Brandon didn't even bother to show up. Didn't call, either. One by one, members of the Alliance drifted out of their stores and into mine, chattering about this and that—the kind of day they had, the Arts Festival, rude customers, plans for that evening . . .

I got caught up in the chatter, so it took a little while to process what was happening. By the time I did, the scents of caramelized sugar and cinnamon oil made the late lunch I'd wolfed down turn over in my stomach. Thirty-nine years old, and I felt like a sixteen-year-old waiting for her date to the prom. Instead of Prince Charming, I'd somehow managed to pick a frog.

Again.

Being stood up isn't a new experience for me, but that's not something I'm proud of. Not that it happens with regularity, mind you. But it has happened before. Shane Clements stood me up for Homecoming during my sophomore year of high school. Kelley Jackson left me waiting with a steaming pan of lasagna and five pounds of chips and dip one Super Bowl Sunday during college. And Roger, the ex-husband I try not to think about, had forgotten plans we made more times than I can count. But for some reason, I hadn't expected Brandon to be that kind of guy. I guess I'm just naïve.

Since I knew Brandon would never forget the meeting or lose track of time for something this important, the only other option available was that he'd had a change of heart. I don't know why I was surprised.

I'd spent a good thirty minutes fighting to get my hair lying flat—at least in the front where I could see it. I'd dug out a pair of heels, left over from my days as a corporate attorney, from the back of my closet and stuffed my poor, protesting feet into them. I'd run an iron over the wrinkles in my good black pants—and all because I thought Brandon would actually keep his promise.

Annoyed almost beyond words, I shut and locked the front door and started through the kitchen toward the stairs. If Brandon came late, he could let himself in the back way.

I was about to head upstairs when I caught a flash of movement out of the corner of my eye. My heart went into overdrive as I let myself outside. Maybe Brandon had come after all.

Thanks to the steep canyon walls and narrow valley floor, the streets of old-town Paradise are barely wide enough for a couple of cars to scrape past each other. Especially when the town is filled with tourists, parking areas are hard to come by and stringently regulated. To make life easier for shop owners, small parking areas are carved into the spaces between shops up and down the street. To keep the town beautiful for tourists, the parking areas are also cleverly disguised as mini-parks, complete with benches and flower-filled planters.

Divinity shares one of these flowery parking lots with a neighbor up the hill, so there was a good chance the shadow belonged to a passerby or a customer at Picture Perfect. I stepped into the gathering shadows anyway and tried to make Brandon appear. I was already limping, thanks to the heels, and I wondered how I'd make the walk from here to Romano's and maintain my dignity.

It had been a warm day, but cool air from the nearby mountains brushed the evening with a hint of autumn, and the golden shimmer of aspens made the hillside look as if someone had poured peanut-brittle syrup over everything. The hills were so beautiful, they almost took my breath away.

I couldn't make Brandon miraculously materialize out of thin air, so I turned back toward the candy kitchen. A figure loomed in the doorway. I let out a little cry of alarm, and Stella Farmer moved farther into the light so I could see her.

"Abby? Are you all right?"

Clasping a hand to my chest, I grabbed the back of a park bench to keep from falling. "I'm fine. You just startled me. I didn't see you standing there."

Stella's lips curved slightly. She's a tall, sturdy woman with mint-green eyes and firm, broad hands. The only time she's not wearing jeans and a man's shirt with the tails out is when she's in the church, and that only happens when there's a funeral.

"Sorry," she said, and she almost looked as if she meant it. "I've been looking all over for you. We need to talk before you go inside."

Stella is one of the town's strongest opponents to changing the Arts Festival. I'd already heard what she had to say more than once, and talking to her about it right now wasn't high on my list of priorities. "The meeting's about to start," I said. "Can it wait?"

The half-smile that had been playing at the corners of her mouth faded. "I'm afraid not. Duncan and I have been taking a straw poll, and we're concerned. I hope you're prepared to stand with us at the city council meeting next week."

I was annoyed with Brandon, but that didn't mean I'd turn on him in a fit of feminine spite. I shoved past her into the kitchen, picked up a tray of cream-cheese mints from the counter, and headed for the back staircase. "You know how I feel about this, Stella. You're wasting your breath."

"I know," Stella said, trailing behind me, "but have you really thought this through?"

"Of course I have. Not that my opinion matters. I don't have a vote, remember?"

"No, but you're a member of the Alliance. If we present a united front, the city council will have to take notice."

I laughed in disbelief and turned back to look at her. "You

don't really expect to get everyone on the Alliance to agree with you?"

"We can try." Stella glanced up the stairs over my shoulder and lowered her voice. "Look, Abby, I know Brandon's been paying attention to you the last little while, and believe me I know how seductive something like that can be. But don't let it go to your head, and for God's sake, don't let it affect your business judgment."

I've never been a violent person, but the pitying smile on her face made me itch to wipe it right off again. "I haven't based my decision on hormones, Stella. Now, if you'll excuse me—"

She snagged my sleeve to keep me from leaving. "Your Aunt Grace would never have approved of this ridiculous idea."

"Aunt Grace would have been first in line to vote yes," I assured her, "and I'm more than capable of making this decision without your help."

Stella leaned in closer, and something flashed in her eyes that left me feeling a little nervous. "Decisions like this need to be made with the *whole* business community in mind. Some shops might do all right if we cut off traffic for nearly a week, but what about those of us who don't sell little trinkets and candy? What are we going to do if access is shut down for four days?"

We'd been over this ground a million times before, and I had no patience with it now. "Maybe you should take another look at the proposal," I said. "Brandon's planning to set up parking lots on the edge of town, and there'll be shuttle service every fifteen minutes to the shopping district. If I remember right, you'll have a shuttle stop twenty feet from your door. How much closer do you need it to be?"

Stella's eyes narrowed. "You're assuming that Kevin Horvath will agree to rent that stretch of land to the city for the parking lot. Do you know something I don't?"

"No, but Kevin's not unreasonable." At least he wasn't *most* of the time. "And we'll find out in a few minutes, I'm sure."

Stella gave another dismissive flick of her wrist. "You know what Brandon is trying to do, don't you?"

"Expand the Arts Festival?"

"He's *trying* to put us out of business," Stella snarled. "And if this idiotic measure passes, he just might get his wish."

That accusation nearly knocked me off my feet. "Why on earth would Brandon want to put you out of business?"

Even though she was a step or two below me, Stella lifted her nose and managed to look down it at me. Her mouth puckered as if she'd just swallowed a handful of Sour Patch candy. "Because he can't stand the fact that we're doing well."

I laughed. I couldn't help myself. "Oh, please, Stella. You and Brandon aren't in competition with each other. You don't even sell the same kind of merchandise."

"No, but Duncan and I have one of the prime locations in town. Brandon has made it quite clear that he'd like to relocate." She arched an eyebrow. "Need I say more?"

Retail space downtown *is* at a premium, and property values have shot up in the past few years, but her suggestion was so outlandish I nearly choked. I thought about Brandon's claim that no one took him seriously and wondered if he knew just how wrong he was. "Even if what you say is true," I said, struggling for patience, "Brandon would never deliberately put another store out of business."

Stella's expression grew grim. "If you believe that, you don't really know Brandon. He's ambitious, Abby. He's trying to dig a foothold here in Paradise, and he's using the rest of you to do his dirty work."

This conversation was so far beyond ridiculous I couldn't believe we were having it. I climbed a few more steps. "Even if Brandon *does* have some nefarious plan up his sleeve— which he doesn't—there are more effective ways to plot a takeover."

"Not if he wants to fit in when it's all said and done. And not if he wants to keep his more . . . gullible . . . friends from seeing what's right in front of their noses." Stella stepped onto the landing, and her smile turned sugary sweet. "Frankly, I'd be offended if I were you, Abby. But, then, maybe you don't mind being manipulated."

Since the year I turned ten, my mother has been warning

me to hold my tongue when I'm angry. It's probably good advice, but I'm not known for taking advice—good or otherwise—and sugarcoating my words when I'm upset has never been my style. "I don't know about that," I said. "But I definitely resent the way you're trying to manipulate me right now."

Stella's voice grew whisper-quiet. "I'm not manipulating you, Abby. I'm giving you a friendly warning. If you don't wake up soon, you'll regret it."

A chill inched up my spine, but I wasn't going to let Stella intimidate me. "Don't you think you're being a little overly dramatic? My suggestion for you is to talk to Brandon and then really listen to what he says. I'm sure he could set your mind at ease."

"I couldn't do that, even if I wanted to," she said. "He's not here."

Hearing someone else mention it made my stomach knot with worry. Brandon might stand me up, but he would never forget tonight's meeting. It was too important to him. I'd already wasted enough time talking to Stella, so I mumbled an excuse and climbed the rest of the stairs. To my surprise, the crowd was standing-room-only.

If Brandon was coming, he'd better get here soon.

Abandoning Stella by the door, I found space on the goody table for the mints and wedged myself into a conversation with Rachel Summers and Gavin Trotter. I've known Rachel for years, although we've never really been friends. She graduated from high school two years ahead of me, and now she runs a shop a few doors down called Candlewyck. The business seems to be doing well, but Rachel's just biding her time there until someone discovers her and whisks her away to a career as a plus-size model.

Gavin's a former high school football coach who settled in Paradise about five years ago to run a sporting goods store. He's opinionated and a little rough around the edges, but he's a nice enough guy, and I'd rather talk about ice hockey than listen to Stella any longer.

Keeping one eye on the door in case Brandon showed up, I indulged in small talk with Rachel and Gavin until Duncan

Farmer squaddled up to the front of the room and started the meeting.

Two hours of name-calling and accusations later, I shut the door behind the last of the stragglers and turned off the light. Only a few stray pieces of candy remained on the table upstairs, a fact that left me feeling hopeful about the future, but Brandon never had put in an appearance, and that worried me.

It was after ten o'clock by then, and I was more than half-convinced something had happened to him. I just couldn't imagine why else he'd miss the meeting—even if he had wanted to avoid dinner with me.

Acting on impulse, I ran up the outside steps to my apartment, changed into more sensible shoes, and hurried outside again. A cool breeze was blowing into town from the mountain valleys, and it only took a few minutes for me to regret coming outside without a sweatshirt, but Man About Town was only a couple of blocks away, and I didn't plan to be outside long.

Man About Town takes up all of a two-story building built around the turn of the last century. For fifty years or so, the J.C. Penney store did business there. Since then, half a dozen tenants had moved in and out, but Man About Town fits in so neatly, it's easy to forget it hasn't been there forever.

I half-expected to find lights on and Brandon hard at work, but the windows were dark, the store looked deserted. I checked out the cars parked nearby, but I couldn't see Brandon's 4Runner anywhere, so I turned toward home.

Paradise at night is a great place to be. City ordinances ban the use of neon lights, so the sky looms huge and black overhead. On clear nights like this one, the stars look like powdered sugar sprinkled on a velvet background. A few stragglers were making their way home from the meeting, and cars lined the streets in front of restaurants and nightclubs. Even though I was by myself, I didn't really feel alone.

I was just passing the art emporium when I heard the roar of an engine and saw lights sweep across the side of a nearby building. An instant later, a red Dodge pickup pulled out of the small parking strip between the emporium and the used book store. With a squeal of tires, it shot onto the street and disappeared around the corner, but not before I saw the customized license plate that belonged to my brother.

That was just strange enough to pull my attention back to the moment. I hadn't noticed Wyatt at the meeting, but maybe I'd just missed him in the confusion. His absence wasn't nearly as unsettling as Brandon's, so I decided not to worry about it and tossed around the idea of driving over to Brandon's condo to make sure he was all right.

But what if he *had* had second thoughts about taking me to dinner? Even worse, what if he was there with some other woman? I didn't think I could bear the humiliation of that, so in spite of my vaguely unsettled feelings, I told myself to wait until tomorrow. No doubt Brandon would show up at Divinity early in the morning wearing an embarrassed grin and brandishing some lame excuse. I'd pretend not to forgive him just long enough to convince us both that I wasn't a pushover. He'd tease me for a while, and we'd be right back where we'd left off by nightfall.

Having decided that, I hurried home again. I've been living in this upstairs apartment since my marriage fell apart. While I was floundering, looking for a place to get back on my feet, Aunt Grace had come to the rescue, just like she had so many times in the past.

The apartment is a far cry from the Sacramento condo I shared with Roger while I thought we were happy. There's not a stick of furniture that matches any other in the whole place. Everything I own is secondhand, a castoff from friends or relatives. I have Aunt Grace's old plaid sofa-bed and Uncle Butch's dinged-up coffee table in the living room. Near the door is the hideous space-age chair that used to belong to my parents. In the bedroom, I sleep on my grandmother's bed and keep my clothes in a dresser that came from the Goodwill. By themselves, the pieces are wretched, but together they suit me in some strange way I can't explain.

Upstairs, I changed into flannel pajama pants and a T-shirt, opened my window an inch or two so I could listen to the crickets, and made cocoa the old-fashioned way with actual milk. I dropped in a homemade marshmallow and curled up in bed with one of Aunt Grace's books to bone up on how to make hazelnut and cherry caramels.

If you've never had a homemade marshmallow, you don't know what you're missing. It differs as much in taste and texture from the store-bought variety as milk chocolate from dark. In ancient Egypt, marshmallow was made by squeezing sap from the mallow plant and mixing it with nuts and honey. It was considered such a delicacy that it was reserved for gods and royalty—a far cry from today when we pass out handfuls to kids so they can incinerate them over campfires.

These days, even Aunt Grace's recipe calls for gelatin instead of sap, but on a chilly autumn night when you're nursing hurt feelings, it can make you feel better, if not exactly like royalty.

I pulled the covers up to my chin and tried to pay attention to what I was reading, but exhaustion got the best of me before I could even finish half the cocoa. I'm still not sure what woke me first—the sound of sirens or the smell of smoke. It took me a few seconds to piece the stinging odor of burning wood and the stench of an electrical fire together with the shouts of people on the streets.

Confused and still not fully awake, I staggered into the kitchen to see if I'd turned off the stove. The second time I banged into the wall and sent pain shooting through my hip and shoulder, I woke up enough to realize the apartment wasn't engulfed in flames.

Stuffing my feet into slippers, I raced down the stairs and onto the street. Outside, the smell of burning wood eclipsed everything else, and an eerie red glow painted the night sky. Obviously, the fire was close but, luckily, coming from somewhere else.

The wail of sirens calling the volunteer fire department to duty stopped suddenly, and the sudden silence chilled me to the bone. A couple of cars shot past, and Lydia Cole, who lives above the bakery on the next block, streaked by wearing a pair of cow-patterned pajama pants.

With my heart in my throat, I set off after her. Someone in town was in trouble, and a sick feeling lodged in the pit of my stomach. The fact that the small crowd was moving toward Man About Town only made it worse. I picked up the pace and ran, full-out, slippers flapping against my feet, and my throat burning from exertion and the smoke. The closer I drew to Brandon's store, the harder it was to delude myself.

Flames shot into the sky. Wood popped and crackled as it burned. My nose stung, my eyes burned, and the smoke made it hard to breathe. Glass from an upstairs window shattered, and a woman's scream pierced the night.

I could only wrap my arms around myself and watch in horrified disbelief as the upper floor crumbled, and the fire consumed Brandon's store right before my eyes.

Chapter 3

By two o'clock in the morning, the excitement was over. I wandered home, climbed back into bed, and lay staring at the ceiling for a couple of hours before finally giving up on the idea of sleep. I couldn't concentrate enough to read, and even with satellite TV—the only hope for clear reception in our little valley—there was nothing on worth watching. After what seemed like a long time, I dressed and went downstairs to Divinity's candy kitchen.

Aunt Grace used to always say that when she had a case of jangled nerves, nothing soothed her like a session at the stove. I don't know about that, but I did have a couple of orders to fill, so I decided to do something productive with my time.

I'd just finished coarsely chopping enough hazelnuts to keep everyone in Paradise happy when I saw a familiar red truck pull into the parking strip. Seeing Wyatt in town almost before sunrise was even stranger than seeing him driving around late at night. He parked, taking up at least two spots, and would have climbed the stairs to my apartment if I hadn't banged on the window to get his attention.

When he saw me waving at him through the glass, he pivoted on his heel and strode across the narrow parking strip.

He's five years older than I am, and if you ask me, he looks every minute of his forty-four years, plus a few. I like to think the years have been a little kinder to me, but I'm probably just deluding myself.

He was dressed for work in jeans, a T-shirt, and a ratty pair of cowboy boots his wife has thrown away twice. Wyatt has rescued them both times. That ought to tell you something about him.

Throwing open the kitchen door, he came inside wearing a deep scowl that was almost hidden by the thick swag of mustache he's been cultivating since the summer he turned eighteen. "You're up early."

I pulled bags of dried cherries from the cupboard and carried them to the chopping block. "Couldn't sleep."

"Yeah? Well, I guess that means you've heard."

"About the fire?" I nodded sadly. "I was there half the night. I still can't believe it."

Wyatt hooked one of the stools and dragged it across the room so he could talk to me. "It's a damn mess, that's for sure. The guys have been over there all night trying to make sure the fire's completely out."

The blaze must have sent our volunteer fire crew into shock. They're used to the occasional brush fire, but Paradise has never had a fire like this. I yawned hard enough to bring tears to my eyes and nodded toward the coffeemaker on the far counter. "I just made a fresh pot," I said. "Pour me a cup, would you?"

Wyatt almost got to his feet, but he stopped and shot a skeptical glance across the room. "Is it real coffee or that sugary crap you like so much?"

"Don't get your boxers in a bunch. It's regular, and it's strong. It won't hurt a bit."

He made a face at me. I tore open a package of cherries and dumped them onto the board. "Any idea what Brandon's going to do now? It didn't look like there was much left last night."

"There's *nothing* left." Wyatt filled two cups, handed me one, and turned his attention to one of the two refrigerators humming away on the other side of the kitchen. We keep candy supplies in the new one and personal items in the white Frigidaire that's as old as I am.

He dug around in the old fridge for a few minutes and finally emerged holding a container of shrimp fried rice left over from lunch at the Lantern Palace. Sniffing the rice to make sure it was still edible, he pulled a fork from a drawer. "Looks to me like Mills has lost everything. If you ask me, it couldn't have happened to a more deserving guy."

I stopped chopping so I could gape at him. "That's a horrible thing to say. Why do you dislike him so much anyway?"

"Because he's an asshole." Wyatt shoveled rice into his mouth and spoke around it. "He probably started the fire himself."

"That's not funny."

"It wasn't meant to be. I wouldn't put anything past him."

I gave the cherries a vicious whack with my knife and glared at my brother. "What are you doing in town so early anyway? What's the matter? Didn't Elizabeth fix your breakfast?"

Something flashed across his face, and his mouth thinned. "I heard about the fire. Thought maybe I'd come see how bad it was."

Wyatt and Elizabeth live several miles out of town—just far enough to make a person think twice about driving back and forth without a good reason. Someone must have called mighty early for Wyatt to be in town at this hour. "Well, I guess that proves that the grapevine is alive and well," I said. "Do you mind me asking who was up making phone calls in the middle of the night?"

"Nate Svboda."

Nate's been a friend of Wyatt's since high school. He's also a patrol officer with the Paradise police department. "Why would Nate call you in the middle of all that trouble just to tell you about the fire?"

"It wasn't in the middle of all the trouble. The fire was mostly out when he called."

"So he called you in the middle of the night?"

"I didn't say that."

He didn't have to. I abandoned the cherries and carried sugar and the creamer to the table where mounds of old-fashioned stick candy waited to be bundled into gift jars and tied with raffia ribbon. I don't care how old people get, they still seem to love those candy sticks, and the jars filled with them are one of our best-selling items during the summer months.

"It's barely six-thirty now," I pointed out. "It takes at least half an hour to get to town from the ranch, and obviously this wasn't your first stop."

"So?"

"So why did Nate think it was so important to call you?"

Irritation flashed in my brother's eyes. "How should I know?"

"You didn't ask?"

"I was tired."

I shook my head firmly. "No way. The last time I called before sunup you nearly took my head off, and I'm your sister. Are you telling me that after dealing with the fire for half the night, Nate called you just because? And that you didn't mind?"

Growling, Wyatt tossed his fork onto the table. "What the hell is this? The third degree? Nate called me. Leave it at that."

His reaction stunned me. Wyatt's an open book. Honest as they come. Sometimes almost too honest. He says what he thinks, and he means what he says. I couldn't remember a single time in our adult lives when he'd told me anything but the unvarnished truth, even when I wished he would. I couldn't prove he was lying now, but I would have bet a prime-rib dinner at the Timberline Grill that he was.

He was also spoiling for a fight, but giving him one wouldn't accomplish anything. I kicked my feet onto a chair and gave a nonchalant shrug. "Well, Nate's a weird duck. So what did he say, anyway? Do they know how the fire started?"

Wyatt dragged his gaze away from my face slowly and went back to attacking the fried rice. "They're not absolutely certain yet, but Nate thinks somebody set it deliberately."

I sat up sharply. "He thinks it was arson?"

"That's what he said."

"But why? Who'd do something like that?"

Wyatt scraped the bottom of the container and licked a few grains of rice from his fork. "I don't know. Somebody with a bone to pick, I suppose."

"A bone to pick with Brandon?"

Wyatt slanted an annoyed glance at me. "That'd be my guess."

"Yeah, but who?"

"How the hell would I know? Brandon's pissed off so many people, it could have been just about anybody."

"I know a few people were upset over the Arts Festival, but *that's* certainly no reason to do something so horrible."

"I never said it was over that."

"Then what?"

Wyatt rested his elbows on the table and cradled his coffee mug in his hands. "Maybe some poor jerk found out his wife was fooling around on him."

I laughed uneasily. "Come on, Wyatt. I know Brandon dates a lot, but he doesn't mess around with other men's wives."

Wyatt met my gaze steadily. "You want to put money on that?"

"Of course not."

"You're sure? I could use a new stereo for the truck."

I'd always had strong opinions about fidelity, and learning about Roger's affair had only made them stronger, but even I wouldn't convict Brandon on my brother's say-so. "That's a pretty ugly thing to say. Can you prove it?"

"I'm sure I could."

"Then do it. Who has he been seeing?"

An odd expression inched across Wyatt's face. "It's not my place to say."

"You can't make an accusation like that without proof to back it up."

"Oh, there's plenty to back it up. Believe me."

"Well, I hope you're wrong. And I hope Nate's wrong about the arson."

Wyatt fixed me with a steady stare. "Why do you care? What's Brandon Mills to you?"

I hadn't told him about my so-called date with Brandon, and I sure didn't want to mention it now. "He's a friend," I said. "And besides that, he's a human being. Last time I heard, people were supposed to be innocent until proven guilty. If you can't prove that he was sleeping around, you shouldn't spread rumors."

"It's not a rumor."

"Well, *I've* never heard anything about him sleeping with married women."

"That's because you're new in town."

I kicked my feet from the chair and glared at him. "That was a rude thing to say. I'm not new around here."

"Might as well be." Wyatt reached for the hazelnut creamer, sniffed, and put it back with a grimace. "You can't leave town for twenty years and expect everything to be the same when you finally drag yourself back. Life doesn't work that way."

Like it or not, he was right about that. I'd received a warm welcome from some of the people I'd known before I left, but there were some who still held me at arm's length, and a few others who acted as if I'd committed treason by leaving. I was counting on the uncertain ones warming up once they realized I was back to stay, and I told myself the others weren't worth worrying about.

"I understand why people might not confide in me," I assured him, putting my feet back on the chair. "What I don't understand is why they'd choose *you*."

With a laugh, Wyatt propped his feet onto the last empty chair. We were mirror images of the same reflection, except that he's a foot taller, and I don't have a mustache. "What can I say? I'm just the kind of guy folks trust, I guess."

I made a face to show what I thought of that, but I couldn't stop thinking about his accusations. I knew firsthand the depth of pain and anger a person could feel in the face of infidelity. I'd felt plenty of both after walking in on Roger and his new girlfriend. But to burn down an entire building and wipe out a man's life work? That kind of anger was beyond me.

To soothe my irritated nerves, I slid grape, cinnamon, cherry, lemon, and orange sticks into a jar. "Well, whoever set the fire—assuming anybody did—I'm sure somebody will have seen something. You can't sneeze in this town without somebody knowing about it." I wedged in root beer, butterscotch, and watermelon. "You were there last night. Did you see anybody hanging around?"

Wyatt lifted his gaze away from what I was doing. "I was where?"

"On Forest Street. I saw you pulling out."

"What in the hell were you doing on Forest Street? I thought you had a meeting."

"This was after the meeting, and I wanted some exercise. So did you?"

"Did I what?"

"Did you see anybody hanging around Man About Town?"

His shoulders stiffened noticeably. "How would I know? I wasn't there."

"Of course you were. I *saw* you."

"No you didn't."

Was he trying to drive me crazy? "I know your truck, Wyatt."

"Apparently, you don't."

Telling me I'm wrong when I *know* I'm right is guaranteed to set me off. I pushed a licorice stick into the jar with a little too much force and felt it crack in my hand. I removed the broken candy and tossed it into the table. "I *saw* your truck pulling out of the parking lot."

"There are probably a hundred other trucks just like it around here. I don't know who you saw last night, but it wasn't me, okay?"

No, it wasn't okay. There might have been a hundred Dodge trucks around Paradise, but they weren't all red, and only one has a license plate that reads EARP.

But Wyatt was finished talking. He shot to his feet and fished keys from his pocket. "I gotta go," he snarled. "It's getting late." He was gone before I could even come up with a way to make him stay.

I stared at the door after he left, listening to the sound of his footsteps on the asphalt and trying to believe what he'd told me. Trouble was, I knew what I'd seen.

Wyatt had been near Man About Town last night and he was lying about it this morning. I couldn't imagine why, but whatever his reasons, I knew they couldn't be good.

Chapter 4

My conversation with Wyatt preyed on my mind while I finished packaging the candy jars, but no matter how I replayed the words, they still meant trouble. Hoping to ward off the headache I could feel coming on, I swallowed a couple of ibuprofen and called Brandon's home number.

Yeah, I was still irritated and hurt over being stood up, but I'm an adult. Tragedy trumps hurt feelings any day of the week.

His answering machine clicked on after five rings, but I hate answering machines, so I hung up and tried his cell phone. One brief ring later, an automated voice informed me that the customer I wanted was either unavailable or out of the calling area.

That might have raised a warning flag if I'd lived in the city, but cell-phone coverage in the mountains is always spotty. He could have been passing Winegar's Market, where the signal disappears for three blocks. He might have been standing in the shadow of City Hall, where the signal comes and goes like the flashing stoplight on Bear Hollow Road.

It had been half a day since I last talked with Brandon, and while that wasn't unusual under normal circumstances, the past twelve hours had been anything but normal. On impulse,

I locked up the kitchen and set off for Man About Town—
what was left of it, anyway. Brandon was probably already
there, I told myself. He'd be surveying the damage, talking
with his insurance agent, and trying to get his life back in
gear. Maybe I couldn't raise him on the phone, but I could
track him down in person and offer to help. It was the least I
could do.

I wasn't the only person in Paradise walking the streets so
early in the morning, either. By the time I reached Forest
Street, the crowd had grown almost dense—by Paradise
standards, anyway. Sadly, the devastation seemed even more
complete in the daylight than it had looked the night before.
All that remained of Brandon's store was one partial wall of
bricks. The rest had been reduced to a smoking rubble.

My stomach knotted and my heart hung in my chest,
heavy and sore. I couldn't even imagine what I would do or
how I would feel in Brandon's place. I jostled through the
crowd and battled a growing irritation. How many of these
people were there out of genuine concern? How many out of
morbid curiosity?

At the far end of the block I spotted a couple of SUVs
bearing the logos of Denver television stations, and my heart
sank a little lower. It must have been a slow news day in the
city if our fire rated coverage, but I wondered if Brandon
would be grateful for or annoyed by the attention.

I strolled through the crowd for a few minutes, occasionally glancing at the ruins and picking up stray bits of conversation. People were speculating like crazy, tossing around
theories about how the fire started that ranged everywhere
from faulty wiring in the old building to a cigarette thrown
from a passing car. I took it as a positive sign that Nate's
arson theory wasn't being widely circulated. Brandon didn't
need that headache on top of everything else.

When I spotted Lydia Cole, no longer wearing cow paja-
mas, in a small cluster of people up ahead, I started toward
her. I was only a few feet away when Lydia shifted position
and Stella Farmer's frosted hairdo loomed into view. Grind-
ing to a sudden halt, I decided to ask the stern-faced cop
standing a few feet away if he'd seen Brandon anywhere.

A few of the guys I knew when I was younger have grown

up to be members of Paradise's finest, but there are plenty of others who aren't familiar to me. This guy belonged in the second group. I'd never seen him before, but everything about him—from his close-cropped brown hair, to the moustache drooping over his lips, to the mirrors on his sunglass lenses—gave him away. Plus, he was inside the police barricade, leaning against the trunk of a cruiser. He crossed one cowboy boot over the other, and he cradled a steaming cup of coffee in a giant paw.

In sheer size alone, he was intimidating. The disapproving expression on his face didn't help. "Excuse me, Officer," I said. "I wonder if you could tell me where to find Brandon Mills?"

He stared at me for a full minute without answering, and every second that passed made me a little more uncomfortable. Like I said, he was a big man, probably in his late forties, and the badge pinned to his jacket labeled him P. Jawarski. He was every bit as tall as Brandon, but without any of the charm. I could have brought peanut brittle to the hard-crack stage in the time it took him to form his reply. "Sorry. I can't let anybody over there."

"I don't really want to go over there," I assured him. "But I'm a friend of Brandon's, and I want to make sure he's okay. And I'd like to help if I can."

A muscle in his jaw twitched. "Help?"

I nodded slowly and wondered if he was just distracted or if he really was having trouble understanding simple words. "Help," I said. "You know . . . that thing people do when someone else is in trouble?"

Jawarski nudged the sunglasses down on his nose and looked at me over the tops of the lenses. "There's nothing you can do, ma'am. Just go on home and let the authorities take care of things around here."

It was the look that bothered me. I'd seen plenty like it during my marriage and a bunch more at the law firm in Sacramento. It might be the twenty-first century, but the world is still filled with men who treat women as if we're objects incapable of coherent thought. Jawarski's look practically screamed "don't worry your pretty little head about it," and that's not an attitude I'm fond of.

I squared up and glared back at him. "I'm not offering to clear rubble," I said. "And I have no intention of getting in the way of your investigation. I'm just trying to find a friend and offer moral support."

"Not necessary."

"Excuse me, but don't you think Brandon should be the one to decide that?"

Jawarski tugged the glasses a little farther down on his nose, exposing a pair of unfriendly blue eyes. "I think, ma'am, that you should go on about your business. We'll do whatever needs to be done here."

I know an immovable object when I run into one. I grew up with Wyatt, remember? So I decided to switch tactics. "Okay. That's fine. Could you just tell me where to find Nate Svboda then?"

Somehow, those cold blue eyes grew even less friendly. "What do you want with him?"

"With all due respect, Officer . . . Jawarski, is it? That's something I'd rather discuss with Nate—if you don't mind."

It was pretty obvious he *did* mind, but he didn't say so. His lips curled into an antagonistic smile, and he squared up in front of me into a cop stance. "Nate's a little busy at the moment. Why don't I have him contact you as soon as he's free?"

I was already feeling frustrated, and Jawarski's bullishness didn't help. I was all ready to launch into an argument when the cameraman from a nearby news crew shifted his camera toward us, probably hoping to catch a bit of spice for the evening news. A blond man standing beside me jerked backward to avoid the camera shot, then turned and plowed straight into me as if he didn't even see me standing there. He crunched my toe underfoot and plunged into the crowd with nothing more than a mumbled apology. He was built like the Stay Puft Marshmallow Man, and my toe began to throb painfully.

"Hey!" I shouted after him, but he didn't bother looking back. I rubbed my tender shoulder and scowled at the scuff mark on my shoe. "Jerk." To add insult to injury, I turned back to offer my next argument and caught sight of P. Jawarski's broad shoulders disappearing into the crowd across the street. "It's not a win if you run away," I shouted after him.

I don't know if he heard me or not. He didn't let on.

Fine. Without him there to stop me, I scooted past the barricade and climbed onto the bumper of the police car. The slight advantage I gained didn't net many results. I was just pondering the pros and cons of climbing a little higher when a woman's voice sounded behind me. "Abby? What are you doing?"

With a muffled scream, I jumped from the car and turned to find Rachel Summers scowling at me from the legal side of the barricade. I don't think I've mentioned how exquisitely beautiful Rachel is or how much I envy her. If she is spun sugar, I'm a sugar cube.

Her dark hair is blunt cut in the latest style, and I'm pretty sure she spends hours every morning getting that casually tousled look just right. I've tried to achieve the same effect, but no matter how much product I apply or time I spend, my hair looks as if I haven't brushed it.

Rachel was dressed for success this morning in a pair of tailored black slacks, stiletto-heeled boots, and a black leather jacket over a cotton-candy pink shell, and I'm almost positive she was angling to get herself into the camera shot. "What are you doing?" she asked again.

I think she was talking to me, but I couldn't be sure. Her eyes were focused on the reporter. "Looking for Brandon. Have you seen him?"

"Brandon?" She seemed almost confused by my question for half a second, then her attention seemed to snap into focus. "I just got here a few minutes ago. It's a nightmare, isn't it?"

"That's one word for it," I agreed. "Have you—"

"I guess this is one way to get out of a lease, huh?" she asked, cutting me off. "A bit melodramatic, but effective."

My mouth snapped shut on the rest of the question I was about to ask, and I tugged her as far away from the camera as I could get her. "What are you talking about? Brandon didn't want out of his lease. He loves that building."

"That old thing?" Rachel angled a glance at me. "You're not serious, are you?"

"It was a beautiful building," I insisted. "And Brandon thought so, too."

Rachel laughed. When she realized I wasn't laughing with her, she sobered. "You're serious, aren't you? Does this mean he hasn't talked to you about letting go of your location?"

"Of course he hasn't."

"Then you must be the only one he's missed."

I didn't like the sound of that. "Do you know that for a fact, or is that just a rumor you've heard around somewhere?"

Rachel shrugged. "I know for a fact that he talked to me. And to Tony Pizzo and Corelle Davies. As for the rest . . ." She swept an arm toward the crowd. "Ask them yourself."

"No, thanks." Not just now, anyway. "So where is he? Do you know?"

Rachel glanced hopefully toward the camera. "I haven't seen him. In fact, I don't think anybody's seen him since yesterday. That's what I heard, anyway." Smoke rose from a hot spot in the rubble, and Rachel shuddered. "I heard one of the guys over there saying they still hadn't found him. This is all too weird, isn't it? First the fire, then Brandon disappearing. I don't like it."

"He hasn't disappeared," I said firmly. "I'm sure in all the confusion—"

She cut me off again. "Maybe he did, Abby. Maybe he didn't mean for the fire to get so far out of control. Maybe he took off when he realized how bad it really was. They're ninety-nine-percent certain it was arson, you know."

The knot in my stomach tightened, but I wasn't going to let myself get caught up in gossip and speculation. I needed facts, and those were sorely lacking. "Ninety-nine percent? Where did you hear that?"

"Somewhere. It doesn't matter, does it?"

"I think it does. Accusing Brandon of setting the fire is serious. Why would he do that?"

Rachel rubbed fingers against thumb in the universal sign for money. "Why else? Insurance."

"He wouldn't do something this stupid just to break his lease, and he certainly doesn't need the money."

"Are you sure about that?"

"Of course, and so should you be. Brandon has never acted like someone in financial trouble."

Her glossy pink lips curved into a patient smile. "How do people in financial trouble act?"

"I don't know. Worried. Frantic. Desperate."

"Desperate enough to torch their business for the insurance?"

I tried to laugh off the suggestion. "You know what I mean. If Brandon was desperate for money, he sure hid it well. Maybe the fire *was* arson, but it was probably started by some derelict."

Rachel gave me a *get real* look. "Yeah. Because we have such a huge homeless problem here in Paradise."

"All it takes is one."

"One more than we have. I'm telling you, Abby, Brandon's not here. Knowing him, he'll show up in a day or two with an airtight alibi so nobody can accuse him of anything."

First Wyatt. Now Rachel. Was I the only one who didn't think Brandon was that devious? Apparently so.

Rachel's chocolate-colored eyes filled with pity. "You're surprised, aren't you? Well, don't feel too bad. You don't know Brandon as well as the rest of us do. He's a smooth operator. Besides, I never said he did it, just that it's possible."

"That's bad enough."

She waved off my concerns with one perfectly manicured hand. "Relax, Abby. The police will figure everything out, and we'll know soon enough. Meanwhile, don't lose sleep over it. Brandon will come out of this just fine. Trust me."

I nodded mutely, but only because I couldn't figure out what to say, and Rachel's attention was almost immediately caught by something she found more interesting.

"Oh! There's Eleanor Douglas. I need to ask her about ordering a turkey for Thanksgiving. Want to come with me?"

I shook my head quickly. "No, thanks."

"You're sure? They've been getting fewer and fewer every year at the butcher shop. Last year I was two days late and ended up having to buy a frozen one."

Which didn't seem like it should rate higher than Brandon's tragedy on her scale of concerns, but who was I to judge? "I'm positive," I said. "You go ahead. I need to get back to the store in a few minutes, anyway."

Rachel flung a smile in my direction and took off after Eleanor, but my conversation with her left me more uneasy than ever. Talk like that could be dangerous. People hear things. Before you know it, "maybe" becomes "definitely," and something that never happened is being passed around as gospel truth. Wherever Brandon was, he didn't need to deal with a damaged reputation when he came back.

On my own again, I spent the next fifteen minutes looking for Brandon, but Rachel had been right about one thing. Nobody had seen him, and nobody had even heard of anyone who had. I desperately wanted her to be right about something else, too. I wanted Brandon to show up with a story that would explain everything.

But no matter how many times I reassured myself, I couldn't shake the feeling that something was horribly wrong.

•

Chapter 5

At ten minutes before ten, I stood on the sidewalk in front of Divinity, clutching the key in my hand and trying to pull myself together. Since 1960, Divinity had provided Aunt Grace with a home away from home. It had been a source of comfort and security for her, and I wanted it to be the same for me.

Divinity is actually quite a large store—big enough to divide into sections, with old-fashioned candy in one area, homemade confections in another, and manufactured favorites ordered from suppliers in a third. It's more than just a candy store, really. A few years ago, Aunt Grace ripped out one set of shelves and put Divinity through some massive renovations. She bought a four-burner coffeemaker, installed a soft-drink machine, and created a small seating area where folks could come and sit for a spell. She always did whatever it took to make Divinity a success, from the moment she conceived of the idea to open her own business to the day she died.

She'd been a pioneer back in the sixties, applying for—and getting—a loan at a time when banks didn't loan money to women without a man to back them. Hers was a grand legacy, and I wanted desperately to carry it on.

Over the years, Aunt Grace had established a number of traditions at Divinity, and I loved them all. But I think my favorite was the seasonal display window made entirely of candy. Grace had been a genius at designing the windows. Her designs were intricate, delicate, and whimsical. My efforts fell far short of the standard she'd set, but I was giving it my all.

Just a few weeks ago, I'd put up the autumn display window. I'd spent two months conceiving of the idea and more than a week putting it together, and even I had to admit that the end result wasn't all that bad.

I'd covered the floor with a mosaic of leaves made of candy chips in autumn colors, created a "blackboard" of licorice and chalk markings of powdered sugar. I'd spent two nights creating school books out of fruit leather and then positioned a few glass jars filled with orange and lemon drops, cinnamon bears, and red, orange, yellow, and green fruit jellies.

In the center of the display, perched atop a tray made of silver dragées, sat the pièce de résistance—Divinity's specialty candy apples, made from Grace's personal recipe. They're made by dipping a Granny Smith apple into alternating coats of caramel and three kinds of chocolate, then rolling them in nuts or crushed hard candies. They take time and patience to make, but the end result is well worth it.

I wondered what Aunt Grace would have said about the morning's events. Surely even she would have caught on to the lies Wyatt had been telling. And what would she have said about Brandon?

In the stillness of the morning, I could almost hear the click of tongue against teeth and see the roll of her always expressive violet eyes. *Innocent until proven guilty, Abby. Isn't that what you learned in law school?*

Yes it was, Aunt Grace.

Smiling at my flight of fancy, I unlocked the front door and flipped on the light switch. Shelves filled with sparkling glass jars lined one long wall behind a long glass counter and an antique brass cash register. Those jars are filled with everything from gummy candy to horehound drops. We boast the largest (and most colorful) selection in the Rocky Mountain West.

The glass canisters on the counter winked in the sudden flare of the lamp and the black-and-white checkerboard floor gleamed. For just a second, the rush of excitement I used to feel as a kid filled me, and with it came one brief moment filled with infinite possibilities. Coming to see Aunt Grace had always made me believe that anything was possible. Adjusting to a world without her wasn't easy.

With a sigh, I opened the small safe in the storage room where I keep just enough cash on hand to open the register each morning, then carried the cash drawer into the store and slipped it into the register minutes before my first customer of the day came through the door.

A small, but steady stream of people followed all day, but everybody wanted to talk about the fire, where they were when they first heard the news, and what they said to their spouse or significant other at the time. When I still hadn't heard from Brandon by noon, I tried both of his numbers again, then packaged a box of the jelly assortment for Miss Lela's Piano Studio, checked my e-mail, and sketched a few ideas for the website I plan to set up one of these days.

Since it was a cool, dry day—perfect for making candy— I decided to get a jump start on Halloween and gathered the ingredients for cinnamon cat lollipops. The lack of humidity in Paradise is one of the things that makes it such a good location for candy making. It may take a little longer to bring the syrup to a boil because of the altitude, but there are only a few days each year when the sugar will actually absorb enough moisture from the air to ruin the candy.

Within minutes, I had sugar, corn syrup, water, cinnamon oil, and food coloring on the counter. I was just starting to measure ingredients when my cousin Karen arrived to work the afternoon shift.

Karen's one of those people who seems to know everything about everything. Want to know how to treat a bee sting, stop a migraine, or keep your skin smooth? Karen's the one you should call. She also knows where to find the best price for everything from gas to ground beef, and who fits where in any family tree. She has a serious sugar addiction, but you'd never know it because she's skinny as a rail. She's actually a few years younger than I am, but I never can remember exactly how many years it is.

It would probably have made more sense for Aunt Grace to leave Divinity to Karen, but Karen swears she only wants the part-time income and very little of the responsibility. She seems content to work whenever her kids aren't practicing something or competing somewhere. Frankly, I'd like to know where she gets her energy. I'd bottle it and sell it over the counter.

She inherited her auburn hair from her father's side of the family, but her hazel eyes and high cheekbones are pure Shaw. True to form, she burst into the kitchen as if someone had pumped her engine full of something before dawn. "So . . ." she said, tossing her keys onto the table. "Brandon Mills burned down Man About Town so he could get his hands on the insurance money, huh?

Et tu, Karen? Scowling, I slipped a gold-edged Divinity apron over my head and cinched the ties around my waist. "Why is everyone so determined to believe the worst? The store burned down. That's all I know for sure. Anything else is gossip and hearsay."

Karen hitched her narrow backside onto one of the stools we keep near the window. "I guess that means you don't think he did it?"

"No, I don't." I measured ingredients and put the pan on the flame. "You know Brandon. He's not the type to do something like that."

"What type is that?"

I frowned up at her. "The arsonist type. The type who'd commit a felony and take a chance on hurting another human being or damaging someone's property for the sake of a little money."

Karen shrugged and dug a huckleberry drop from the sample bowl. "If he did it, it wouldn't have been for a *little* money. I hear the insurance on that building will pay off more than a million dollars if Brandon can prove that he's innocent."

"Which he will."

"I don't know, Abby. The longer he stays away, the harder it's going to be."

That brought my head up with a snap. "He still hasn't been found?"

"Not yet."

That vague sense of uneasiness I'd been feeling all day took on sharp definition. "You don't think something happened to him, do you?"

"To Brandon?" Karen filled the pocket of her smock with fruit drops and smiled reassurance. "I'm sure he's just fine. You know what a charmed life he leads. He's like a cat with nine lives."

I stopped working so I could look at her. "Are we talking about the same Brandon? I've never seen that side of him."

"Well, it's there. The man has been skating around trouble since the day he walked into this town. It's a miracle that some jealous husband hasn't come gunning for him, you know?"

Heat wafting up from the burner scorched my hand and reminded me to stir if I didn't want to toss out the whole batch. "That's almost exactly what Wyatt said, but if that's true, why don't I know about it?"

"Maybe Brandon doesn't want you to know. You two have been getting pretty friendly lately."

"Isn't that all the more reason for one of *you* to tell me?"

Karen crossed her legs and set one foot bouncing slightly. "Would you have listened?"

I shrugged off the question. "That's entirely beside the point. You still could have said something. Do you know for sure that Brandon sleeps with married women, or are you just responding to rumor?"

"Mostly rumor," Karen admitted. "And I didn't say anything because it never occurred to me that you'd take Brandon seriously. I didn't think I needed to worry." She stopped jiggling her foot and lanced me with a look. "I *don't* need to worry, do I?"

I turned my attention back to the pan. "What Brandon does is his business."

Karen scowled at me. "You're such a bad liar. You're dying to know. Admit it."

"I'm mildly curious, that's all. Maybe it would help the police figure out who set the fire."

Snorting a laugh, Karen hopped from her stool and pulled a Diet Pepsi out of the Frigidaire. "You knowing who Brandon sleeps with is *not* going to help the police figure out what happened last night. If you want my opinion, Brandon did it. Brandon's hurt a lot of people in Paradise, Abby. You'll be smart to keep your guard up around him."

"My guard is up," I assured her. But even after she swept off to help a customer, leaving me alone, all I could think about was how different the Brandon I knew was from the Brandon everyone else was talking about.

I swept sugar crystals from the sides of my pan with a wet brush and tried to imagine Aunt Grace working at my side, watching me, cautioning patience, reminding me that cooking anything requires patience and love. This kitchen had been an almost sacred place to her, and the utensils she kept here were symbols of her religion. I still hadn't achieved that level of Zen in the kitchen, but at least some of the panic I'd felt right after Aunt Grace's death was disappearing.

I worked steadily, trying to keep my mind centered on what I was doing by whispering bits of candy-making advice that I remembered Aunt Grace sharing. But no matter how hard I tried to focus, I caught myself staring out the window, first expecting Brandon to come down the hill, then, as the morning wore on, hoping that he would.

By three o'clock I had six dozen shiny red-cat lollipops cooling in molds on the counter. The pleasant scent of cinnamon lingered in my hair and permeated my clothes. Just as I filled the sink and began cleaning up, the back door of Picture Perfect opened and Dooley Jorgensen stepped outside into the bright afternoon sunshine.

Dooley is a tall man in his early sixties with a slight paunch and a shock of hair that I think used to be blond. It's pure silver now and his most recent haircut left it standing straight up on his head. His complexion is naturally ruddy, which makes him look as if he's always short of breath. About ten years ago, he retired and came to Paradise to open a camera store.

He was a great friend to Aunt Grace, and after her first

stay in the hospital began checking on her twice a day to make sure she was all right. He doesn't need to check on me, but he has taken me under his wing anyway and crosses the narrow patch of pavement separating our stores whenever the mood strikes him. Apparently, it struck him now.

Wearing an unusually grim expression, he strode across the parking lot and let himself inside. The buttons on his shirt were being strained almost to the breaking point, and a dark stain made me suspect he'd sent someone out to pick up breakfast burritos again.

"Well," he said, closing the door behind him, "this is quite a day isn't it?"

"That's an understatement." I slid the pan, measuring cups, and utensils into the sink and jerked my head toward the refrigerator. "There's a Coke if you want one."

There's always a Coke in the fridge for Dooley, but part of the game we play includes making the offer. He'd rather die than help himself without an invitation.

With a sigh so heavy it hurt *my* lungs, he found a can in the fridge and cracked it open. "I just came from talking with Nick Peretti," he said after downing half the can. "He says they're pretty sure they've got the fire out completely, so that's good news, eh?"

Nick's a transplant from St. Louis and the captain of our volunteer fire crew, but even with his pre-Paradise experience I don't think he's ever battled a blaze like the one we'd just had. "That is good news," I agreed. "Any idea how much damage there is to the buildings on either side?"

"None, thank the good Lord." Dooley took another long swig and let out a deeply satisfied breath. He crushed the can in his fist and lobbed it toward the garbage can. "Nick says that when they realized they couldn't save Man About Town, they focused on keeping the rest of the block safe. Walt and Becky both suffered a little smoke damage, but their stores are structurally sound."

Walt Neebling and Becky Trotter own the shoe store and jewelry emporium that flank Man About Town on either side, and I was happy to hear that their stores had been spared. "At least nobody else lost much," I said. "I hope they all have good insurance."

Dooley propped one elbow on the windowsill behind him and leaned back to get comfortable. "Walt and Becky do. I guess Brandon does, too—not that it'll do him much good now."

I left the pan to soak and scowled at Dooley as I stuffed unused lollipop sticks into the supply cupboard. "Don't get too caught up in the gossip, Dooley. I know what people are saying, but I'm sure Brandon didn't set that fire. Getting back on his feet is going to be tough enough. He doesn't need to worry about his reputation in the process."

When Dooley didn't answer, I turned to find him staring at me as if I'd grown a third eye. "You haven't heard, have you, pumpkin?"

The endearment made me nervous. Dooley doesn't use them except on special occasions, and those occasions are almost never good. Though I suspected I really didn't want the answer, I felt compelled to ask, "Heard what?"

His pale brows knit in consternation. "They found a body under the rubble, Abby. Whoever set that blaze is not only guilty of arson, but murder, too."

A body. Murder. At Man About Town.

I stared at Dooley for a long time, trying to process what he'd just told me and trying even harder to make him wrong. I would have told him he was, if I'd been able to make my voice work.

"Nobody's seen Brandon yet," Dooley went on as if I wanted to hear more. "Folks are speculating that the body is his. But whether he's the one who's dead or the one who set the fire, insurance isn't going be much good to him."

I wanted to point a third possibility—that Brandon might be out there somewhere, whole, healthy, and innocent, but I couldn't get those words out, either.

I just wasn't sure which possibility frightened me more—Brandon dead, or Brandon guilty of murder.

Chapter 6

My eyes blurred, my breath burned my lungs, and my stomach hurt as if I'd been doing sit-ups all morning. "How soon will we know for sure?" I demanded when I could speak again.

"I wish I knew." Kindness filled Dooley's eyes, and he inched closer. He hovered a few feet away, looking as if he thought he needed to do something but not at all sure what that something might be. "The police have taken the body to the morgue, and I guess somebody will make an official identification. Word is that the fella they found is wearing Brandon's ring, so I think we can probably predict what they're going to tell us."

I squeezed a few words out around the giant jawbreaker in my throat. "Where did you hear about the body?"

He shifted his weight from foot to foot and raked those kind eyes across my face. "I'm sorry, Abby. I know you don't want to believe it—"

"This isn't the time to pat me on the head and try to make me feel better," I snapped. "I need answers. Who told you? Someone who knows what they're talking about? Or is this just the latest gossip on the street?"

Dooley's gaze dropped to the tips of his fingers, then shot back up to lock on mine. "Sloan Williamson told me."

Sloan is the owner/editor of the *Paradise Post*, and while those credentials don't necessarily guarantee the man's honesty, Sloan simply isn't the kind of man to run wild with rumors. He wouldn't have said anything to Dooley unless he had a source to back it up.

So did that mean that Brandon was dead? My knees buckled and I sank onto a nearby stool to keep myself off the floor.

"I wouldn't have said anything," Dooley said after a few minutes, "but I know you and Brandon were friendly. I didn't want you to read about it in tonight's special edition."

I nodded my thanks. "Do they know who set the fire?"

"Not yet, but they'll figure it out. It's just a matter of time." His pudgy face creased with concern, and he put an awkward but gentle hand on my shoulder. "You going to be okay, kid?"

I nodded again, but I don't think either of us believed it. One after another, questions raced through my head. Had Brandon set the fire, or was someone else responsible? If he did it, what possible reason could he have had? Had he been in financial trouble? Wouldn't I have known about it if he had?

Tears threatened, but I fought them back. Between the divorce and Aunt Grace's death, I'd spent far too much time crying in the past year, and I hate crying. I hate that my nose gets stuffy and my eyes hurt. I hate that it leaves me feeling emotionally drained when I'm through. Breaking down hadn't solved a single problem in my past, and it sure hadn't made my situation better. Only hard work and determination had done that.

I focused on the questions and locked away the emotion. Why had Brandon asked me to spend the evening with him if he was planning to set his store on fire? I was sure he wouldn't have . . . unless he was thinking of using me as an alibi. Romano's wasn't far from Man About Town. He could have easily excused himself to use the men's room, slipped out the back door, started the fire, and returned to dinner with me none the wiser.

But if that's what he'd been planning, why had he changed his mind? Why stand me up and wait until later, when nobody was around? Had he suffered an attack of conscience? Or had something else changed his mind? If *he* hadn't set the fire, someone else had. But who would have wanted to hurt him? And why?

"I know he was here yesterday," Dooley said, pulling me back to the moment. "I'm sure the police will know that, too. They'll want to know what the two of you talked about."

"He didn't say anything unusual," I said. "We talked about last night's meeting and the Arts Festival, that's all." I rubbed my forehead with the tips of my fingers and tried to get the world to make sense again. "I almost wish he *had* said something strange. It might help me understand what's happening."

Acting almost relieved to hear that I didn't know anything, Dooley patted my shoulder again. "Well, then, that's all right. Just watch out for yourself, pumpkin. I don't want you to be hurt by this mess."

I managed a weak smile. "Thanks, Dooley, but I'll be okay." And I knew I would be eventually. Sure, I was hurting right now, but if nothing else, the past year had taught me how resilient human beings really are.

Dooley pulled me into a clumsy hug, then released me and stuffed his hands into his pockets. "You'll let me know if you need anything?"

"Of course."

"I mean it. I'm here if you need me."

"I know, Dooley. Thank you. But I'll be okay once the shock wears off. Karen's here, so I won't be alone."

He nodded, but turned back at the door. "You know where to find me if you need anything."

After Dooley let himself out, I spent a few minutes staring at the rows of lollipops and thinking about what he'd told me. I tried again to argue myself out of believing it, but Dooley wouldn't have said a word if he didn't believe it was true. Only a fool could have misread his concern for me.

After a long time, I tossed my apron onto the counter, left the hot kitchen, and stepped outside into the sunlight. A dark blue sky stretched between the mountains, and a light breeze had already cleared away the worst of the smoke. It was a perfect fall day, and I found myself hoping that Brandon would be around to see more days like it. Even more, I wished that I'd spent more time enjoying the ones we'd had.

I sank onto the park bench outside the door and tilted my head back so I could feel the sun on my face. Until the day she died, Aunt Grace had sworn that this bench was the perfect place to solve all of life's problems. I don't know if it's that powerful, but it is a pleasant place to sit. I can see what's happening in my little corner of the world, and the southern exposure catches the sunlight most of the time. That makes it nice in the cooler months, but the thick stand of aspen trees separating Divinity and the shops on the hill behind provides shade when I want it in the summer.

I don't know how long I sat there alternating between the hope that Brandon was still alive and the almost overwhelming certainty that he wasn't, before I felt a shadow pass over me. I opened my eyes just as the sound of footsteps clattering down the steep stairs leading up to Bear Hollow Road reached me.

During tourist season, those stairs are used all day and night by people walking between the downtown district and the hotels and rental condos on the hill. I rarely pay much attention to passersby then, but since we were in the middle of a lull and there was a good chance I'd know whoever was about to walk past me, I opened my eyes and squinted into the sunlight to get a look . . .

. . . and immediately wished I hadn't.

Before I could pretend to be asleep, Jawarski reached the bottom of the steps, saw me watching, and pivoted toward me. "It's Ms. Shaw, isn't it?"

People never call me that in Paradise. It's Abby. Sometimes Abigail. Never Ms. Shaw. We're just not that formal here. In fact, the only time anybody had been that formal with me was during my marriage while I was practicing law with Roger. Hearing the cop use it now made me sit up sharply, ready to face the judge and argue my case, I guess. I didn't like it. Wincing a little, I nodded. "Abby, please."

"If you prefer." He took a couple of steps closer and

scowled down at me. "You look upset. Is everything all right?"

Considering everything that had happened this morning, it struck me as a stupid question, but I decided not to say so. Instead, I nodded and looked away. "It will be."

From the corner of my eye, I saw him tugging off his sunglasses, and those ice-blue eyes of his bored straight into me. "If there's something wrong—"

I blurted a harsh laugh. "Of course there's something wrong. I just heard that a good friend of mine might be dead, and I'm having a little trouble adjusting to the idea, but it's nothing for you to worry about."

"You're talking about Brandon Mills?"

"Unless there's been another death in Paradise within the past few hours." Was he really that dense, or was he just trying to get me talking? I didn't like either option, but it occurred to me that the man could serve a purpose, so I tried not to let him see my irritation. "Does this mean you've identified the body as Brandon's?"

He shook his head and hung his glasses from the neck of his shirt, apparently settling in for a little while. "We haven't made a positive identification yet. Do you mind telling me how you heard about this? That information hasn't been released to the public yet."

"Paradise is a small town," I said with a shrug. "Word gets around."

He made a face and hooked his thumbs into his back pockets. "I'm starting to figure that out. I suppose it's too much to hope that you'll tell me where the word came from?"

"Sorry. Do you know yet who set the fire?"

"It's early, still. We don't know much of anything." He came closer and propped one foot on the bench beside me. "Actually, I'm hoping you can help me with that."

"Me?" I nearly fell off my perch. "How?"

"You and Mr. Mills are friends, isn't that right?"

"That's right."

"And you saw him yesterday?"

"For a few minutes in the afternoon."

He pulled a notebook and pen from his shirt pocket, and

the brief glimpse of humanity he'd revealed faded. "Would you mind telling me what you talked about?"

"Nothing important."

"Why don't you let me be the judge of that?" His face was an expressionless mask, his movements slow and cautious.

I worked up another shrug and scooted over on the bench so he could sit if he wanted. I thought that might help to convince him that I wasn't trying to hide anything. "All right. What do you want to know?"

He ignored my invitation. "What time did you see Brandon yesterday?"

"He stopped by around two in the afternoon and left about an hour later."

"An hour? At a candy store. He must have quite a sweet tooth."

Was that sarcasm I heard in his voice? I couldn't be sure. I decided to ignore it and just be honest. "He didn't buy anything," I said. "Brandon's a friend. He had a cup of coffee and then tasted some candy for me."

"So it was a social visit."

"Yes. I told you, we're friends."

"So you did." He made a note and asked, "Do you know where he was going when he left?"

"He didn't say. I assumed he was going back to work."

"Have you heard from him since that time?"

I shook my head. "Not a word. From what I hear, nobody has. Do all these questions mean that he's *not* the person you found inside the store?"

Jawarski shook his head. "It doesn't mean anything, Ms. Shaw. I'm just trying to cover my bases. What did the two of you talk about while he was here?"

"We talked about a lot of things."

"Name one."

"The Downtown Alliance meeting. Brandon was looking forward to that so he could win votes for the Arts Festival proposal."

"But he didn't show up at the meeting?"

"No, he didn't."

"And did that surprise you?"

"Very much. The Arts Festival is very important to him. He'd been looking forward to getting things settled."

Jawarski dragged another cold blue glance across my face. "Did you notice anything strange in his behavior? Did he seem worried while he was here? Or maybe agitated?"

"If you're wondering whether he set the fire, he didn't. He's not the type to do something that destructive. Besides, he loved that building, and he knows every minute of its history."

Jawarski leveled me with a glance. "Well, that's a compelling argument, Ms. Shaw, but do you have any actual proof to go along with that?"

He laid on sarcasm as thick as the chocolate on Aunt Grace's toffee squares. I ignored it and flashed a tight smile. "Look, I know that's not enough to prove Brandon innocent, but if you're really interested in his state of mind, you should know a little more than just how he felt yesterday."

"And you can tell me that?"

"I can tell you some things that might help."

"You intend to help me build my case?"

He was starting to irritate me, but I tried to maintain my cool and lifted one shoulder. "No, but I'm familiar with how the law works. I was an attorney for ten years before I came here."

"Is that right?" One eyebrow arched to match the mountain peak behind him. "Criminal law?"

"Corporate."

"You represent someone involved in this case?"

I was tempted to say yes, but anyone with a brain the size of a Jelly Belly could prove I was lying in about ten seconds. Jawarski might get there even sooner. "No, but—"

"So you have no professional interest in the case."

"No, but—"

"Then you won't mind if I treat you like a civilian."

"Of course not."

He started to look away, then checked himself. "You left the law to sell candy?"

I wasn't about to go into the gory details that drove me to take such a drastic step. Jawarski didn't need to know about my ex-husband's affair and the career crisis that had brought me here. I gave another shrug. "In a manner of speaking. Let me ask you something, Jawarski . . . do you know Brandon? Have you ever met him?"

"Can't say that I have."

"Then you don't know what kind of person he is."

"Afraid not."

"Well, I do. If necessary, I'd testify in a court of law as a character witness. He *didn't* set that fire."

Jawarski studied the toe of his boot for a long moment. "I understand your concern," he said at last, "but your gut feeling about what Brandon did or didn't do last night doesn't give me much to go on, does it? If you had some actual proof, that'd be a different story."

"I don't have actual proof, but I did see him yesterday afternoon, and he was in good spirits. He was laughing. Looking forward to last night's meeting. He even—" I cut myself off, suddenly a little embarrassed to talk about our plans. But maybe the fact that Brandon had made a date with someone would make Jawarski think twice. "We made plans," I said. "We were going to dinner together after the meeting."

Surprise darted through Jawarski's cold blue eyes. "You had a date?"

"I guess you could call it that. Whatever it was, he didn't show up for that, either. I thought maybe he'd changed his mind. Now I wonder if he was in trouble."

"How did you feel about that?"

"I just told you. I thought he'd changed his mind."

"You were angry?"

Was he trying to pin last night's fire on *me*? I sat up a little straighter. "I wasn't happy, but I wasn't angry, either. Brandon and I are friends, that's all. When he didn't show up here, I went upstairs."

"Did anybody see you there?"

"Plenty of people did. I talked with Stella Farmer on my way in. She wasn't any too pleased with Brandon at the time, either. And I stood next to Rachel Summers and Gavin Trotter most of the night."

"And then what?"

I hesitated over the next part, but what if someone had seen me? "I went out for a walk," I admitted. "I ended up walking past Man About Town while I was out. I was getting worried about Brandon, and I thought maybe something had happened to him."

"You were alone?"

The sun inched higher in the sky and turned Jawarski into a hulking silhouette. Using one hand, I shielded my eyes so I could see him. "Unfortunately, yes."

"What did you do there?"

"Nothing. I walked past, that's all. The building was dark, and Brandon's car wasn't anywhere around, so I just kept walking."

His face gave nothing away, so I couldn't tell whether he believed me or not. "Did you see anyone else in the area?"

I hesitated for no longer than a heartbeat. "Not a soul." Maybe I *should* have mentioned seeing Wyatt's truck, but I knew that my brother had nothing to do with the fire, and I saw no reason to raise questions in Jawarski's mind.

That eyebrow winged upward again. "Nobody?"

Did he know something already? My palms grew clammy, but I stuck to my story. "I saw a few people walking home from the meeting, but I didn't see anybody around Man About Town."

"Where did you go from there?"

"Home."

"And where is that?"

I jerked a thumb over my shoulder. "I live here. There's an apartment above the shop."

"You live alone?"

"At the moment."

"So no one can vouch for you?"

"No, but I don't see why anyone would need to."

Jawarski scribbled another note before he looked at me. "We have a dead body on our hands, Ms. Shaw. I'm trying to determine the extent of Brandon Mills' involvement in the fire. By your own admission, you're well acquainted with Mr. Mills, and you had reason to be upset with him yesterday."

"Not *that* upset."

"I find it a little difficult to believe that he stood you up, but you didn't care."

"Well of course I cared, but I'm not crazy!" I folded my arms, realized I'd assumed a defensive posture, and dropped them to my sides. "I was a little hurt at first, but that's all. When he wasn't at the meeting, I got worried and walked past the store to see if he was there. He wasn't. I came home. End of story. I didn't set the fire and kill somebody in the process just to get back at him over a missed plate of pasta."

One corner of Jawarski's mouth curved, but he kept his opinion to himself. "Is there anyone else you can think of who might have wanted to hurt Mr. Mills?"

I'm not even going to pretend I wasn't relieved that we were moving on. I thought about all the whispers I'd heard in the past few hours, but that's all they were. I still didn't know anything. "I don't know," I said. "I thought everyone liked him."

"And you don't have any reason to believe he might have set the fire himself?"

"No."

Jawarski stared me down. I stared back. After a few minutes, he stuffed the notebook and pen into his pocket and shoved a business card at me. "If you remember anything else about last night or anything Brandon said in recent days that might shed some light on this case, I want you to call me."

I took the card without looking at it. "Sure."

"Is that a promise?"

"Sure. Why not?" But I think we both knew I was lying.

I wasn't sure what was going on inside Jawarski's head, but I didn't trust him. He hadn't come right out and accused me of anything, but he didn't trust me, either. If I was smart—and I like to think I am—I'd fly beneath his radar for a few days. The less attention I called to myself, the better off I'd be. But I'm a Shaw and, much as I hate to admit it, we just aren't known for staying on the sidelines—even when that's exactly what we should do.

Chapter 7

My concentration level was at an all-time low for the rest of the day. I tried not to let Jawarski's questions bother me, but that was easier said than done. Did he seriously suspect me of setting the fire, or was he just digging to see what he came up with?

When six o'clock finally rolled around, I locked up the store, fired up my Jetta, and drove across town to Lorena's, a little hole-in-the-wall restaurant that's one of my favorite places on earth. When we were kids, Mama and Daddy brought Wyatt and me here at least once a month. Now that I'm back in Paradise, it's where I go when I want comfort food and space to think.

The gravel parking lot was packed, so I wedged the Jetta between two dirty pickup trucks and hurried through the evening chill toward the low-slung cinder-block building. Inside, the *Ranchera* blaring from the jukebox and the familiar spicy scents coming from the kitchen had exactly the effect I'd hoped they would. I could feel the tension slipping from my shoulders, and I knew everything would be all right—at least for the next hour.

When I was finally seated at a small table in the corner, I closed my eyes and listened to the chatter from countless conversations underscored by the ceaseless clinking of dishes and cutlery. Weariness tugged at my eyelids and made my muscles ache, and I edged into the corner, hoping that no one would notice me.

I didn't even bother looking at the menu. I already knew what I wanted. On a night like this, cheese enchiladas in flour tortillas were the only appropriate choice. It might not be low-cal, low-fat, or low-carb, but after one bite, none of those things matter anyway.

After several minutes, a harried waitress shoved a pitcher of ice water, chips, and salsa onto the table, then disappeared into the crowd without a word. Even though I wasn't thirsty, I filled my glass and turned it in circles so I could watch the patterns it made.

Voices rose and fell all around me as people talked about the kind of day they'd had, what they planned to order, trouble they'd had with children, parents, and bosses. Here and there, mixed up in the normal everyday conversations, I could hear people talking about the fire in low tones.

I thought about the body they'd found in the rubble and felt anger stirring. I wasn't sure what upset me most, people speculating about who'd been killed and why, or those who didn't even register the death as important.

It seemed so wrong to spend time living, laughing, loving, hating, crying, struggling with failure, and enjoying the headiness of success, and then to fade off the radar screen of life as if you'd never even been here. And if it *was* Brandon, even the life's work that might once have testified of his existence was gone. He had no children. No family that I knew of. No one to mourn his passing except a handful of friends.

I pondered the unfairness of it all until the waitress returned to take my order, but before I could tell her what I wanted, a familiar voice rumbled from somewhere behind her, and she left me again. This time, I followed her and found my brother stuffed into a tiny two-person booth next to the kitchen.

Two empty bottles of Dos Equis littered the table in front of him, and a third, half-full, sat in front of his usual large combination plate. He barked a request for more chili verde.

The waitress turned and plowed straight into me in her hurry to get away.

I didn't blame her. Wyatt can be a real pain in the ass when he's in a mood. When she was gone, I moved closer to the table. "What are you doing here?"

He glanced up, but there was no surprise in his expression. But if he saw me come in, why hadn't he said hello? His gaze dropped almost the instant it touched my face. "Eating. What about you?"

"I just got here," I said. "You should have let me know you were coming. I'd have come with you."

He shrugged away the suggestion. "Too late now,"

"Yeah, I guess. Where are Elizabeth and the kids?"

"Home."

"So why aren't you there with them?"

He shot an unreadable look in my general direction and reached for his beer. "Because I'm here."

Yep, he was in a mood all right, but it had been years since he'd been able to intimidate me. "You have a meeting or something?"

"Something like that." He cut into a chili verde burrito, paused with the fork halfway to his mouth, and ran a look from my head to toe. "You need something?"

"Yeah." I knew I wouldn't get an invitation, so I didn't wait for one. Sliding into the booth, I mooched a chip from the bowl in front of him. "Why are you acting so weird? What's up with you?"

He snorted softly. "What makes you think anything's up?"

"Well, for one thing, you're not acting like yourself. Unless you drove home and came back, you've been in town all day, and now you're here having dinner alone. What's the matter, you and Elizabeth fighting or something?"

I meant it as a joke. Their marriage isn't perfect, but I've never seen a better one. When they argue, it's never serious, and it never lasts. I expected Wyatt to laugh.

He didn't.

"Why don't you mind your own business?" he snarled.

My heart dropped like a stone. "Are you and Elizabeth having some kind of trouble?"

Deliberately ignoring my question, Wyatt shoved food into his mouth and chewed slowly.

"You are, aren't you? What's going on?"

Wyatt wiped his mouth with his napkin and held back a belch. "Nothing."

"Why don't you just tell me?"

"Why should I?"

Obstinate ass. "Because I'm your sister. I care about you."

He blinked once. Maybe that meant that I was getting through. "Well good. But that doesn't mean I'm going to talk about it."

"Come on, Wyatt. You don't have to be so tough all the time. Everybody needs someone to talk to when things get rough. Trust me, I know."

He lifted his gaze again. Something had shifted in his expression, but I still couldn't tell what he was feeling. "Okay," he said after a lengthy silence, "so things aren't going so well right now, and I'm staying in town for a few days. Is that what you wanted to hear?"

My mouth fell open before I could stop it. "You're separated—"

"Temporarily."

"But why?"

He stabbed his fork into the burrito and ripped off a piece. "That's between Elizabeth and me."

I wanted to argue, but since I hadn't shared the gory details when my marriage was failing, I bit my tongue and nodded. "I'm sorry, Wyatt. Are you doing okay?"

"That depends on how you define 'okay.' If it's having a roof over your head and clean underwear, then sure, I'm fine."

"Wyatt—"

He cut me off impatiently. "I don't want to talk about it. You're welcome to sit here if you want to, but not if you want to drag my life over the coals while you eat."

I was dying of curiosity, but I'd been in the hot seat plenty of times, and I knew how uncomfortable it could get. Our waitress came toddling back, so I forced a grudging nod and ordered the enchiladas. When she left again, I folded my hands on the tabletop and looked my brother in the eye.

"Just tell me one thing—did you leave her, or did she kick you out?"

"What difference does it make?"

"It makes a big difference."

He ripped off a piece of tortilla and used it to spoon up a mound of rice and beans. "She kicked me out."

"Why? What did you do?"

His brows crashed together in a scowl, and he let out a breath heavy with exasperation. "Which part of 'I don't want to talk about it' do you not understand?"

"But you and Elizabeth?—" I broke off with a shake of my head. "The two of you have always seemed so perfect together."

"Well, things aren't always what they seem. You should know that."

I didn't need the reminder. Then again, maybe I did. My own marriage had seemed solid to those on the outside looking in. Even I'd missed the first two years' worth of warning signs, and I'd been there for every minute of the trouble. Well, except for the part where Roger brought his pregnant girlfriend home for a romp in my bedroom. I was only there for the last three minutes of that.

But that was *my* marriage. Wyatt has adored Elizabeth since junior high school. There's no way I'd believe he cheated on her, and Elizabeth . . . well, she's choir director at Shepherd of the Hills church, for heaven's sake. She's not the type to have an affair. But what else could have been bad enough to split them up?

"Is it money?"

Wyatt ignored me.

"The kids? Did something happen with one of them?"

"The kids are fine."

"Her parents," I said around another chip. "They're interfering again, aren't they?"

Wyatt downed the rest of his beer and pushed the bottle aside. "Her parents aren't the problem. Just leave it alone, okay? What's going on with that fire, anyway? I heard they found a body."

I nodded and decided to back off for now. I could always drive out and visit Elizabeth. She'd probably tell me what was going on. "Yeah," I said. "They did, but they haven't identified it yet."

"They don't have any idea who it is?"

I couldn't bring myself to repeat aloud what Dooley had said about Brandon's ring, so I shook my head and said, "Not yet."

"Brandon still missing?"

"As far as I know."

Wyatt scooped up another mouthful of rice and beans. "You think it's him?"

"How would I know?"

His gaze shot to mine as the waitress slid a hot plate in front of me. "I'm just making conversation, Abs. Don't be so touchy."

But I *was* touchy. And I wasn't even sure why. My feelings were as fragile as a batch of divinity—all frothy and without substance. Apply heat or pressure for too long, and they might just collapse in on me.

I shook my head and dug into my food with all the grace of a bull moose, but that's the good thing about eating with your brother. You don't have to be ladylike. "I'm not the only one who's touchy tonight, you know. I don't want to talk about Brandon. You don't want to talk about Elizabeth. What's left?"

Wyatt shook his head and slid down a few inches on his tailbone. "Thanksgiving dinner with Mom and Dad?"

After Mom lost the sight in one eye and Dad's arthritis started bothering him all the time, my parents had moved off the mountain and into Denver. That was three years ago, but Mom's still going through withdrawal at being so far away, and she lives for the holidays when the whole family is together again.

"Now *there's* a subject," I said with a laugh, then sobered slightly and asked, "Do they know?"

"About me and Elizabeth?" Wyatt shook his head. "Not yet. I'm still trying to figure out how to tell them."

That was a problem I could relate to. Dad's one of those parents who doesn't handle failure well, and Mom sails through life clutching to the belief that her children are superior in some way to the rest of the world. Letting either of them down is tough.

I swallowed a mouthful of cheese and smiled encouragement. "You'll figure it out. Maybe you and Elizabeth will work things out before you see them, and it won't even be an issue."

"Yeah." He slid down another inch. "Maybe."

I think the dejected look on his face worried me more than anything he'd said or done all day. Wyatt's perennially upbeat. Almost annoyingly so. If he's feeling that far down about something, it's big. We sat in silence while I wolfed down the rest of my enchilada, but he stood before I even swallowed the last bite and tossed a tip onto the table. In a rare burst of generosity, Wyatt picked up the tab for both our meals and led the way outside.

Pleasantly full, I trailed him across the parking lot toward the truck I'd somehow missed when I came in. He unlocked the door and turned to face me. "Now what?"

"Where are you staying?"

"I've got a room."

"A room? Where?"

He watched a shiny new Blazer slow and turn into the parking lot before he answered. "At the High Country Inn."

The High Country isn't a bad motel. He'd probably be comfortable there for a few days, but I hated to think of him alone. Wyatt's the gregarious sort. He's best when he's with people. "You can stay with me if you want. The couch folds out into a bed."

"You and me together in that little apartment of yours?" Wyatt gave an exaggerated shudder and grinned for the first time all night as the Blazer's lights swept across us. "Thanks, Abs, but I'm okay where I am."

The apartment isn't that little, but I couldn't picture us sharing the space, either. Still, it might be better than leaving Wyatt to rattle around on his own. "Are you sure? It might help to be around someone."

He swung up into the cab of his truck and smiled down at me. "Don't worry about me, sis. I'll work through this and be just fine."

"I know you will. You're a Shaw."

"Damn straight. Now go home. Get some sleep. Take care of things down at the store." He cranked the engine to life, shut the door, and rolled down the window. "You've got enough to deal with. You don't need to get all bent out of shape over my little problems."

Except his "little" problems weren't so little.

He put the truck into gear and backed past me, then shot out of the parking lot with a spray of gravel that made him seem about sixteen again.

I stood staring after him and tried to believe that everything would be all right. But the year I'd just gone through made it hard to believe. My divorce had started the chain of events still in motion. Aunt Grace's death had left us all reeling. I wondered what was coming next, and how long it would take us to get over it.

Chapter 8

Wyatt's taillights disappeared around the corner and all at once I realized that I was alone in a dark parking lot. Not a comfortable place to be, considering that someone had been killed less than two miles from here within the past twenty-four hours.

All the worry I'd been feeling for Wyatt morphed into irritation that he could drive off and leave me alone. Some gentleman. Mom would be so proud.

As I pivoted toward the Jetta, I caught a quick, shadowy movement out of the corner of my eye. My heart shot into my throat, and all my senses went to high alert. I could feel the hair on my arms, and the night sounds suddenly seemed amplified. Somewhere, buried deep beneath the soothing song of crickets and the whoosh of cars coming from the next street over, I heard the soft scuff of a foot on gravel.

My breath caught in my throat, and I tried to figure out whether I was closer to the Jetta or the door of Lorena's. To reach either one, I'd have to pass a row of darkened cars, any one of which might be hiding someone. The only other option was to run for the road, but I hadn't seen a car pass since Wyatt left and, let's face it, I'm not the fastest runner in the world.

Making a silent vow to buy a membership at the health club, I dug the keys out of my pocket and threaded them through my fingers. I felt nominally better with some kind of defense. Taking a deep breath for courage, I decided to make a run for the restaurant. If there was trouble lurking out here, and I could get close enough, maybe someone inside would hear me screaming for help.

I took one step, then another, reminding myself that I'd grown up with a brother, and I'd taken countless self-defense courses in Sacramento. The trouble was, I'd never had to put any of the tips I'd learned into practice, so all those techniques were as rusty as my candy-making skills.

Another footstep caught my ear, and the shadow loomed into my path. I held back a scream and tried to think. Not so easy when your lungs have collapsed and your heart is slamming against your rib cage.

"Ms. Shaw?" A familiar voice cut through the panic. "I thought that was you."

"Jawarski?" My relief was so strong, it was all I could do not to belt him. He was dressed casually in jeans and a blue denim shirt with some kind of logo on the pocket. "What are you doing creeping around in the dark like that?"

"I didn't know I was."

"Well, you were." With the panic abated, I took a good look around and decided he must have come in the Blazer I'd noticed earlier. Since there seemed to be nothing more to say, I started past him toward my car. "Well, good night, Jawarski. Enjoy your dinner."

"Ms. Shaw?"

"Yes?" I stopped walking and turned back to face him.

"I thought you might be interested to know that we got the preliminary lab reports back."

He certainly knew how to get my attention. "And?"

"The victim has been positively identified. It was Brandon Mills, Ms. Shaw. There's no doubt."

I'd been half-expecting this, but actually hearing the words spoken aloud hit me hard. My knees buckled, and I sank onto the bumper of a nearby truck. "Do you know how he died?"

Jawarski watched me closely, but I wasn't sure if he

wanted to make sure I was all right or decide whether I was guilty. "Preliminary reports show smoke in his lungs, which means he was still alive when the fire started. Right now, it looks like maybe that's what got him, but we won't know for sure until the autopsy is completed."

Everything inside me recoiled at the thought of Brandon alive while the fire raged. "How long will it take to do the autopsy?"

"A week. Maybe longer."

It was too dark to see, but I stared at the spot where my fingernails should have been, trying to absorb the news. "So he wasn't murdered before the fire was set."

"No, ma'am."

My head swam with images. I wondered if Brandon had been aware of what was happening to him, and I prayed that he hadn't. I remembered his laugh and thought about how kind he'd been to me the day Aunt Grace died. He'd come to the hospital when he realized how seriously ill she was, and he'd been there with me as I'd made that endless round of calls to tell people she was gone. When spreading the news overwhelmed me, he'd gently taken the phone away and spoken the words I couldn't get out. Now, someone else would be going through that particular hell, but I didn't know who would fill that role. I didn't even know who they'd call.

It was all I could do to force out my next question. "Do you have any idea who did this to him?"

"We don't have a clear picture of what happened yet, but we'll get there." Jawarski's voice sounded almost kind.

"Good. Just let me know what I can do to help. I know that some people think he set that fire himself, but I don't believe it. He had nothing to gain by doing that, and everything to lose."

"Maybe he needed the insurance money."

"No. The store was doing well. *He* was doing well. Someone else is responsible for setting that fire. I just hope you're not going to take the easy way out and blame him."

Jawarski shifted so that he was standing in the glow of a nearby light. In that setting he seemed younger than I'd first thought. Early forties, maybe. Not much older than I am. "Who do *you* think did it?" he asked.

I shrugged. "I don't know. Brandon had some minor disagreements with people over the Arts Festival, but nothing anyone would kill him over."

"You might be surprised what some people consider worth killing over. And for the record, withholding information won't help."

He was making me uncomfortable, but I still didn't want to tell him about seeing Wyatt's truck that night. "I'm not withholding information," I insisted. "If I seem distracted, it's only natural. You've just confirmed that a friend of mine is dead. In the very next breath, you accused him of arson and attempted insurance fraud. It's not an easy thing to take in."

"I didn't accuse Brandon of anything," Jawarski corrected me. "I suggested the possibility."

"It's *not* a possibility."

His lips curved slightly. "Loyalty is a good quality in a friend. I hope yours isn't misplaced." His gaze flickered toward the street, then back to my face.

Heat rushed into my cheeks, and I said a silent prayer of gratitude for the darkness. "I've told you everything I know, Jawarski. Why wouldn't I?"

The moon drifted behind a cloud and dropped us both into shadow. Jawarski shifted again, this time leaning against the truck bed with his legs stretched out in front of him. "I don't know. Maybe you're trying to protect someone, but if that's what you're doing, you're making a big mistake."

"Well, you can relax. I'm not covering for anybody. I just don't know anything."

And it was *true,* I told myself. Whatever Wyatt was doing in Paradise last night, it had nothing to do with the fire or Brandon's death.

Jawarski remained silent for a long time, then finally pushed to his feet again and towered over me. "So who was the guy you were talking to when I drove in?"

"My brother."

"Your brother?"

"Don't sound so shocked, Jawarski. I come from a regular family. I even have parents."

"I'll make a note of that. This brother of yours lives nearby?"

"That depends on how you define 'nearby.' He and his wife have some property about twenty miles out of town." I almost left it at that, but if Jawarski started asking around, he could probably find out the rest. Besides, maybe I could convince him that I wasn't trying to hide useful information. "He's staying here in Paradise for the time being, though. He and his wife are going through a trial separation."

I couldn't see Jawarski's expression, but I could feel him turning toward me. "How long has that been going on?"

"Hey! I don't mind answering questions about the fire and Brandon, but don't you think you're stepping over the line here? Wyatt and Elizabeth have nothing to do with any of that."

"You're sure about that?"

Why did everyone keep asking how sure I was? "Of course I'm sure. Wyatt hardly knew Brandon, and I don't think Elizabeth ever met him."

"Maybe you don't know as much about your brother and his wife as you think you do."

I shot a glance at him, but I couldn't see his face. "What's that supposed to mean?"

"It means, Ms. Shaw, that I have a witness who saw your brother's truck on Forest Street less than an hour before the fire broke out. I have two more who are willing to testify that your brother threatened Mr. Mills earlier that day. Now it could be that your brother is a witness. Maybe he's more deeply involved than that. Either way, if you know anything at all, I suggest you tell me."

I'm no good at taking advice from annoying cops, either. "That's insane," I snapped. "Wyatt didn't threaten Brandon. Why would he?"

"According to my witnesses, Wyatt wasn't exactly thrilled about the attention Brandon was paying to his wife."

"To Elizabeth?" I barked a disbelieving laugh. "Have you ever met my sister-in-law?"

"Not yet, but I intend to."

"She's not the type to fool around on her husband."

"What type is that, Ms. Shaw?"

"She's director of her church choir, for heaven's sake!"

"I hate to burst your bubble, but that's no guarantee of sainthood."

Well, of course not. But Brandon and *Elizabeth?* Impossible! At least I thought so until I remembered the look on Wyatt's face earlier and thought about the mood he'd been in all day. He'd been so careful to avoid my questions, so determined to convince me he wasn't in Paradise the night of the fire.

My stomach turned over and bile rose in my throat. "You're wrong."

"Am I? I'll tell you how it looks to me, Ms. Shaw. It wouldn't take much at all to make me believe that your brother killed Brandon Mills and tried to make it look like an accident. It wouldn't take a whole lot more to convince me that you're helping him cover his tracks, and that makes you an accomplice to murder."

The blood in my veins turned to ice. Outrage swelled up inside me, but cold, stark fear was a whole lot stronger. "What about all the other people who were angry with Brandon? Are you accusing all of them of murder, too?"

"What other people?"

"Duncan and Stella Farmer, for starters. Stella came right out and accused Brandon of trying to destroy their business."

"Did she? When was that?"

"Before the Alliance meeting."

"Did anyone else hear her?"

"Are you accusing me of making it up?"

"Not at all. I just want to get my facts straight. Who else?"

"Half the city council and a long list of people in the Alliance. I haven't talked to a single person all day who isn't convinced that Brandon set the fire to collect on his insurance—"

"And yet you steadfastly defend his honor."

"At least he had some."

"I guess we'll see, won't we?" Jawarski took one last

look at the street. "I'm sorry for your loss, Ms. Shaw. I'll be in touch." And before I could respond, he turned away and strolled across the parking lot as if he didn't have a care in the world.

For the second time that night, I was left staring at the empty parking lot, but this time I hurried to the Jetta, locked myself inside, and cranked up the heat. Jawarski's accusation had chilled me to the bone, and it was going to take more than a few blasts of hot air to make me feel better.

Chapter 9

I woke up the next day a few minutes after nine, neck kinked, head pounding, eyes so tired they hurt. After Jawarski disappeared, I'd driven straight to the High Country Inn and circled the parking lot looking for Wyatt's truck. It hadn't taken long to figure out he wasn't there.

The desk clerk had been no help. I'd tried everything I could think of to get him to talk, but none of my attempts had done any good. All I'd managed to do was annoy him, almost to the point of calling the police to get rid of me. To avoid another conversation with Jawarski, I left, still without knowing whether Wyatt was a registered guest or not.

Back home, I laid awake for hours thinking about Wyatt and Elizabeth. Brandon and the fire. Jawarski and his half-baked theories. Questions circled relentlessly through my mind, but the answers eluded me. Brandon was dead, there was no doubt about that. Did someone in Paradise have a motive to kill him? I didn't want to believe it, but, still, doubts lingered.

With a heavy sigh, I glanced at the calendar, realized that it was the second Wednesday of the month, and dragged myself out of bed. The second Wednesday meant it was book club day at Divinity, and I wasn't anywhere near ready for the ladies to start arriving.

I showered and dressed quickly, then raced downstairs to make coffee and throw together two trays of assorted candies for the meeting. The ladies of the Paradise Pageturners left the selection up to me each month, and I tried to give them a few old favorites and a few new varieties to try each time.

This month, I'd decided on hazelnut cherry caramels, almond butter crunch, Irish Creme truffles, candied citrus peel, pralines, and Hawaiian bonbons made of white chocolate, macadamia nuts, flaked coconut, and orange zest.

I'd just finished arranging the candies on two of Aunt Grace's antique crystal dishes when Meena Driggs, this year's book club president, marched through the front door. Meena's probably in her late fifties, short, dark-haired and serious-faced. She's one of those super-organized people who seems to get everything done with time to spare, and she has no patience with people who can't keep up. I fell into that category this morning, based on the disapproving glance she swept across the small room on the east side of the building.

Back in the early days, that room was the original holding cell for the territorial jail. Rumor has it that a few famous visitors passed time in there, but I don't know how true that is.

With its bare brick walls and uneven flagstone floor, the room has a lot of old-fashioned charm. The bars on the windows are gone, and sunlight streams into the room now through high, wide windows. It's just large enough to hold a small table and a dozen folding chairs, and still leave room for customers to browse. Some year, when I have enough money, I'd like to open up a wall and create an outdoor seating area in the shade of the aspen trees.

But first, I needed to set up the room for this morning's meeting.

"You're running behind?" Meena asked, her thin mouth turned down in a scowl.

"Only a few minutes. I'll have everything set up before the others get here."

I trotted off to the supply cupboard, pulled out a table-cloth and the silver tray for the coffee service, then scrounged napkins and spoons from the drawer. By the time I carried everything back to the meeting room, Meena had already dragged a few chairs into a semicircle and stood surveying her handiwork. "This had better not be a waste of time."

Smiling encouragement, I deposited the things I held on a chair and smoothed the cloth over the table. "Of course it won't be. Why are you even worried about that?"

Meena centered the tray on the table and shot me a look. "Surely you've noticed how people have been acting since the fire. Everyone's racing around like chickens with their heads cut off. Nobody seems to be able to focus on anything."

"That's because there's been a murder," an imperial sounding voice announced from the doorway. I turned to find Nicolette Wilkes, tall, blonde, and leggy, watching us. She shrugged out of her full-length suit jacket and tossed it over the back of a chair as if it hadn't cost more money than I'll make this quarter. "People are always fascinated by scandal, Meena. Surely you know that. And especially something like this . . ."

Meena snorted disapproval and wiggled impatient fingers at me for the silverware. "I don't know what's so fascinating about it. It seems pretty obvious what happened."

I looked up from the halfhearted effort I was making at folding napkins. "Oh? What do you think happened?"

"What else? Brandon set the fire and got caught in it."

Nicolette's laugh bounced around the empty room. "You'd *like* to think it happened that way. It would appeal to your sense of order, and everything could be tidied up and fit into a neat little box. But what if that's *not* what happened? What if somebody else set the fire?"

"Don't be silly," Meena scoffed. "Who else would?"

I steeled myself, either for the jealous-lover explanation or the mention of Wyatt's name, but Nicolette didn't suggest either one. "Maybe that girl he had working over there. She's an odd one, if you ask me."

"Chelsea?" Her name popped out before I could stop it.

Nicolette nodded. "Don't you think she's a little strange?"

Meena snatched the napkins out of my hand and began folding them herself. "She's not strange, she's just young. Young and impressionable."

"Oh, please! She's spooky, that's what she is." Nicolette draped herself artfully in a folding chair and slipped a praline from the candy dish. She popped it into her mouth and closed her eyes briefly in appreciation. "I don't know why Brandon let her stay around," she said. "I'm not sure she ever actually *did* anything around there."

"I'm sure she did plenty," Meena said with a scowl at the uneven number of pralines. "And she's hardly the first person I'd suspect of murder. She seemed quite loyal to Brandon, if you ask me."

I made a mental note to replenish the praline supply before the rest of the group arrived. "So who would you suspect?"

"Me?" Meena glanced up sharply, almost surprised by the question.

The bell over the door tinkled, and a heavyset blond man stepped inside. I acknowledged his presence, but I wanted to hear the rest of the conversation, so I didn't rush off to help him.

"I told you." Meena gave the last napkin a twitch. "It must have been Brandon who set the fire. And if he didn't do it, then I don't know who. It's hard to believe anyone from Paradise could have done such a thing."

"Well, you just might have to believe it," Nicolette said, her beautiful face smug. "Life doesn't always line up in neat little rows, Meena. Sometimes it gets messy."

"I'm well aware of that, and I resent your tone. The point I'm trying to make is that Brandon was an unknown quantity. We don't have any idea what made him tick, now do we?"

The bell jangled again, this time to signal the arrival of several book club members, including Rachel Summers, who breezed inside wearing a pair of brilliant turquoise pants and a matching sweater. Bangles jingled on both wrists, and rings of various sizes winked from her fingers. If she didn't get noticed, it certainly wouldn't be her fault.

Deciding I'd dawdled long enough, I scurried off to finish making coffee while the ladies of the club settled in and my lone male customer strolled slowly up and down the aisles. I was just pouring the last of the coffee into a carafe when I heard a footstep and looked up to find Rachel watching me.

"I guess Meena probably sent you to find out where this was?" I said with a nod toward the tray.

"I volunteered." Rachel glanced over her shoulder, then leaned across the counter and lowered her voice to a near-whisper. "I feel terrible about what I said yesterday. I had no idea—"

"Don't worry about it," I said, forcing a smile I didn't feel. "Neither of us had any idea what really happened."

Rachel nodded gratefully, but the clouds didn't leave her eyes. "How's Wyatt? Have you seen him?"

The question made my blood run cold. "I saw him last night. Why?"

"I've heard that the police suspect him of starting the fire."

"And you believe it?"

Her gaze dropped to her fingertips, and the cold water in my veins turn to ice.

"Come on, Rachel. You've known Wyatt since you were kids. You know he's not violent."

"I don't know what to believe. All I *do* know is that the police have been asking a lot of questions about him."

"What kinds of questions?"

"Whether or not I saw him the night of the murder. Whether or not I ever heard him threaten Brandon. I don't know what to tell them, Abby. I can't believe Wyatt would do something like this, but I don't want to get myself in any trouble."

I started to tell her that trouble isn't contagious but stopped myself. Maybe it is. "Questions don't mean he's guilty," I said. "What did you tell them?"

She watched a couple stroll past on the sidewalk before muttering, "I don't know if I should tell you."

"I think Wyatt has the right to know what's being said about him, don't you?"

"I don't know."

"What if you were being accused of something you didn't do? Wouldn't you want to know what people were saying so you could defend yourself?"

Rachel nodded slowly, but I could tell she still wasn't convinced.

But that only made me more determined to get answers. I stole a glance at my meandering customer, decided he was fine on his own for a while longer, and let myself out from behind the counter so I could talk to Rachel face-to-face. "You might as well just tell me what you said to the police. You know I'm not going to leave you alone until you do."

"What could I tell them?" she asked grudgingly. "I don't know anything."

"Maybe that's because there's nothing to tell."

Rachel's gaze narrowed even further. "Well, of course *you'd* feel that way. You always have thought that the sun rose and set on Wyatt."

"He's my big brother. What can I say?"

Laughter erupted from the meeting room and Rachel reached instinctively for the coffee tray. "Look, you're right. I *have* known Wyatt forever. And yes, it's hard to believe that he could do something like this. But *somebody* killed Brandon, and I don't know who else it could have been."

"So Wyatt's guilty by default? Meanwhile, whoever really did this is wandering around the streets of Paradise without a care in the world."

Rachel's lips thinned. "I didn't say Wyatt was guilty by default, but he hated Brandon. Everybody knows that."

I wanted to say that I didn't, but that wouldn't have been entirely true. "Do you know what happened to make Wyatt hate Brandon?"

She pulled the tray toward her, and I watched as her eyes went blank. "Why don't you ask Wyatt?"

"I have. He's not talking. Please, Rachel. We're talking about my brother. I need to help him if I can."

Rachel rolled her eyes, but I sensed her weakening. "I'm not even sure I know the whole story."

"Then tell me what you do know."

She hesitated a moment more, then put down the tray and

folded her arms in front of her. "I don't know much, but it started about the time Brandon came to town. Wyatt and a few others were trying to bring in a gun show, and Brandon stopped it. I think Wyatt felt as if he'd been publicly humiliated, but Brandon didn't care. The whole thing has just sort of snowballed since then." Rachel broke off with a shake of her head and stared into a jar filled with jawbreakers to avoid looking at me. "Look, I know he's your brother and everything, and it's not as if I think he did it in cold blood. But you know what a hothead he is."

"A hothead? *Wyatt*?"

"Have you forgotten what he did to Tommy Jerrick at Homecoming?"

"That was *thirty years* ago."

"Memories last a long time. But that's not the only thing. You haven't been around. You don't know what he's like. He's . . . well, he's got an attitude, Abby. I'm sorry, but he does."

"There's a big difference between having an attitude and committing cold-blooded murder."

"I know that, but he has a history. He got so upset with Darren Broadbent over some rusty old cars in that field out by Wyatt's place, Darren had to call the cops. And you know how he is with Elizabeth. I mean, there are times when I actually feel sorry for her."

"Sorry? For *Elizabeth*? That's utterly ridiculous. Wyatt adores her."

Rachel's lips curved, but there was no warmth in her smile. "Wyatt is extremely jealous of her, I know that. He can't stand it when she goes anywhere or does anything without him."

I've never even seen a hint of jealousy from Wyatt, but then I've only really seen them together on holidays and my few rare visits home. A seed of doubt took root, but I shook it off. Though I couldn't imagine it of Elizabeth, if she *was* screwing around on him, maybe Wyatt had good reason to be jealous. Lord knows I'd been madder than a wet hen when I found out about Roger's affair.

"Wyatt doesn't try to restrict Elizabeth's activities," I

said, trying to reason through my confusion. "She's involved in just about everything."

The blond man left the store, and I had one brief pang of guilt for ignoring him. But my need to hear what Rachel had to say was a lot stronger.

"Elizabeth's a strong woman," Rachel agreed, "but even she can't stand up against it forever. I'm not sure I could put up with everything she does from Wyatt."

I was beginning to feel as if I'd stepped into an alternate universe, but Rachel looked so serious, I couldn't just dismiss what she was saying. "So tell me about these jealous episodes of his. What has he done? What has he said? I need specifics, Rachel, not just vague accusations."

Rachel gave that some thought. Just when I'd about convinced myself she was making up the whole thing, she spoke again. "Well, there was one time when we were getting ready for a church supper. Wyatt came storming into the gymnasium looking like he was about ready to explode. He walked right up to Elizabeth, grabbed her by the arm, and dragged her out of there like a rag doll."

Unbelievable. And yet . . . "Do you know why?"

Rachel's brows beetled over her nose. "Does it matter why? There's no excuse for treating a woman like that."

"I never said there was," I assured her quickly. "I just wondered if you knew what prompted it. I'm assuming he had a reason, right or wrong."

"If he did, Elizabeth didn't tell me what it was. She came back inside about ten minutes later and tried to act like nothing had ever happened."

"And you didn't ask her?"

"It was none of my business."

Right. "So was that the only time?"

Her lips pursed so tightly, tiny lines formed around them. "Of course not. She's dropped out of the book club, and she's stopped scrapbooking—and not because she's not interested, either. I don't know what's going on with Wyatt lately, but you're probably the only person in town who doesn't think he's at least capable of doing Brandon in."

Exhibiting the worst possible timing in the world, Meena stepped into the doorway and scowled at both of us. "Do you mind, Rachel? Some of us have places to be when we're through here."

Rachel jumped about a foot and dragged the tray off the counter. "I need to go." She started across the room, then checked herself and made eye contact with me. "Be careful, okay Abby? Don't let Wyatt drag you into this."

But Rachel's warning came too late. I was already in the middle, and I'd stay there as long as my brother was suspected of murder.

Chapter 10

Shortly after six o'clock that evening, I stepped out of Divinity and locked the door behind me. My neck and shoulders ached with the effort of keeping a smile on my face all day long, and a dull ache throbbed just behind my eyes. Clouds had rolled into the valley while I worked, and now they hung low and menacing along the tops of the mountains, matching my mood exactly. A stiff wind set the hanging planters along the street swinging, and I shivered as I tucked my deposit bag under my arm and turned toward the bank.

The lobby was already closed, but there's a teller window in the foyer that stays open until eight o'clock on weekdays. Usually, there's a long line when I get there, but tonight only one other person stood in the lobby.

Iris Quinn is a small woman of about sixty, with a wide smile, teeth too large for her face, and graying hair that hangs to the middle of her back. I don't think I've ever seen her when she wasn't wearing a cardigan, no matter what the weather. She runs Once Upon A Crime, a mystery book store on the next street over. She's not a pretty woman, but she's friendly and intelligent, and nobody knows their product the way Iris knows mystery books.

When the teller passed back her receipt, Iris tucked it into the shapeless leather bag on her shoulder and stepped away from the window. Today's cardigan was a dull gold. A pair of glasses dangled carelessly from the neck of her blouse. Without them, her eyes had a vague, unfocused look that disappeared the instant she saw me. "Why, Abby! Just the person I was hoping to see."

I'd been dealing with people all day, some of whom actually wanted to buy candy, some of whom were just morbidly curious about my brother's part in the fire. Iris's effusive greeting left me a little off-balance.

I took her place at the window and pushed my bag through the opening. "What can I do for you, Iris?"

"I need a couple of those gift baskets of yours for a book signing next Wednesday. Am I too late to order them?"

"Of course not. Do you want me to include anything special?"

A smile fluttered around her mouth. "Whatever you think a best-selling mystery author would like. Maybe some of those caramels Grace used to make, and that apricot almond bark is heavenly. If you have any in stock, put some of that in."

I didn't, but I could make some easily enough, so I nodded. "Sure. No problem. Anything else?"

"Whatever you think is best. I'll leave that up to you. I just want to make a good impression." Her smile faded, and she glanced over her shoulder. "Not that there's much we can do around here right now to make a good impression on anyone."

I wasn't sure what to say to that, so I said nothing at all.

Iris didn't seem to notice. "It's terrible about Brandon, isn't it? He was so young. Not even fifty, was he?"

"Forty-two."

"Such a shame. So do you think he was murdered? Or do you think he set the fire himself?"

"I don't particularly like either option," I admitted, "but I guess it had to be one or the other."

"Yes, I suppose you're right." She dug into her purse, pulled out a pot of lip balm, and spent a few seconds smoothing some over her lips. The pungent aroma of menthol filled the lobby and made my nose sting. "It's just so hard to believe. Murder. Here in Paradise. Although I guess Brandon did have his share of enemies."

I wondered if she was talking about the angry husband of some phantom married lover, or if she actually knew something. "He had enemies?"

"Don't we all?"

"I'd like to think I don't," I said with a weak smile. "But maybe you're right. Do you know who Brandon's enemies were?"

"Me?" She let out a laugh that was surprisingly girlish. "No. But it wouldn't surprise me to find out that he'd left a trail of unhappy people behind him. You know how much he liked to argue. I swear, sometimes it seemed like his greatest joy in life was goading people into fighting with him."

It wasn't the most flattering description I'd ever heard, but it was probably accurate. "Yeah, but those arguments were always over little things. Unimportant things."

"That depends on who you are, doesn't it? What seems like nothing to one person might mean life and death to someone else. You never know what might push someone over the edge. Even the mildest person in the world can snap under the right conditions."

I studied her plain face carefully, but I didn't think she was making veiled hints about Wyatt. I might not see my brother as the powder-keg-ready-to-explode that Rachel described, but even I know he's not mild. But if she wasn't talking about Wyatt, who was she thinking of? "Do you know something I don't?"

Iris's narrow eyes shuttered, and she turned toward the door. "Oh, now, Abby. What could I possibly know? I hardly even knew Brandon except to speak to."

I trailed her outside into the rising wind. "Look, I know you probably don't want to say the wrong thing about an innocent person, but the police think Wyatt's responsible for the fire and Brandon's death. He's not, of course, but if you know anything that might help, please tell me."

Iris stopped near the curb and turned. "I can't help you, Abby. I really can't. You should just leave things alone. Let the authorities figure this out. That's what they get paid for."

"My brother is in trouble," I argued. "I can't just sit around and do nothing."

The wind picked up Iris's hair and tossed it about her head. She tugged the edges of her shapeless sweater together and held them there. "Oh, all right. It's probably nothing, but if you get me involved in this thing, I'll never forgive you. I saw Brandon a few days ago, and something about that afternoon has been troubling me ever since."

"Why? What happened?"

"I saw him talking to someone. Arguing, really. And it wasn't just your run-of-the-mill argument. I can't put my finger on it, but they both seemed extremely angry. You might even say dangerously so."

My heart jumped into my throat. "Did you hear what they were arguing about?"

"I was too far away. By the time I got closer, the other man was gone. To be honest, the whole thing made me quite uncomfortable. I worried a little about what I should say to Brandon, but it didn't really matter since I'm not sure he even realized I was there."

"He didn't see you?"

"Oh, yes. We even spoke for a few minutes. But I don't think he was really aware of me, even then. He was too distracted."

"So who was he arguing with?"

"I don't have a clue." She made a vain attempt to control her hair, but it did no good. "I only saw him from behind, but there wasn't anything familiar about him."

"Did you notice anything unusual?"

She gave that some thought, but shook her head. "No. Sorry. He was medium height, medium build. You know . . . ordinary. He was wearing one of those stocking caps the kids all wear these days, so I can't even tell you what color his hair was."

"You think he was young?"

Iris shook her head thoughtfully. "No. He didn't seem like a young man, but I don't know why I feel that way. Young people move differently. This man was more . . . solid." She flashed an embarrassed smile. "Not much help, is it?"

"It's more than I knew ten minutes ago. I don't suppose you've told Detective Jawarski about this?"

Her eyes grew round and solemn. "I didn't see much point in doing that. After all, I don't know anything, *really*."

"Maybe not, but you might help take some of the suspicion off Wyatt."

"Maybe." Iris glanced up the street, chewing the corner of her lip. "Brandon is—*was* a bit mysterious, don't you think?"

"Do you?"

"I do. Think about it, Abby. What do you know about him, really? Where did he come from?"

"Texas."

"What part?"

I started to answer, realized I didn't know, and shut my mouth.

"What about his people? Do you know anything about them?"

"No," I admitted slowly, "but—"

Iris patted my arm. "Don't feel bad. I don't think anybody knows. Brandon never really shared much of himself with any of us."

"So you think this man may have been someone from Brandon's past?"

"It's possible, isn't it?"

"Yeah, but probably a little too convenient." I could just imagine how the police would react if I tried to convince them that a mysterious stranger from Brandon's past had set the fire. Jawarski would probably lock me up just for that.

"It's also possible," Iris said, more to herself than to me, "that Brandon set the fire himself, don't you think?"

I shook my head firmly. "People keep saying that, but he had no reason to set the fire. It's not like he needed the money."

"What if he did?"

"But he didn't."

"Maybe he didn't admit it," Iris said with a sly smile, "but I've heard rumors. Several of us have. That's one of the reasons so many people opposed the idea of expanding the Arts Festival. Folks thought that Brandon was more interested in lining his own pockets than doing what's best for the whole town."

Little prickles of discomfort raced up my spine. Ever since I was a little kid, I've hated feeling left out, and nothing's changed just because I'm an adult. Logically, I know that a person can't live away for twenty years, then come home again and expect everything to be the way it was, but that doesn't stop me from wishing. I hated feeling like the one girl who didn't get invited to the party, and I wondered how long it would take me to earn my way back into the inner circle, or if I ever would.

"I don't get it," I said. "How would the Arts Festival put money in Brandon's pockets?"

"Kickbacks."

"What?"

"That's the rumor." Iris found her glasses on their chain and spent a minute situating them on her face. "I don't know anything for sure, of course, but there has been talk that Brandon is overdrawn at the bank. I've even heard that some of his payroll checks have bounced in the past couple of months. But there's no telling whether or not that's true."

I scrambled to take in everything she was telling me. I'd always thought that Brandon was doing well at Man About Town, and this image just didn't fit with what I knew. "Who told you that he'd been bouncing checks?"

"You know how talk is. I don't remember where I heard it now, but I think it came from a reliable source." The clock at City Hall interrupted her, chiming the half hour. Iris looked up with a start, and her entire demeanor changed. "Six-thirty already? Oh, dear. I'm sorry, Abby. I hate to just toss all of this at you and run, but Carma will be wondering where I am. You know how she is."

I managed a weak smile. Neither Iris nor Carma has ever admitted that they're more than business partners and roommates, but I think almost everyone in town understands what's what. Some people accept it. Some don't. Same as anywhere else, I guess.

Carma is a notorious worrywart who comes unglued when Iris isn't where Carma expects her to be. Iris would never stick around to talk to me if she thought Carma was fretting.

"Just try not to worry about Wyatt," she said. "Things have a way of working out."

It was an optimistic outlook, but I was having a little trouble sharing it. All the possibilities were making my head spin. Had Brandon been the charming, friendly, funny man I thought I knew? Or a scheming stranger with a mysterious past? I wondered if I would ever know.

Chapter 11

I was still puzzling over my conversations with Rachel and Iris the next afternoon when I pulled up in front of the sprawling old farmhouse that had belonged to Elizabeth's family for four generations. The storm that had blown into the valley yesterday had settled in heavily, and the sky had darkened to an ominous slate gray. In the distance, thunder rumbled, and I could smell ozone spiking the air as I got out of my car.

A tray of caramel apples sat on the seat beside me, a treat for my nieces and nephews. Aunt Grace's apples had always been a particular favorite of mine, and I thought they might help the kids get through this difficult time—and earn me some good-aunt points at the same time. After all, Wyatt's kids barely knew me.

My own fault. I'm the one who left for college and never came back. I'm the one who let enthusiasm for my new life eclipse the old one. My nonexistent relationship with my nieces and nephews would take more than a few caramel apples to fix, but they were a start.

Elizabeth must have seen me coming because the door flew open before I was even up the steps to the front porch. With her sandy-red hair piled carelessly on top of her head, her face scrubbed clean, and one of Wyatt's T-shirts swimming on her, she looked scarcely older than her teenage daughters.

She held the door open with one hand and watched me clatter onto the old wooden porch, struggling not to spill the goodies I held. "You should have called before you drove all the way out here," she said, taking the tray out of my hands. "Wyatt's not here."

I shook the rain from my hair and pretended not to notice that she didn't seem all that pleased to see me. "That's okay. I came to talk to you."

"What for?"

"We're family. Do I need a reason?"

Elizabeth blocked the doorway for a minute longer, then, without a word, turned away to let me inside. The screen door banged shut behind me, and I closed the door against the storm. The big country kitchen had always felt warm and welcoming before. Today, it seemed cold and lifeless. I wondered if I was feeling the void caused by Wyatt's absence, or if there was something else at work here.

Elizabeth stood in front of the refrigerator, arms folded high on her chest, her eyes narrowed uncertainly. The muffled pounding of bass from a stereo overhead told me that at least one of my twin nieces was home. I glanced into the living room to make sure neither of the boys was in there, then tossed off a grin to break the tension and jerked my head toward the ceiling. "Dana or Danielle?"

"Both. They're punishing me."

Punishing her? Interesting. Did that mean the girls weren't on board with their parents' separation? I thought it might be a trifle crass to badger her with questions right off the bat, so I made myself comfortable at the table and tried some small talk. "Where are the boys?"

"Wyatt picked them up a couple of hours ago. He was going to take all the kids to dinner, but the girls aren't speaking to him, either."

Okay. If she wasn't going to pretend that everything was normal, I wouldn't, either. "What's going on around here, Elizabeth?"

She turned a tight scowl in my direction. "You don't know?"

"I've heard a few rumors. I'd rather hear the truth from you."

"You're Wyatt's sister. Why don't you ask him?"

"I have. He's not saying much."

"Really?" Elizabeth let out a skeletal laugh and mumbled, "That's a first."

"It doesn't take a rocket scientist to figure out that there's some bitterness here. So what's the deal?"

Elizabeth's mouth pinched. "There's no deal. We're just working a few things out, that's all."

"What things?"

"That's a little personal, isn't it? That's between Wyatt and me."

"Not anymore, it's not. Or haven't you heard what's been happening in town?"

"It's nothing. All marriages have trouble now and then."

"Yeah, but not like this. For twenty years you and Wyatt have had the best marriage I've ever seen. Now, suddenly, he's moved out, and you're here raising the kids on your own. Rumors are flying all over town. A man's dead, and the police think Wyatt's responsible. How much more would it take for you to think there's something we should be talking about?"

Elizabeth's jaw clenched and unclenched while she fought with herself over whether to talk to me or kick me out. I've seen her get stubborn with Wyatt and he usually caves in, but I am a whole lot more patient than my brother.

She stared into my eyes, trying to make me back down. I stared back, watching for the flicker that meant she was losing focus. It finally came, and a minute later she gave in. "You don't understand," she said. "It's not what anybody thinks."

"Okay. What is it?"

"You don't give up, do you?"

"Not when something's important to me. So tell me. *Please*. Why do people think Wyatt killed Brandon Mills?"

Elizabeth plowed her fingers through her hair, pulling locks of it from the clip that held it up. "Sometimes I hate the way the people in this town think everything is their business. We can't even have an argument without people thinking they have the right to comment."

"Yeah, well, that's the hell of a small town," I told her. "At least people care. If I'd been living here, maybe somebody would have told me about Roger and WhatsHerFace when they first started playing around. And that might have saved me the trouble of catching them making whoopee on my bedroom floor."

Her gaze flashed to mine, but I couldn't read the emotions there. "Yeah. Maybe. But then the whole town would have kept scorecards while you battled through the divorce."

That put a knot in my stomach. "Is that what you're doing? Getting a divorce?"

She sighed, but the wind rattled the window behind her and drowned out the sound. "Ask Wyatt."

"I thought *you* kicked *him* out."

"I did. But only because he wouldn't stop—" She cut herself off with a shake of her head and pulled two bottles from the fridge. "Do you want a beer? I think I need one."

I didn't, but I nodded, thinking it might help loosen her up.

She carried the bottles to the table and handed one to me. "I know finding out about Roger's affair was hard, Abby. I can't even imagine what you went through. But do you have any idea how hard it is to be accused of something you *didn't* do?"

I uncapped my bottle and took a sip. "Is that what happened?"

She nodded miserably. "After twenty years, you'd think my word would count for something, wouldn't you? But nothing I say makes any difference. He's convinced I'm lying, and the kids are half-convinced he's right. They're so confused right now, they don't know whether to pet the horse or saddle the dog."

"He's been talking to the kids about this?" Had he lost his mind?

Rain spattered against the window. Elizabeth glanced at it and shook her head. "No. He's not that far gone, I guess. But the kids hear things. You can't keep anything secret around here. And they're not babies. They're smart enough to figure out what's going on."

"So you *weren't* having an affair with Brandon?"

Elizabeth's eyes flew wide and indignation brought her face to life. "Absolutely not. Did you even think I *was*?"

"No. But how could Wyatt believe the rumors are true? He adores you. It doesn't make any sense."

"If you can figure out what's going on inside his head, you're a smarter woman than I am. I've been trying for months, and the only thing I can figure out is that he's having a midlife crisis. But if that's the case, I wish he'd just go out and buy a Porsche or something. Bankruptcy would be easier to handle than this."

She opened her bottle, but instead of drinking she focused on the metal cap as if it held clues to Wyatt's odd behavior. "There are times," she said after a minute, "when I've wondered if it has something to do with your divorce. Not that I'm blaming you or anything," she assured me quickly, "but I think finding out about Roger really bothered him. He couldn't figure out how you didn't know. I mean, Roger had been seeing that girl for what—a year?"

Now *there* was a subject I loved talking about, but I couldn't very well shut down if I wanted Elizabeth to talk to me. I watched the trees in the yard bending under the onslaught of the storm and said, "Eighteen months."

"And you really didn't have a clue?"

I'd asked myself the same question a thousand times, but the answer kept changing. "It's hard to explain," I told her. "Looking back, I can see all kinds of clues, but at the time I didn't see a thing. I guess maybe I didn't want to know."

"It's that part that I think bothers Wyatt the most. I think he started stewing on it—you know how he does."

I nodded slowly. That made sense, but according to Rachel there'd been trouble between Elizabeth and Wyatt for longer than I'd been divorced. "So you think he just imagined all of this?"

"What else could have happened?"

I hesitated to ask the next question, but I had to. Skimming over the rough parts wouldn't help anybody. "Has he ever hurt you, Elizabeth?"

She gaped at me. "Who? Wyatt?"

"Has he?"

"Are you asking if he's ever hit me?"

"Hit you. Shoved you. Dragged you out of the church like a rag doll."

"Is that a serious question?"

"I'm afraid so."

She barked a laugh and sat back hard in her chair. "Someone actually told you that Wyatt dragged me out of the church like a rag doll?"

"Someone mentioned it."

"Oh, this is unbelievable. Who was it?"

It wasn't exactly loyalty to Rachel that kept me silent. I just didn't think dropping her name would be the smartest move considering Elizabeth's current mood. "I don't remember who it was," I said. "And it really doesn't matter. The point is that people are talking about it. Did it happen, or didn't it?"

"No, it didn't happen. At least not the way you're making it sound."

"Then how?"

She let out a huge sigh and crossed her legs. "I shouldn't even dignify that question with an answer."

"You have to dignify it, Elizabeth. This isn't a game we're playing. You might be pissed off as hell at Wyatt right now, but do you really want the father of your children in prison for murder?" She didn't say anything, so I pressed a little harder. "How did it happen? Be honest with me."

"It happened," she said, "because he found out I'd lied to him."

Her voice was so low, I wasn't sure I'd heard her right. "You lied to him? About what?"

The lights flickered, and the music overhead went strangely quiet. "It was stupid, really. A stupid decision on my part. I would have taken it back if I could have, and I'd have done everything differently. But hindsight is always twenty-twenty, isn't it?"

"What did you lie about?"

"I had coffee with Brandon a few times. That's all. Just coffee. I don't know why. We'd been working together on a project—I can't even remember what it was now. Anyway, we got to talking. You know how you do. One thing led to another, and I came home late a couple of times. Nothing happened," she assured me quickly. "We just lost track of time. Maybe I should have told Wyatt the truth, but it didn't seem like a good idea at the time."

"So you lied."

She nodded miserably. "I told him I'd been talking, but I didn't tell him with who. And then a little while later I realized that Brandon was expecting more out of the relationship than I was. The minute I realized that, I put at end to it. But by that time it was too late to tell Wyatt the truth."

"It's never too late to tell the truth," I said. My voice sounded pinched and disapproving, but I couldn't change that.

Elizabeth's eyes pleaded with me to understand, but I was having trouble doing that. Maybe she hadn't had sex with Brandon, but there'd obviously been an emotional connection between them. Sometimes emotional intimacy is more threatening than physical. *Any* kind of infidelity leaves a nasty taste in my mouth.

"How did Wyatt find out?"

"One of his buddies saw us having coffee and, of course, he couldn't wait to let Wyatt know."

"I guess somebody had to."

Elizabeth glowered at me. "*Did* they?"

"Wyatt deserved to know."

"Know what? Nothing was going on. They should have just left well enough alone."

"You were seeing another man and lying to your husband about it," I pointed out. "Maybe you didn't see it as wrong, but obviously other people did."

"I *wasn't* having an affair."

"Maybe not technically, but what you were doing must have felt wrong or you would told Wyatt about it yourself."

She reached for the bottle in front of her. "I should have known you'd take Wyatt's side in this."

Maybe she should have. Frankly, I couldn't decide what I was feeling. I was angry for Wyatt and furious with myself. It wasn't that I'd ever expected my friendship with Brandon to turn into something more, but I'd sure been blinded by his charm. It was particularly galling to realize that, like Elizabeth, I'd actually thought that I had my eyes wide open the whole time Brandon had been busy pulling the wool down over them.

"When did all this happen?"

"A couple of years ago."

"That long ago? Well then why did you kick Wyatt out now?"

"I asked him to leave because he can't seem to get over it. He doesn't trust me, and he's always calling to check up on me. I'm sorry that I hurt him. Really, I am. And I've given up almost everything I used to do, hoping that seeing me here with the kids will make him feel better. But nothing helps, and I can't spend the rest of my life doing penance for one stupid mistake. I just can't live that way."

I tried like hell not to let my lousy marriage infect theirs, but I just couldn't convince myself that Elizabeth was the victim here. "I don't understand," I said. "If this is all old news, why do the police think Wyatt suddenly went off the deep end?"

Elizabeth hesitated over that one. "Because Brandon called me last week," she admitted after a long time. "He said he had something important to talk to me about, and he asked me to meet him for coffee."

"And you *agreed*?"

"He sounded upset."

Until that moment, I'd always thought of Elizabeth as an intelligent woman. "When did *that* happen?"

She looked miserable. "The day of the fire."

My whole system recoiled as if she'd tossed a pot of icy water into my face. Did that mean Brandon stood me up so he could meet my sister-in-law? That felt wrong on about a dozen different levels. "What time did you meet him?"

"It was about seven, I guess. We thought it would be safe since everyone would be at the meeting." The lights flickered again, and Elizabeth pulled two candles from the junk drawer. "It wasn't what you're thinking, Abby. He said he needed help with something. Something important."

I wanted to slap a little common sense into her, but I was probably too late. "So was it all that important?"

"I don't know. He was waiting outside in the parking lot when I got there and said he had to meet somebody else instead."

I could have told her not to feel bad. That was more than he'd done for me. "So you didn't actually talk to him?"

She shook her head. "I wouldn't even have met him if he hadn't sounded so strange when he called. I really believed he needed my help."

If Brandon was in trouble, why would he turn to *her* for help? A selfish little voice inside wondered *Why not me?* But I ignored it. The point was that Brandon had called Elizabeth, a married woman whose husband wasn't exactly Father Peace. He must have known that meeting her would mean trouble, so why her? "You have no idea what he wanted help with?"

"None. He said he'd tell me later, and then he left. I came home. The next thing I knew, that idiot Nate Svboda was on the phone telling Wyatt about the fire."

I guess I had my answer about that middle-of-the-night phone call. Nate must have known about Elizabeth's relationship with Brandon, but it rankled that Wyatt would tell Nate and not say a word to me.

"Why did Nate think Wyatt should know about the fire?"

"How should I know? Maybe so he could celebrate." Bitterness filled her voice and pinched her expression, but I still couldn't work up a lot of sympathy for her.

I had to force out my next question. "Do *you* think Wyatt killed Brandon?"

Elizabeth lifted her chin and looked me square in the eye. "Honestly? I don't know. I don't want to think so, but there are times when I wonder. He didn't come home until late that night, and he refused to tell me where he'd been. He's always had a temper. You know that. But lately . . ." She let her voice trail away.

I could have said a thousand different things, but I didn't want to make it easy on her, so we sat there listening to the wind blow. Part of me wished that I'd left well enough alone. That I'd stayed back at Divinity stocking the shelves, ordering supplies, trying new recipes, or trying to perfect the old. Maybe that's why Aunt Grace thought spending time in the candy kitchen was so therapeutic.

"Look," Elizabeth said after a while. "I know I made a mistake getting so involved with Brandon. I just kept telling myself that we were friends. It didn't seem right for Wyatt to dictate who I could and couldn't be friends with. But I guess you're right. I lied to him. That has to mean something, doesn't it?"

I certainly thought so. Her involvement with Brandon and her lack of faith in Wyatt suddenly made me itchy to get away. At least now I understood all the sly glances and thinly veiled hints I'd been tripping over in town. I could even understand, in a twisted sort of way, why Jawarski considered my brother a suspect.

Standing abruptly, I turned toward the door. "What time is Wyatt bringing the boys back?"

"By eight. They have school tomorrow. Do you want me to tell him to call you?"

I shook my head. "He won't do it, and if he knows I've been talking to you, he'll work even harder to avoid me when I call him. I'd rather catch him off-guard."

I told myself that Elizabeth couldn't really doubt Wyatt's innocence. If she had, she wouldn't have let him take the boys. Whatever her faults, she's always been a good mother. But my visit with her had left me melancholy.

As I started to step outside again, one more question occurred to me. "Did Brandon ever tell you anything about his past? Where he came from? His family?"

Elizabeth looked startled, but she shook her head. "He never talked about the past with me. Only the future."

After she shut the door between us, I wondered if she and Wyatt would get past this. Part of me hoped they would, but if he couldn't forgive her and move on with their lives, I'd understand completely. I'd been there and done that, and I had the emotional scars to prove it. The truth was, I didn't know if *I'd* be able to look at her the same way after this, and I didn't know what any of this would do to the kids.

Hunching my shoulders against the driving rain, I tried not to slip in the mud as I ran for the Jetta. For the first time

ever, I felt a flash of relief that Roger and I hadn't had children. I'd wanted children of my own so desperately for a
while, the relief I felt now seemed wrong. But I was relieved.
Maybe we'd made a mess of our marriage, but at least the
only people we'd damaged had been ourselves.

I wished I could say the same thing for Wyatt and
Elizabeth.

Chapter 12

Rain-drenched and aching inside, I leaned my forehead against the Jetta's steering wheel and tried to ignore the guilt I felt over not saying hello to Dana and Danielle while I was inside. I probably should have gone upstairs and spent a few minutes, but they weren't even speaking to their own parents, and they hardly knew me. I wasn't sure I could give them what they needed right now, but I was pretty sure caramel apples weren't going to be enough.

Sheets of water ran down the windshield and the rain-heavy air landed hard in my lungs. Anger made it even more difficult to breathe. After a while, I realized that Elizabeth was probably watching me, and the overwhelming need to get away before Wyatt came back washed away everything else.

I needed to talk to him, but not here.

Battling a headache, I started the car, shifted into reverse, and stomped on the gas. My tires spun in the mud for a few seconds, then caught and shot me backwards toward the road. I had half a second to enjoy the satisfaction before my neck snapped forward, and the horrifying sounds of metal and shattering glass filled the car. A sharp pain ping-ponged around inside my head, and my neck felt as if someone had tried to wring it.

I shoved the gear shift into park and glanced at the dashboard clock, thinking that Wyatt must have come back a few minutes early. Great. If I thought he'd been in a foul mood before, just wait. On the plus side, maybe I wouldn't have to explain why I was here—at least at first. He'd be too busy yelling at me.

I fumbled for the door handle just as a pair of denim-clad legs appeared in my window and a deep voice demanded, "What in the hell do you think you're doing?"

I'm sure it occurred to me on some level that the voice was too deep to be Wyatt's, but I shrugged it off. I opened the door, misjudged the distance, and bashed it straight into the legs in front of me. With a groan, I shut it again and rolled down the window. "Look, I'm sorry, but don't wig out on me, okay? I didn't see you back there."

"How could you see me, Ms. Shaw? You didn't even look."

Recognition froze me solid. I swore under my breath and felt the half-bottle of beer I'd swallowed in Elizabeth's kitchen churning in my stomach. I craned to see out my rear window and realized that I'd bashed in the front of an obviously new Blazer belonging to one very unhappy cop.

Those aren't ideal circumstances, no matter who you are. They're even worse when the cop thinks you're an accessory to murder. I'd have crawled into a hole gladly if one had opened up for me. The thought crossed my mind to put the Jetta into gear and make a run for it, but that might be a little difficult with Jawarski's Chevy attached to my bumper.

Upstairs, the blind in the twins' bedroom twitched. That meant that at least one of my young, impressionable nieces was watching, so I gathered as much dignity as I could and hauled myself back out into the rain. "There's no need to get nasty, Jawarski. I didn't hit you on purpose."

"For your sake, I hope not. You want to tell me where you were going in such a hurry?"

"Home," I said, doing my best not to breathe on him. "It's been a long day, and I'm cold, wet, and tired. You want to tell me what you're doing here?"

"Not especially." He strolled to the back of my car and looked at the damage. "Have you ever thought of looking over your shoulder before you step on the gas?"

Deep down inside, a voice whispered not to antagonize him, but that cautious voice has never had a lot of influence over me. "Novel concept," I said around a pseudo-sweet smile. "I'll have to try it one of these days."

The look he shot me could have carved stone. "All I can say is you'd better have insurance."

Rain plastered my hair to my head and water snaked down my neck, soaking my clothes. "Well, of course I do," I snapped. "I'm not completely irresponsible." I jerked my head toward the house where Elizabeth had appeared in the open doorway, watching us. "Do you mind if I get in out of the rain, or is keeping me out here part of my punishment?"

He rolled his eyes and waved me off.

I started away, but that stupid inner voice of mine reminded me that I had caused the accident. Impatient with myself for feeling guilty, I turned back toward him. My feet slipped on the mud, and only a miracle kept me from landing on my butt. "You might as well come with me. There's nothing you can do out here except get yourself worked up."

He didn't even look at me. "I'll be fine."

"Suit yourself. Do you want me to call somebody?"

"Sure. How about your insurance agent?"

"First thing in the morning. Don't worry so much, Jawarski. Your Blazer will be like new in no time."

I sloshed toward the house, toed off my muddy shoes, and slipped past Elizabeth into the kitchen for the second time in less than an hour. She shooed me down the hall into the bathroom, disappeared for a minute, and returned with one of Wyatt's clean T-shirts. Grudgingly grateful, I toweled my hair dry, stripped off my wet blouse, and slipped the T-shirt over my head. My jeans were soaked through, but I wasn't about to lose those with Jawarski lurking about.

The homey scents of detergent and bleach filled the air around me, and sadness crept into my heart. Why would a woman who had all of this let herself be taken in by a man like Brandon? Hadn't Wyatt loved her enough? Or had he loved her too much? Maybe this wasn't the life she really wanted, although twenty years seemed like a long time to pretend.

Tired and confused, I tossed the towel over the side of the bathtub, and skimmed a glance at my reflection in the mirror. My hair stuck out at all angles, and my face looked as pale as powdered sugar. Good thing I wasn't trying to impress anybody.

Back in the kitchen, Elizabeth had made fresh coffee, and a waterlogged Jawarski sat at the table, his face tight, his expression pinched. Neither spoke when I entered the room, and I wondered if they'd fallen silent when they heard me coming or if they were both trying to pretend he wasn't here to dig at her secrets.

I didn't want to sit with Jawarski, but I wasn't going to stand up all night, either. Pretending a nonchalance I didn't feel, I dragged a chair from the table and plopped myself into it.

He grunted and slid a glance in my direction. "Don't get any big ideas about leaving. The sheriff's department is sending someone to investigate."

"It's a fender bender."

"It's an accident, and I'm a member of the police department. We'll go by the book, Ms. Shaw."

"Fine." I accepted a cup of coffee from Elizabeth. The heat on my hands made me realize just how cold I really was. When I saw that the beer bottles had mysteriously disappeared, I flashed a silent thank-you at my sister-in-law. Realizing that I might still have alcohol on my breath, I lunged forward and pulled a bag of tortilla chips from the counter. Half a beer might not register on a Breathalyzer, but why take chances?

Besides, it was already after eight o'clock, and I was starving. I tend to eat under stress, which may explain the extra baggage I'm carrying on my hips, and I was definitely under stress now. "How long do you think we'll have to stay here?"

Jawarski scowled at the mug he cradled between both hands. "I have no idea."

He fell silent again, and I decided not to push him into conversation. But the dark looks he lasered at me from under that thick swag of eyebrows said more than enough. Elizabeth excused herself to check on the girls. I chewed a few chips and watched the second hand on the kitchen clock go around in circles. I lasted ten solid minutes before I just couldn't stand the silence any longer.

"Look," I said, "I'm sorry. I didn't mean to hit you."

Jawarski dragged his gaze away from the window and settled it on me with all the enthusiasm of a kid who's just been given a plate of Brussels sprouts.

"It was an accident," I said. "By definition, that's something that doesn't happen on purpose."

"Ms. Shaw—"

"Would you please call me Abby? Ms. Shaw is way too formal."

He didn't make any promises.

"I was upset," I explained.

"Did it ever occur to you that that might not be the best time to get behind the wheel?"

"I didn't think about that. I just want to get out of here—" I cut myself off before I could say anything about Wyatt and finished with a lame, "—and back to the store."

"The store?" Jawarski looked skeptical. "You have some kind of candy emergency going on down there?"

He really was unlikable. I muttered a sullen, "No."

"You're still trying to protect your brother?"

"My brother doesn't need protection."

"Ah. I see. You still don't think he did it."

"No, I do not."

"Well, I'm sorry, Ms. Shaw, but the evidence is piling up."

"Evidence that Wyatt murdered Brandon?"

Jawarski dipped his massive head.

"I don't believe it."

He shrugged that set of broad, rain-drenched shoulders. "As long as the district attorney and a jury believe it, that's all I need."

I had the almost irresistible urge to belt him, but I figured that wouldn't do much to help Wyatt. Or me. I balled my hands into fists and dug fingernails into my palms so hard I wouldn't have been surprised to find out I'd drawn blood.

"Do you even care about finding the truth, or are you just on a witch-hunt?"

"Of course I'm after the truth. I'm hot on its trail."

"I'll bet you are. What kind of evidence do you have against my brother?"

"Enough. He isn't helping his case any by refusing to talk with me."

Even I knew that avoiding the police was a stupid move. "You haven't talked to him yet?"

"Not for lack of trying. I came here tonight because I had reason to believe he would be here at eight o'clock." He shot a pointed look at the clock, then zapped me with the same look. "Obviously, he's changed his mind."

"The only evidence you could possibly have against Wyatt is circumstantial. That doesn't mean a whole lot in a case like this. You could probably find as much evidence on anyone else in town if you looked hard enough."

"I doubt that."

"Have you tried? What about your original theory that Brandon set the fire himself? What happened to that?"

"You told me yourself that it was impossible."

"You stopped pursuing that idea because I said to? In that case, stop trying to prove Wyatt guilty."

He actually laughed—almost. It was really more like a curl of the lip, but it made him look almost human. "So now you *want* Brandon to be the one who set the fire?"

Better him than Wyatt, I guess. I almost said so aloud, but I couldn't. "It wasn't either of them. Wyatt's not a murderer, and Brandon wasn't facing some kind of ruin that drove him to arson. I wish you'd at least consider the possibility that someone else is guilty."

He curved his lip again. "For the record, Ms. Shaw, you really don't know what I'm considering, do you? I understand that you believe someone else is responsible for the fire and the death of Mr. Mills, but what you believe doesn't do me a whole lot of good. Unless you can prove your theories, that's all they are."

"Proving that somebody didn't do a thing isn't exactly easy," I pointed out. "I mean Brandon is— He *is* . . . dead." I forced my emotions aside and tried to remain logical. Getting emotional wouldn't accomplish anything. "And there was a fire. And we know that *somebody* set it. I don't know how to prove Wyatt *didn't* do it without proving that someone else did."

Jawarski inclined his head an inch or two.

"What about the dog?" Elizabeth asked from the doorway.

I jumped at the sound of her voice. Jawarski looked equally startled. And confused. "You think the dog set the fire?" he asked.

Elizabeth rolled her eyes. "Of course not. But don't you think it's strange that he wasn't with Brandon at the time?"

In all the excitement I'd forgotten about Max, but Elizabeth was right. Brandon had never gone anywhere without him. It had never occurred to me that he might not have been with Brandon that night. "If he wasn't with Brandon," I said, "where was he?"

"Across town with Chelsea Jenkins."

It took a second for that to sink in. I shot a glance at Jawarski, but he was no help. "He was *what*?" I demanded.

"Across town at Chelsea Jenkins's apartment." Elizabeth found some *con queso* dip in the refrigerator and pushed it toward me. "I talked to her this morning, and she told me she has him."

I dragged the jar closer and plunged a chip into the cheese dip. I didn't let myself ask why Elizabeth had been chatting with Chelsea. I was afraid she might tell me. "Did she say how she got him?"

"Only that Brandon asked her to watch him."

"Impossible. When Brandon mountain-biked, Max ran beside him. When he dated, Max chaperoned. I never knew Brandon to leave Max with someone else. Not for any reason. If Chelsea has him . . ." My brain went into high gear, trying to process all of this at once. Chelsea was young, but to the extent Brandon had a right arm at the store, she'd been it. Even so, she'd never been in charge of Max. At least not that I knew about. True, I'd learned quite a few things in the past couple of days that I hadn't known before, but I could more easily imagine Brandon trying to sleep with my sister-in-law than I could believe him asking Chelsea to take Max somewhere.

So why *did* Chelsea have Max? Was she capable of arson? Of murder? Did she even have a motive? Were a couple of bounced payroll checks enough?

The doorbell rang, announcing the arrival of the sheriff's deputy, putting everything else on hold. We trooped onto the porch, answered questions, and filled out paperwork while the rain slowed and eventually stopped. It took so long, it was dark by the time the deputy wrote out a ticket, which I accepted with as much dignity as I could muster.

While Elizabeth, Jawarski, and the deputy looked on, I put my car in gear and backed carefully out of the driveway. I'd lost a taillight in the accident, and my rear bumper was hanging at an angle as I rolled away. All in all, not my best night, but I wasn't worried about the ticket, the damage to my car, or even the increasing grumble coming from my stomach.

All I could think about was Chelsea Jenkins—and Max.

Chapter 13

". . . I don't know what that girl was thinking," Karen said, pulling a box of lemon drops from the supply cupboard. "I've told her over and over again, make sure you lock the door behind you when you come in from school. Even Paradise isn't completely safe anymore. Wouldn't you think an eleven-year-old girl would be just a little nervous after there's been a murder in the neighborhood?"

I nodded, only half-listening to the chatter that had been running nonstop for the past two hours. I love Karen. Really. She's my cousin, and she's saved my hide more than once in the past six months. She's also the closest thing I have to a sister. But I don't understand the need to let every single thought that passes through her head slip out from between her lips.

She stopped working and turned to look at me. "Well, wouldn't you?"

Apparently, she expected an answer this time. Who knew? Most of the morning's nonstop "conversation" hadn't needed any input from me—a good thing since I'd been too busy puzzling about how Chelsea had ended up with Max and wondering if Jawarski had talked to her yet.

When Karen gave an exaggerated sigh, I met her gaze and

tried to look connected. "Paige is young. Maybe she doesn't really understand what happened."

"Oh, she understands all right." Karen shoved the box at me and turned back to rummage for more. "Sergio and I had a long talk with her about it, and she fully comprehends that Brandon has been killed. She just doesn't think that murder is any big deal, and do you know why?" She whipped around again, this time holding a box of licorice pastels. My brief input into the conversation was no longer required. "Television, that's what's behind it. She sees so much violence and death on the damn boob tube, she's immune to it. I swear I'm going to have Sergio get rid of the TV for good. This weekend."

I nodded and scooped lemon drops into the gift basket I was filling. I'd always thought of Chelsea Jenkins as sort of a dim bulb, but what if I'd been wrong?

"I mean it," Karen warned, watching my reaction carefully. "Out it goes." Closing the storage room door with a bang, she came to stand in front of me, hands on hips, round face puckered by a deep, disapproving scowl. "All right, what is it?"

"What's what?"

"What has you so distracted this morning? You've hardly heard a word I've said. So what are you thinking about? The fire again?"

"In a way," I admitted. "What do you know about Chelsea Jenkins?"

"About Chelsea?" Looking intrigued, Karen rescued a couple of pecan delights from the cooling tray and handed one to me. "She's an odd girl, but I've told you that before. Why are you asking now?"

"Do you think she's capable of murder?"

Karen recoiled slightly. "Chelsea? Are you serious?"

I shrugged. "I don't know, but Elizabeth says that Chelsea has Brandon's dog. No matter how hard I try, I can't make that make sense to me."

Stern-faced, Karen sat across from me. "Why does it have to make sense to you?"

I nibbled at one edge of the candy and spent a few seconds savoring the buttery taste on my tongue. "Because Wyatt's in trouble," I said at last, "and *something* about this whole stupid mess needs to make sense before he's out of trouble again."

"I understand that, but it's not your job to get him out of trouble."

"Who else will do it if I don't?"

Impatience flashed across Karen's face. "Oh, I don't know, maybe the police. Last time I looked, investigating murder fell under their jurisdiction."

"Has it escaped your notice that the police think he's guilty?"

"They think it's possible," Karen corrected me. She shifted, hit the table with her knee, and set a stack of air-tight containers filled with peanut brittle teetering. "But that doesn't mean they've stopped investigating."

Since Karen didn't notice, I leaned up to steady the brittle before it fell. "You don't know that. Have you heard one other person named as a suspect? I sure haven't."

"No, but I haven't spent a lot of time talking to the police about the case, either." She uncapped a container and snitched a piece of brittle. If we kept eating inventory at this rate, neither of us would fit into a thing in our closets. "Look," she said, "I understand that you're worried about Wyatt, but getting involved in a murder investigation just isn't something normal, sane people do."

"I know that. And if my brother wasn't the only suspect, believe me, I wouldn't go anywhere near the case. But he is. Frankly, I'm surprised that you aren't as eager to clear his name as I am. You have children to think about. It won't do them any good to have a convicted felon in the family."

Karen's eyes narrowed dangerously. "That's playing dirty. Of course I want Wyatt cleared, and not just for the kids' sake. I'm just worried about how involved you're getting, that's all. I mean, it's not as if you know what you're doing."

"I know how to ask questions."

Karen's face clouded with irritation. "Tracking down a murderer isn't like making candy, Abby. There's no recipe to follow, and if you make a mistake, you can't just toss the mess into the trash."

More than a little irritated myself, I waved away her

objections. "I haven't always needed to follow a recipe to get through the day," I reminded her sharply.

"That's true. But just look how your life turned out then."

She couldn't have hurt me more if she'd slapped me. I moved the peanut brittle out of her reach and dumped pastels into the gift basket in front of me. "Are you going to answer my question or not?"

"And encourage you? Not a chance."

"Come on, Karen. Just tell me what you know about Chelsea Jenkins. I promise I won't get myself into some kind of trouble. I just want to know why Brandon left his dog with her, that's all. And don't tell me you don't know, because I won't believe you. You know everything."

"Not everything," she said, but it was a token protest only. The twinkle of pleasure in her eyes left no doubt in my mind.

"Okay, then, tell me what you do know. She's not from around here originally, even I know that."

"No, she's not. If I remember right, she moved here shortly after Brandon did."

"Do you know where she's from?"

"Somewhere in the Midwest, I think. Illinois, maybe?" Wrinkles creased Karen's forehead. "I really don't know a lot about her, Abby. That's the truth. Do you seriously think she might have started the fire?"

"I think it's possible."

"But why?"

"That," I admitted, "is the million-dollar question. Do you know where she lives?"

"No."

"Can you find out?"

"No."

"Karen—"

"No, Abby. No. You are not one of Charlie's Angels. You own a candy shop."

"I know that, but—"

"Well, what if Chelsea is the murderer? How will you protect yourself if she tries to hurt you? Fling peanut brittle at her?"

"I'll figure that out."

"How? Brandon couldn't."

I'll admit that made my pulse stutter, but I wasn't ready to back down. "Fine. Then I'll find out from someone else."

Anger flared in Karen's eyes. "And do what?"

"I'll know that after I talk to her."

"Oh, now *there's* a convincing argument. Why didn't you just say that in the first place? You're being stupid, Abby. I don't want any part of this." Karen turned away as if she thought the conversation was over.

I barely resisted the urge to fling peanut brittle at *her*. "All I want is to find out why she has Max," I shouted, but the bell over the front door rang, and Richie Bellieu sashayed into the shop. My heart dropped, and I knew the argument was over—at least for now.

Unlike Iris, who keeps her sexuality a secret, Richie practically flaunts his. Arms wide, spiked hair bobbing a little with each step, he rushed Karen and swept her into a huge hug. "Karen, darling," he said, making kissing motions at the air near her cheeks, "don't you look fabulous this morning?" He spotted me in the kitchen and wriggled his fingers over Karen's shoulders. "Abby, that sweatshirt is *so* your color."

Yeah. Gray. I swallowed my temporary defeat and forced a smile. "Morning, Richie. How can we help you?"

He released Karen and pressed a hand to his chest. "I desperately need your help. We have a huge group coming to stay at the B and B this weekend, and we're out of *everything*. I need something to fill the dishes in each of the guest rooms, and I need something terribly special for the lobby and the lounge." He lowered his voice half a decibel and dragged Karen away. "I'm not supposed to say anything, but these people are from Hollywood. They told Dylan they're coming to scout a location for a new movie, so naturally I want everything to be just perfect when they get here."

His voice trailed away as they turned the corner, and the last thing I saw was the triumphant gleam on Karen's face. She should have known better.

Giving up just isn't something I do.

Karen managed to dodge my questions for the rest of the afternoon. I spent some time trying to find a line on Chelsea

Jenkins, but she wasn't listed in the phone book, and none of the people I called knew where to find her. Apparently, my sister-in-law was the only person around who knew where Chelsea lived, but Elizabeth wasn't answering the phone—at least not for me.

I tried again, without success, to reach my brother and fielded questions from my mother who called to tell me about a new recipe for pecan logs she'd just found, and to complain that she was having trouble finding Wyatt. Maybe I should have told her what was going on, but I'd had enough trouble telling her when my life fell apart. I didn't want to be the one who told her about Wyatt and Elizabeth, and I hoped she'd never need to know that her baby boy was under suspicion for murder.

A little before six, I left Karen to lock up the shop and set off on foot to make a couple of deliveries. I delivered a candy bouquet to Lois Williamson at the shoe repair shop and dropped three pounds of Divinity's special sparkling hard candy assortment at Curl Up and Dye. Every one of the women who works there (and most of their clientele) is on a perpetual diet, so I don't know where the candy goes, but it disappears like magic every week.

Paisley Pringle bounced around the parlor in a bright yellow sundress and matching flip-flops, trying to convince me that I should let her "do something" to my hair. I don't mean to be rude, but if Paisley's hair is what I can expect for my money, I'll pass. It took almost half an hour, but I finally escaped without a manicure, without a pedicure, without frosted highlights, and without a head full of hair product.

With the rest of the evening to call my own, I decided to stroll past Man About Town again—at least what was left of it. I was halfway there when I noticed a familiar Buick Regal on the street in front of the Paradise Playhouse and decided to make a slight detour.

I'd promised to buy advertising for Divinity in the theater's next playbill, and I really should confirm the arrangement with Vonetta Cummings, the theater manager. But that wasn't the only reason for my visit. Chelsea Jenkins had appeared in a couple of productions at the Playhouse in recent months, and I hoped Vonetta would know where to find her—and that she'd share that information with me.

Posters advertising the theater's next production, *Forever Plaid,* hung in one window; a brightly colored poster listing the season's full schedule hung in the other. I scanned the list quickly and made a mental note to buy tickets to several of the shows.

Inside the deserted lobby, props lined the walls, and the concession stand stood empty, waiting for tonight's crowd. I could hear music and laughter coming from the back of the theater, probably from the rehearsal hall, but Vonetta rarely attends rehearsals, so I decided not to waste my time looking for her there.

I turned in the other direction, passed the ticket window, and walked down the short hallway that leads to Vonetta's small office. Her door was ajar, and I could see her sitting behind the desk, the telephone receiver glued to her ear. She grinned broadly when she saw me and motioned for me to come inside.

There's only one word to describe Vonetta—regal. She's tall, slim, and powerful, always perfectly put together, always clothed in something that celebrates her African-American heritage. Her short black hair may have started turning gray in recent years, but her office hasn't changed a bit.

Scripts, CDs, video tapes, sheet music, and pieces of a hundred different costumes litter almost every inch of the small room, leaving just enough space for Vonetta to squeeze in.

She gestured toward a chair buried beneath a mound of paper, so I moved the stack to the floor and sat. It had been a long time since I'd been here, and old memories came flooding back. My first and last production for the Playhouse was *The King and I.* I'd been one of the nameless wives—a human set prop whose only job was to smile, provide occasional musical backup for the main characters, and look pretty. And I wasn't very good at any of it.

I was only sixteen at the time, and I'd been thrilled to be part of the play—until Vonetta cast me in that nothing role and made Chrissie Montague a dancer. I don't like to think

I'm a sore loser, but that decision effectively ended my career in theater. I'm sure it would have ended anyway. If *The King and I* hadn't done the trick, going away to college and meeting Roger would have. My husband had done his best to eradicate all evidence of my upbringing during the early years of our marriage and I, God help me, had let him.

But like I said, I try never to think about Roger.

After a few minutes Vonetta finished her phone call and beamed at me. "Abby Shaw. I heard you were back in town. I've been meaning to get down there and say hello."

"And I've been meaning to do the same thing. Life gets in the way sometimes."

She nodded and moved a stack of folders from one spot on her desk to another. Vonetta's organized. You'd just never know it to look at her workspace. "I'm sorry about your aunt," she said. "I know how close you were to her."

Even all these months later, it still hurt to think about losing her. I choked out a "Thank you." Vonetta sensed my discomfort and tried to lighten the mood. "So what brings you here? Don't tell me you're thinking about joining us again."

I laughed and shook my head. "Not yet. I'm still trying to get my head above water at the shop."

"Then you've come about the ad space?"

I wagged my head yes-and-no. "I still want to do it," I assured her so she wouldn't misunderstand. "But I need to ask you a big favor."

"Oh?"

"I'm trying to find Chelsea Jenkins. I'm hoping you can help me."

Vonetta's expression didn't change, but the smile faded from her eyes. "Why do you want to find her?"

I shrugged. "I've been thinking about her since the fire. I just want to make sure she's all right."

"Yeah, and I'm Oprah Winfrey," Vonetta said with a sharp laugh. Before she could say more, a digital ring tone sounded, and she scowled at the cell phone on her hip. "Walk with me," she said, rising abruptly. "There's a delivery at the loading dock."

One thing you don't do is argue with Vonetta. Like I said, she's organized, and her days follow a strict timetable. I shot to my feet and followed her out into the hallway. She set off at a rapid clip—another thing about her that hasn't changed.

"Talk to me, child. Why do you really want to find Chelsea?"

"I want to find out what she knows about the fire that killed Brandon Mills."

"And what makes you think she knows anything about it?"

"I just learned that she has his dog, but Brandon never let that dog out of his sight. I want to know why Max wasn't with Brandon when he died."

Vonetta glided through the lobby and then turned down the long, narrow corridor that leads to the dressing rooms on one side and the loading dock on the other. "So she has his dog. What does that have to do with you?"

"The police think my brother killed Brandon. I'm trying to prove that he didn't."

We'd reached the metal doors at the end of the hall. Vonetta stopped walking and turned to face me. "And you think Chelsea will help you do that?"

"That's what I'd like to find out."

"That's a tall order, Abby. I don't know if it's such a good idea."

I started to speak, but Vonetta opened the door and ushered me outside. I waited impatiently while she checked the delivery, signed the shipping bill, and finally came back to talk to me. "I know where to find Chelsea, and I can call her for you if you'd like, but I can't just hand over her address without her consent. We have a responsibility to protect the people who volunteer their time here, and we take it seriously."

"These are unusual circumstances."

"Every circumstance is unusual to the person who needs something." Vonetta had her don't-mess-with-me face on, so I didn't. "I don't know that talking to her is going to help," she warned. "I always understood that she and Brandon were close."

"I'm sure they were. She worked for him for a long time."

"No . . . I mean *close*. If you know what I mean."

Brandon and Chelsea? That was almost as hard to imagine as his relationship with Elizabeth. "Are you sure about that?"

"That's certainly the impression I've had."

Chelsea and Brandon. Was there anyone in town he *hadn't* been with? I was beginning to think five minutes of being special to him were four-and-a-half minutes too long. "Even if they had a relationship," I reasoned, "it still wasn't like Brandon to leave Max with anyone else."

"Not even the woman in his life?"

My laugh echoed around the loading dock. "If there's one thing I've learned in the past few days, it's that Brandon didn't have just one woman in his life."

"Maybe not, but I was under the impression that his relationship with Chelsea was quite serious."

"Serious? Brandon?"

"I was under the impression that they were talking about a more permanent arrangement."

"More permanent?—" I gaped at her. "You mean marriage?" Was that why he'd called Elizabeth? To solicit marriage advice? Considering how cavalier both of their attitudes were toward the institution, he'd probably called the one person in Paradise who'd tell him what he wanted to hear.

But if he'd been thinking about marrying Chelsea Jenkins, what the hell had he been doing flirting with me? I wondered how many other people had known about his relationship with Chelsea, and I hated him fiercely. Or maybe I hated myself for being so naïve.

Vonetta watched me trying to absorb what she'd said, and her expression softened. "I didn't know the young man, but I do know Chelsea. She was head over heels in love with him, that was evident to everyone. The last time I saw her, she was ecstatic because their relationship had turned a corner."

"When was that?"

"Two months ago, maybe. I heard her telling one of the other girls that she'd be married before the end of the year. I drew the only conclusion I could."

"I just never— Brandon never gave a hint of that to me."

"And you knew him well?"

"I thought I did."

"Apparently not, though?"

"Apparently." I chewed a thumbnail while the driver finished unloading his shipment. As I followed Vonetta back into the darkened theater, I asked, "Do you think Chelsea is capable of killing Brandon?"

Vonetta looked at me with genuine surprise. "Chelsea? That girl couldn't hurt a fly."

"Even if she found out that Brandon was being unfaithful to her?"

"Not even then. She's a sensitive girl. Quiet. I don't think she could hurt someone she cared about under any circumstances."

"What about someone she didn't care about?" I muttered, only half-joking.

Vonetta laughed and took my arm for the long trudge back up the corridor. "Only by accident. I'm sure your brother isn't the murderer, but I'm equally sure about Chelsea. I don't know why she has that dog, but she didn't kill Brandon. I'd stake my life on it."

Chapter 14

It was nearly seven o'clock when I left the Playhouse, frustrated by my conversation with Vonetta and several hundred dollars deeper in debt. Vonetta *could* be wrong about Chelsea, but she's such a great judge of character I had trouble patching the holes she'd punched in my theory.

The rich aromas of grilling beef spilled onto the street from the Timberline Grill next door, making my stomach clench and reminding me that I'd skipped lunch. Since it was already dark, I gave up on my stroll past Man About Town and decided to take care of my hunger pangs instead.

I grabbed a Whopper, fries, and a Diet Coke at Burger King and carried everything back to my apartment. While I ate, I made a list of Brandon's friends, their phone numbers and addresses. Surely one of the people on my list would know where to find Chelsea. They might even be able to confirm Vonetta's story.

Maybe I was grasping at straws, but it felt good to be doing something constructive. Maybe Chelsea wasn't capable of murder, but she was the only other person who'd floated to the surface as a possible suspect, and I wasn't ready to let go of her yet.

By the time I polished off the last fry, I had a game plan.

First stop, Urban Ross, Brandon's closest friend. If anybody could identify Iris Quinn's mystery man, set my mind at ease about Brandon and Elizabeth, or corroborate Vonetta's story, Urban was the man.

I thought about calling him, but people can hide too much over the phone. I wanted to see his face while we talked.

I tossed the trash, grabbed a sweatshirt, and headed out the door. The storm had moved out of the valley at last, but the temperature had dropped when the sun went down, and I could see my breath as I walked to my car.

After living in Sacramento for so many years, it felt good to be back where I could enjoy the changing seasons, but I'd forgotten how it feels to live with freezing temperatures in September. I cranked up the heat and set off for Paradise's residential district.

Old maps of Paradise divide the town into distinct sections, with Chinatown running along the creek bed and Swede Alley just above that. Follow Swede Alley half a mile north, and you'll find yourself surrounded by modest single-family houses and apartment buildings. This is where you'll find the schools and all the less glamorous businesses no town can survive without.

I drove until I found the address the phone book had listed for Urban Ross and pulled up in front of a small duplex. One side of the lawn was littered with toys. Urban's black pickup sat in the driveway of the other, right in back of his Harley-Davidson.

I parked on the street and hurried to the door where I could hear the TV playing. The sound died away when I rang the doorbell, and a few seconds later the porch light flared to life.

Urban is short with the solid build of an athlete. His hair has been bleached by the sun through so many seasons most of it is blond, and it hangs to his chin in wild corkscrew curls some women would sell their firstborn to have. He looks like the kind of guy you'd expect to see walking the beach carrying a surfboard, and I've never been sure how he earns his money. I just know that he spends most of his time outdoors.

That's not surprising in a place like Paradise. People flock to these mountains for the sun, the space, and the snow. In the winter, Urban is either on skis or a snowboard. In the summer, he trains on his mountain bike. I'm not sure what he's training for, but it occupies most of his time.

It took him a few seconds to recognize me and usher me inside out of the cold. Declining the offer of a beer, I made myself reasonably comfortable on a sagging couch while he squatted in front of a bicycle wheel and kept doing whatever he'd been doing before I arrived. "I guess you're here about Brandon," he said.

"Yeah. Can we talk?"

"Sure." He flashed a glance up at me. "Sucks, doesn't it?"

"To put it mildly." Now that I was here, I didn't know quite how to get the conversation rolling. I tried to come up with something natural-sounding, but the smooth segue was simply beyond me. Finally, I blurted, "The police think that either my brother killed him or Brandon set the fire and accidentally killed himself in the process."

Urban scowled thoughtfully, but he didn't say a word.

I scooted to the edge of the couch and leaned forward so I could see his face better. "Wyatt didn't do it. You know that, right?"

Urban seemed almost startled by the question. He blinked up at me in confusion. "I suppose not."

"You *suppose* not? Come on! You know my brother, don't you? Whatever issues he had with Brandon, they weren't serious enough to commit murder over."

"Your brother wouldn't be the first man to kill someone over a cheating spouse."

"Elizabeth wasn't cheating—not technically." I caught myself and added, "Unless you know something I don't."

With a shake of his head, Urban stretched his legs out in front of him and set one bare foot jiggling. "Relax. I don't think things ever progressed that far."

"Then what happened?"

The foot stopped moving. "You think I know?"

"I think you know more about Brandon than anyone else."

"I don't know who killed him."

"But you know if he had enemies, don't you? You'd know if there was someone who might have wanted him out of the way?"

Urban grabbed his wrench and tightened a bolt. "You know how Brandon was. Always joking around. Never could take him seriously. But there were times . . ." Urban gave the bolt another turn. "He was different the last few days before the fire, y'know? More serious. Don't you think?"

"I didn't notice."

He thought about that for a minute, then shrugged. "Maybe it was just with me."

"Maybe." I didn't like the direction the conversation was taking, but I needed to know the truth. "Did he give you any idea why he was acting strangely?"

"Not really."

"Not really? Does that mean he did say something?"

"It wasn't what he said, really. It was the way he acted." Urban stood, wiping his hands on the seat of his shorts. "He came over for a beer a couple of nights before the fire. He was kind of . . . I don't know . . . distant, I guess. I'd say something, and he'd respond, but half the time it was like he wasn't really listening. Don't know why, though." He perched on the arm of the couch and smiled down at me sadly. "Wish I did."

"Me, too." We fell silent and sat that way for a while. Urban was the first person in days who hadn't run down Brandon's character and sitting here with him made me remember the good things about our friendship. When I couldn't stand the silence any longer, I said, "I talked with someone a couple of days ago who says she saw Brandon having an argument with a strange man shortly before he died. Do you know anything about that?"

Urban looked at me in surprise. "Not a thing. Any idea who it was?"

"The woman I talked to couldn't see the man's face. Brandon didn't mention an argument to you?"

"No, but he wouldn't have. We're . . . we *were* friends, but we didn't go over every detail of the day when we got together."

"What about money? Did Brandon ever mention having money trouble?"

Urban's eyes narrowed. "Not to me."

"He didn't tell you that his payroll checks were bouncing?"

Urban's gaze shot to mine. "No, but you've sure been busy, haven't you?"

"For all the good it's done. What about his family? Did he ever talk about them?"

"Not really. Why?"

"No one seems to know about his life before he came here."

"That's not unusual," Urban said. "Not in a place like this."

"Maybe not," I conceded, "but someone's going to have to plan a funeral service and decide where he'll be buried. I just wonder who's going to do all of that."

"The police will know."

"Yeah, maybe." I stared around the room and thought how odd it was to find comfort in the presence of a near-stranger.

Urban flicked something only he could see from his shorts. "Hell, I don't know what you want me to say, Abby. You're asking me questions I can't answer. We never talked about stuff like that."

"Then what did you talk about?"

"Stuff." When I didn't move on, he added, "We talked about skiing. About the best hiking trails. Whose turn it was to buy the beer. Sometimes he'd talk about the business, but not often."

"Was he worried about it?"

"Not that I knew of."

"What about Chelsea?"

Urban stopped moving. "What about her?"

"She and Brandon were serious about each other, weren't they?"

A laugh shot out of Urban's mouth. "Brandon and Chelsea? Are you kidding?"

"They weren't a couple?"

He dug a pack of cigarettes from behind a book and held them up, either offering or asking, I wasn't sure which. I waved off the question, and he lit up, inhaling so deeply his face caved in. It made me wonder how he found enough wind to ride his bike. "They weren't a couple," he said when he exhaled. "She's one weird chick."

I sat up straight. "What do you mean?"

"I mean she bugs me. But I guess she never bothered Brandon. He kept her working there."

"Can you give me something specific? What is it about her that bugs you?"

Urban lifted a shoulder. "I don't know. She's different."

Hardly a crime. "This whole town is made up of people who are different," I reminded him.

His lips twitched. "Can't argue with that. All I know is, I would have sent her packing the first time she didn't show up for work."

"The *first* time?"

He took another deep drag from the cigarette and exhaled noisily. "Let's just say she wasn't the most reliable employee in history."

"I knew that much," I admitted. "I never could understand why Brandon didn't fire her. Maybe this explains it."

"Naw, I think he just liked playing big brother or something. It made him feel good to take care of people."

Was that really the reason? I just didn't know. I'd been so hopeful that Urban would know something helpful, but he seemed as confused as I was. "So you think that's why he left Max with her the night he died?"

Urban flicked ash into an overflowing ashtray. "Who told you that?"

"I heard it somewhere."

"Never happened. Brandon never let that dog out of his sight."

"Apparently, he did that night. At least that's the rumor. I'd sure like to find out if it's true or not. Do you have any idea where she lives?"

He gave his head an uncertain shake. "I'm trying to remember if Brandon ever told me, but I don't think so. 'Course he might have, and I just didn't pay attention."

"Do you think one of his other friends would know?"

"You can ask, but I wouldn't hold my breath if I were you. Brandon played his hand close to the vest, you know? He never really opened up a whole lot to anybody."

"So then he could have been madly in love with Chelsea."

Urban nodded thoughtfully. "I guess he could have."

"So if Brandon did leave Max with her, he must have had a good reason. If it wasn't because he was planning to set fire to the store, why do you think he did it?"

Urban's expression grew solemn. He crushed out the cigarette and looked at me. "That's the thing, Abby. He *wouldn't* have done it no matter what the reason. He just wouldn't have left Max behind . . . unless—" He met my gaze, and I could tell he felt as miserable as I did.

My heart slowed, and an empty hole opened up inside my chest. It wasn't easy, but I made myself say aloud what we were both thinking. "Unless he knew he wasn't coming back."

Chapter 15

I was just digging the keys out of my pocket when Karen pulled up in her Subaru the next morning. I'd spent a long time the night before thinking about my conversation with Urban and trying to figure out what I was missing. The nearly sleepless night had left me looking a little like Grandma Shaw—complete with puffy eyes and blotchy skin.

I'd dragged on another sweatshirt and covered my hopeless hair with a baseball cap, but I couldn't hide the rest.

Karen climbed out of her car and gave me a thorough once-over. "You sick or something?"

"Not sick, just tired. I got in late, and I didn't sleep well."

"Oh? Why?"

After our conversation yesterday, I wasn't in the mood for true confessions—or for the lecture that would inevitably follow. I tried changing the subject. "How was Paige when you got home yesterday?"

Karen responded with a suspicious scowl. "Fine. Why?"

"You were worried about her yesterday."

"Yeah . . . and?"

"And she's family. I'm concerned."

Karen snorted a laugh and pushed past me into the kitchen.

"Well I *am*!"

"And I'm Julia Roberts." She nodded toward the rear bumper still dangling from the Jetta. "Did Maggie Sherwood get in touch with you? She called three times after you left yesterday."

Karen might be younger than me, but she has a maternal streak a mile wide. I really hate when she turns it on me. "I'll call her," I promised. "Later. Right now, we need to put the coffee on so it's ready when we open. And the sugar-free section needs some serious attention. I noticed that yesterday."

My cousin didn't take the bait. "Detective Jawarski stopped by last night after you left. He wanted to know if we've seen or heard from Wyatt."

Damn! "What did you tell him?"

"I told him no. What else could I tell him?"

"And that was it?"

"He asked where you were."

"And?—"

"And I said I didn't know. Because I didn't. He wasn't happy."

"Well, since I live to make him smile, I consider that a real tragedy."

Karen stashed her purse in a cupboard and turned back wearing a deep frown. "You're going to get yourself in trouble, Abby."

I didn't want to go there. So I didn't. "After you finish with the sugar-free section, that batch of Halloween lollipops needs to be wrapped. And then maybe you could start washing the jars on the top shelf. Last time I looked, they were covered in fingerprints."

Karen gave me a look cold enough to freeze pipes. "Anything else?"

I shook my head and chewed on a licorice pumpkin. There are just times when you need something substantial. "You haven't found out where I can find Chelsea Jenkins, have you?"

Wearing an expression like the witch in my lollipop mold, Karen tugged her apron from its hook and slipped it over her head. "If the police are going to charge Wyatt with something, don't you think it would be better for him to hire an attorney?"

I saw no reason to admit that Wyatt had no idea what I was doing. I put on my most innocent smile and reached for Aunt Grace's recipe file. "Sure it would, but it would be even better if things didn't get that far in the first place."

"You need to stop playing private detective."

I found the almond toffee recipe and pulled out the card. "I'm asking a few questions, that's all. Trying to get things straightened out in my own head."

"That policeman isn't going to like you snooping around."

"Well I don't like him accusing my brother of murder," I said, heading toward the refrigerator, "so I guess that makes us even."

"Oh you're even, all right. Except *he's* the one with handcuffs and keys to the jail. That tilts the scales in his direction just a little."

I pulled two pounds of butter from the fridge and carried it back to the counter. "It doesn't matter which direction the scales are tilted. Wyatt's my brother, and he's in trouble. I can't just turn my back and pretend I don't notice."

"Is it true what they say about Brandon and Elizabeth?"

I nodded. "But she claims that her relationship with Brandon was strictly platonic."

"And you believe her?"

"I want to."

Karen pulled the keys to the front door from their hook so she could open us for business. "I can't even *imagine* her cheating on Wyatt. That's almost harder than picturing Wyatt as a murderer."

Not for me. I poured sugar into the large measuring cup but stopped short of pouring it into the pan. "She *did* meet Brandon without telling Wyatt about it."

"But nothing happened."

"That's what she says."

"So Wyatt actually does have a motive." Karen caught the look in my eye and added, "I mean, the police think he does."

"But they're wrong."

"I still say you should let the professionals handle it. It's not going to help Wyatt if you end up behind bars."

"I could end up there anyway," I admitted. "Jawarski thinks I'm an accessory for helping Wyatt cover his tracks."

"And you're still snooping around? Are you crazy?"

"No, just determined." I added the sugar to the pan and turned on the flame. "You could save me time by just telling me where Chelsea lives."

"I've already told you, I don't know."

"But you know everything about everyone who works downtown."

"Not everyone."

"Okay. Then tell me this— Did you know that Chelsea and Brandon were engaged?"

Karen pulled back slightly and regarded me through narrowed eyes. "Engaged?"

"That's what Vonetta Cummings says. According to Chelsea, their relationship had just turned a corner, and she planned to be married by the end of the year."

"She's a child! Brandon was a good fifteen years older than she is."

"Oh. Yeah. And you never hear of men getting involved with younger women, do you?"

Karen rolled her eyes and leaned against the counter. "I know it happens all the time. I'm just having a tough time believing it in this case."

"Vonetta believes it."

"And Chelsea supposedly has the dog with her?"

"That's what Elizabeth says. If it's true, maybe the facts speak for themselves."

Karen let out a heavy sigh. "Dammit. Now you've got *me* curious."

She looked so pained, I had to laugh. "Poor Karen. Tell you what— You stop nagging me about getting in trouble, and I'll share everything I find out with you."

She held up both hands and looked horrified. "Don't get me involved. I have kids to think about."

"Relax. Jawarski isn't going to throw you in jail for listening to gossip. If that was a crime, everybody in Paradise would be behind bars."

"All the same—" She stepped into the showroom and busied herself with the coffeemaker. "Isn't there anything I can say that will convince you to stop this?"

I pretended to consider. "Sure. Tell me Wyatt's not a suspect anymore, and I'll back right off."

"That's what I was afraid of." Karen let out another heavy sigh and turned on the coffeemaker. "Try Libby Baker up at Birds of Paradise. I think she's friendly with Chelsea. Maybe she'll know where to find her."

I tried not to grin, but it wasn't easy. I turned on the burner, settled the pan over it, and savored my slight victory. With Karen, they were few and far between, but when they came, they were usually worth waiting for.

A couple of hours later, ten batches of toffee lay in smooth, thin sheets to cool, and I set off up the steps toward Bear Hollow Road. Like most other Rocky Mountain mining towns, Paradise was built in a steep, narrow canyon, and the hills climb sharply as you move away from the heart of the city—too sharply to make the climb an easy one. At various intervals throughout the city, you'll find long, steep sets of stairs leading from one street to the next.

Even with stairs, the climb isn't easy. I was more than a little winded by the time I reached the top. I'm older than I was when I lived here before, and I'd been living almost at sea level for twenty years. My body is still adjusting to the lack of oxygen at this altitude.

Even before I reached Birds of Paradise, I could see Max lying on the sidewalk. Looked like luck was with me for the first time in days.

The dog lurched to his feet when he saw me coming. I just couldn't tell if he was happy to see me or if he thought I looked like lunch.

Now that I knew he really *had* escaped the fire, I was filled with a mixture of relief and sadness. Obviously, Brandon had left him behind that night, but why? Had he really been desperate enough to do something so stupid?

Max watched me carefully. Maybe I was just projecting my own emotions onto him, but I thought he looked sad, and I wondered how much he was able to comprehend. Did he know that Brandon wouldn't be coming back?

Holding out one hand for him to sniff, I inched toward him. "Max? What are you doing, boy?"

He tugged on his leash, and his stubby tail gave a little wag. He didn't seem interested in taking my arm off, so I edged closer and ran my hand across his knobby head. A high-pitched whine filled the air, and he rested his head against my thigh.

In the past few days I'd learned so many things about Brandon, I didn't know how I felt about him anymore, but I didn't have that problem with Max. I don't mind telling you that my heart went out to him. "Oh, you poor thing. You miss him, don't you?"

That little stump gave another twitch just as Chelsea appeared in the doorway. She's twenty-five or so, a little chubby, with a head full of wavy red hair that falls to the center of her back. No matter when I've seen her, she always looks a little disheveled. Today, she was wearing a pair of striped bib overalls over a white tank top and a pair of men's high-top tennis shoes. A shapeless leather purse hung from her shoulder.

Even knowing what I knew, she didn't seem like Brandon's type. But who was I to judge?

Lousy fashion sense didn't stop her from looking me over as if *I* was the one in need of a makeover. I tried to ignore it, but I wondered if she knew that Brandon had been at least mildly interested in me.

"I haven't seen you since the fire," I said when I realized she was waiting for me to say something. "Are you doing okay?"

Her pouty mouth quirked into a half-smile. "I guess. It's just hard, you know?"

"I'm sure it is. The two of you were together for a long time."

She sniffed and, in a surprisingly delicate move, pressed the backs of her fingers to the tip of her nose. Her fingers looked short and stubby, and the ragged fingernails meant that she probably chewed them habitually. "We were together for four years."

Apparently that was longer than he'd been with anyone else. But I *still* couldn't imagine the two of them together.

Max head-butted me so I scratched behind his ears. "I heard that you had Max, but I didn't really believe it until just now. I didn't think Brandon ever went anywhere without him."

Chelsea lowered her hand and dropped her gaze to the dog's head. She didn't offer an explanation, but I wasn't going to let a little thing like that stop me. "So how did you end up with him?"

"Brandon asked me to take him with me when I left work that afternoon," she said matter-of-factly, "so I did."

"Really? How often did he do that?"

"Not very often, but he did sometimes. Why?"

"That surprises me. I didn't think Brandon ever left Max with anyone else."

"Well, he didn't usually. And he wouldn't have trusted Max with just anyone. But we had a special relationship. Away from work. I wasn't just anyone."

"No, I can see that."

"Not many people knew about us. Brandon didn't like to talk about his private life much."

"No, he didn't, but I have heard that the two of you were close. Do you mind if I ask you a couple of questions? I'm having a hard time piecing together what happened that day."

She pulled back ever so slightly. "I guess not."

"Did Brandon tell you why he wanted Max out of the way?"

"No, but he didn't have to. I liked making him happy."

"It didn't strike you as odd? When he asked you, I mean."

"No, it didn't." Chelsea tucked an errant lock of fiery hair behind one ear. "I know what you're getting at. You think this proves that Brandon set the fire, don't you?"

"Not necessarily. Do you?"

Anger flashed in her hazel eyes, and a look of willful determination tightened her face. "Brandon? No way. Man About Town was his life. He wouldn't have done that."

"Then what was he doing at the store that late?"

"I don't know. He didn't tell me."

"He didn't offer *any* explanation about why he wanted you to take Max?"

Chelsea's eyes flashed again. "I told you. No."

"And you didn't ask?"

"Why should I? Brandon and I weren't like that. He didn't have to explain himself to me."

After everything I'd learned in the past few days, I had no doubt Brandon would have preferred a relationship without explanations, and Chelsea was just young enough to let him get away with it. "Of course not," I said, and steered the conversation onto another subject. "I've heard rumors that Brandon was having trouble at the store. Is that true?"

Chelsea shot daggers at me. "What are you trying to do, Abby? Make Brandon look like the bad guy?"

"I'm just trying to find the truth. Is it true that some of your payroll checks bounced?"

She bent to untie Max's leash. "I don't want to talk to you."

"If you really believe that Brandon is innocent, then you have no reason not to tell me. Did some of your payroll checks bounce before Brandon died?"

She straightened slowly. She still didn't look happy, but at least she wasn't running. "A couple did," she admitted. Her tone said it was no big deal, and if she and Brandon were together, maybe it was even true.

"Just a couple?"

"A few, okay? Where did you hear about that anyway? Brandon didn't want anybody to know."

"This is Paradise," I reminded her. "There are no secrets around here."

"Well, it was a temporary problem, and we all knew that. Brandon had some great stuff coming in, and he had plans to expand the store. Things would have gotten better. It always does around the holidays, anyway. He would have made it up to us eventually."

Disappointment took some of the wind out of my sails. I guess I was still hoping that some of the bad things I'd heard about Brandon in the past few days would prove false. I wondered if she believe that Brandon would pay them, or if she just wanted to believe it. I couldn't tell from the expression on her face. "Was he having any other kind of trouble? Was anyone mad at him? Did you hear him arguing with anyone or hear anyone threaten him?"

A sly expression stole across her face. "You don't really want me to answer that, do you?"

Did I? I forced a nod. "I want the truth."

"Even if it means your brother goes to prison?"

"Do you have evidence against him?"

"I know he hated Brandon."

"But he might not have been the only one. I heard that Brandon was arguing with somebody the day before the fire. Do you have any idea who that might have been?"

She picked up a curl and stared at it for a minute. "Lots of people were upset with him over the stupid Arts Festival thing, but you know that."

"Yes, I do, but was anyone upset enough to kill him?"

"Over that? Probably not."

"Over something else then?"

She dropped the curl and spent a minute smoothing it across her shoulder. "I don't know, Abby. Look, I told the police everything I could. Everything I know for sure, anyway. And I really don't want to talk about this anymore. My life's completely messed up thanks to this. Losing Brandon has ruined everything. He's gone, and I'm alone, but I still have rent and other bills to pay, and living in this town isn't cheap. I need a job. Quick. But I'll be lucky to get a job flipping burgers at this time of year. And this . . ."

She gave a sharp tug on the leash, and Max's head snapped up. "This thing eats like a pig. I've spent a fortune already in dog food, which he then poops out all over the lawn for me to pick up and throw away. He spends half the night awake, scratching at the door and whining. My neighbors are pissed off, and the landlord's threatening to evict me."

I looked down into Max's puppy-dog eyes and felt another sharp tug on my heart strings. "I'm sure it will get better," I said, dragging my gaze back to Chelsea's irritated scowl. "Surely the landlord will give you both a little time to adjust."

Her face contorted as if I'd suggested eating worms for breakfast. "No way. I'm not *keeping* him."

"Oh. I thought—" I broke off with a confused laugh. "I just assumed that having him around would be a comfort."

"Well, it's not. Libby's going to drive me to the pound so I can leave him there. I don't know what they'll do with him, but I've had enough."

Her abrupt mood shift stunned me. "But you can't take him to the pound."

"What else am I going to do with him? Brandon didn't have any family, and everybody else is afraid of him."

Until a few minutes ago I would have said that list included me, but Max seemed like a different dog this morning. Not that I wasn't still a little afraid of him. Or maybe respectful was a better word. Max had always been a one-man dog, and I was not that man. "But what if nobody adopts him?"

"Then nobody adopts him, and the pound will do what they do. I *can't* keep him, so unless somebody else wants to take over—" She tilted her head, ran another glance from my head to my toes, and held out the leash. "You want him? Be my guest."

I backed a step away and held up both hands. "No. I didn't mean that. I mean . . . Well, I *can't* have a dog."

"Okay then. But don't be thinking bad things about me for doing what *I* have to do. Nobody else wants him, either."

But the *pound*!

As if on cue, the dog nudged my hand again. A move Chelsea didn't miss. "Look! He likes you."

"He likes me at the moment," I agreed reluctantly. "He's never been this friendly before."

"So it's a sign." She held out the leash again. "Take him."

"But I—"

"Come on! You have that whole place to yourself. No landlord giving orders. No neighbors to get upset if he makes a little noise."

"Yes, but there are health codes I have to consider. I can't have Max around food."

"He could stay outside while you're working, and he'd be happy. You know how much he likes watching what's going on. And he'd keep you safe. He's a terrific watchdog." As if she suddenly remembered that she was grieving, her voice caught, and she blinked away tears. "If I hadn't taken him, nothing would have happened to Brandon. Please? Take him?"

Max's stubby tail wagged slowly, and for a second or two I even imagined he understood what we were talking about. Knowing that I might live to regret it, I took a deep breath and held out my hand. "All right. Leave him with me."

Chelsea's hand shot out with the leash in it. "Oh, this is great. Thank you." She passed the dog off to me and tucked that willful strand of curly red hair behind one ear. "One problem down. You don't happen to have a job opening, do you?"

"Sorry." I tried to look as if I meant it. "If I hear of any, I'll let you know."

"Great. Thanks." She slipped her hands into the pockets of her overalls and backed away. "You'll be fine with Max. Seriously. I mean, he's kind of moody sometimes, but it's not really that bad."

A whole round of warning bells suddenly went off in my head. If he wasn't that bad, why was she so eager to get rid of him? Doberman pinscher. Trained attack dog. *Moody?* "What do you mean, 'moody'?" I called after her, but she'd already put several feet between us.

Waving one hand over her head, she bounced down the hill as if she hadn't a care in the world.

Chapter 16

Trouble hit at exactly three-forty-five on Monday afternoon.

Karen had run to the boutique across the street to negotiate the price of a sweater with Kim-Ly Trang, owner of one of Paradise's trendiest boutiques, which left me in the store by myself. Business had been slow all day, but I didn't know whether that was because Max was on the sidewalk in front of the store, or because nobody in Paradise had a craving for sugar. I didn't want to think that something else might be keeping them away, but the thought crossed my mind that some people might be a tad reluctant to eat something made by the sister of a suspected murderer.

I'd spent the morning making more Halloween candy—licorice and orange lollipops in a variety of shapes and chocolate-covered marshmallow tombstones that I'd ask Karen to decorate later. I was even starting to feel marginally comfortable with the amount of product we had on hand for the upcoming holiday. I'd been surprised to learn that Halloween is the busiest holiday for candy sales—bigger even than Christmas and Easter—with sales topping over two billion dollars every year.

While I didn't expect people to buy their trick-or-treat

goodies from Divinity, I did expect an increase in walk-in business over the next few weeks. Business we'd get, that is, if people weren't afraid to come through the door.

While the candy cooled, I turned my attention to the pre-Christmas inventory Karen and I had managed to avoid all weekend. Sometime within the next six weeks, ski season would come to Paradise, and the usual low humidity would be less dependable as snow came to the mountains. I could count on a few days each month that would be good for making candy, but I wouldn't be able to predict when they'd be. If I didn't build up my inventory soon, I'd almost certainly regret it.

Then there were the display windows to plan—one for Halloween, one for Thanksgiving, and one for the Christmas holiday. Forget about the trouble I could get myself into, I really didn't have the time to rush around Paradise trying to find Brandon's murderer.

I was working on the Halloween sketch when the door flew open so hard it sent the brass bell over it into spasms. Stella Farmer burst inside, eyes flashing, nostrils flaring. She was wearing one of the green smocks from D&S Lighting, and a pair of glasses dangled from a chain around her neck and bounced hard against her breasts as she bore down upon me like a heat-seeking missile. "What in the hell do you think you're doing?"

I don't think I've ever seen Stella so angry, but I didn't want her to think she intimidated me. I stood slowly, trying to keep my movements unhurried and the emotion out of my voice. "Is something wrong, Stella?"

"You're damn right something's wrong. Did you tell the police I murdered Brandon?"

Where had *that* come from? "Of course not. What are you talking about?"

"You didn't give them my name and tell them to talk to me?"

Well, when she put it *that* way . . . I'd almost forgotten, but I had told Jawarski about her.

Her eyes narrowed into thin slits. "It *was* you, wasn't it?"

I stole a glance at Max who lay on the sidewalk, his head down on his paws. No help there. "I never said you murdered

Brandon. I just mentioned that you'd disagreed with him over the Arts Festival. What was I supposed to do? Lie?"

Stella could have tunneled through the mountain with the look she gave me. "I don't expect you to lie, but a little common sense wouldn't hurt. For goodness sakes, Abby, it's only an Arts Festival."

"You didn't feel that way the night of the Alliance meeting."

"Of course I did." She uncapped a dish, fished out a cinnamon disk, and popped it into her mouth. I wondered what she'd do if I waltzed into her store and slipped a light bulb into my pocket, but I didn't ask.

"Okay, sure. I was upset with Brandon," she said. "But being a little annoyed with someone is a far cry from murdering them in cold blood."

"You accused him of trying to put you out of business," I reminded her. "That's not really *a little* annoyed."

She waved one hand expansively. "It was a figure of speech."

I rolled my eyes and the cinnamon disks out of her reach at the same time. "I never said you murdered him, Stella. If you don't like being asked about the wild accusations you toss around, maybe you should be a little more careful about what you say."

A flash of anger lit her eyes. "You're such a little fool, Abby. You really think that Brandon was this great guy who could do no wrong, don't you?"

Oh, if only she knew. "Of course not. I just don't think he could have done all the things he's being accused of doing."

"Then you didn't know him very well."

She was such a mean-spirited, venomous woman, I wondered how poor Duncan had stayed married to her all these years. "This is pointless, Stella. Obviously, you didn't think much of Brandon, but you don't need to run him down now that he's dead. Can't you just let him rest in peace?"

"I'm not the only one who didn't see his shining armor," Stella said, her voice low. "It might surprise you to find out just how some people felt about him."

I'd heard plenty in the past week, but Stella's voice raised the hair on the back of my neck. "Actually, I'm starting to get a pretty good idea. I just don't understand why. Not completely. Why did you think he was trying to put you out of business? What did he do?"

"I told you, I exaggerated. He wasn't trying to put us out of business."

I thought her eyes looked a little wild, but it took me a second to realize that she was afraid. Afraid that I'd find out the truth? That she'd been angry enough with Brandon to kill him?

"You certainly seemed to think otherwise last week," I said again. "I'm sure I'm not the only person who knows that."

She leaned in close, and the light in her eyes died. "Back off, Abby, or you'll wish you had. You're looking in the wrong place."

My heart thumped hard against my chest, and my mouth grew dry, but I didn't want her to know that I was afraid. "Is that a threat?"

"It's just friendly advice." She turned away and yanked open the door with only slightly less force than she'd used coming in. "Just do me a favor. Next time you feel the need to offer up a sacrificial lamb, leave my name out of it."

She stormed out the door, somehow avoiding stepping on Max as she left. I think he twitched an ear, but it was clear that he wouldn't be much use to me in a bad situation.

I could still feel her anger banging off the walls, so I opened the door to let the fresh air in and the evil spirits out. Max tilted his head a little, decided I wasn't worth the effort, and dropped it back onto his paws.

There was more than enough to do inside, but the ability to take a break when I want one is one of the great perks of owning my own business. And I don't mind admitting that Stella's visit had unnerved me.

I sat on the step and scratched Max's ear. "Friendly advice, huh? Friends like that I don't need. I suppose the good news is Jawarski actually listened to me. I just wish he wouldn't tell other people what I say."

Max had no advice for me. Frankly, he didn't even seem concerned.

I watched Stella barrel across the street at the corner and shivered. How seriously should I take her? Was she threatening me, or just trying to protect herself? Brandon would know, but he was the only one.

I moved my hand to Max's neck and rubbed.

"I wish you could talk. I'll bet you could fill in some of the blanks for me."

I didn't expect an answer, but I was still a little disappointed when I didn't get one. "Look," I told him. "It's not that I expect us to get along like Lassie and Timmy or anything, but a little interaction would be nice."

Apparently, he didn't agree.

Standing, I brushed the dirt from the back of my pants and turned toward the door. "Okay, but you know where to find me if you ever want to talk. Right?"

The rest of him didn't move, but the ear I'd been scratching rotated to one side. Maybe it's a sign of my mental state at the time, but I counted that as a good sign.

By evening, I was exhausted, both physically and mentally. I locked up the store and climbed the steps, carrying a couple of lollipops with me. Oh sure, maybe you think it's childish, but adults buy—and eat—sixty-five percent of the candy sold in America, and it's not all exotic gourmet varieties, either.

I wanted nothing more than to take a hot bath and curl up with a good book, but I still hadn't connected with Wyatt, and I wanted to make sure he was still doing all right. I also wanted answers.

I'd been trying for days to reach my brother, but I was finally ready to concede that he wasn't going to pick up the phone, no matter how many times I called. He probably wouldn't come around to visit me, either. No, if I wanted to talk to him, I was going to have to look for him.

Knowing I might live to regret it, I loaded Max into the Jetta and combed the streets of Paradise for well over two hours before conceding defeat. I had no idea where Wyatt was hiding, but if avoiding me was his goal, he was doing a good job.

Upstairs in my apartment again, I threw together a couple of open-faced grilled cheese sandwiches with thick slices of tomato and plenty of garlic salt. Max dropped to the floor and lay there with his nose up against the wooden door.

When the cheese was properly melted, I slid the sandwiches onto a plate, tossed on a handful of chips, and fished a Coke out of the refrigerator, then carried the whole thing to the couch and curled up with the remote.

I spent the next thirty minutes mindlessly flipping through channels. Over a hundred channels, and not a thing on to watch. How pathetic is that?

About that time, I realized that Max was still lying in front of the door waiting for something that was never going to happen, and my heart sank. I coaxed him into the kitchen and opened a can of Mighty Dog beef and chicken, thinking the brand name might encourage him. He looked at the shimmering brown glob for a minute, even sniffed it halfheartedly, then turned and padded back into the living room.

Growing discouraged, I trailed after him with the dish and sat on the floor beside him. "Come on, Max. Eat something. Please?"

He blinked, but that was the extent of his interest.

Far from being a menace, the poor dog had me worried. Where was the dog Chelsea had complained about? The one who ate his weight in dog food and disposed of it on the lawn? If I hadn't known better, I'd swear she'd handed me the wrong leash.

I sat with him until my back started hurting, but even then I couldn't make myself get up and leave. I dragged my sketchbook onto the floor with me and spent some time working on holiday display windows. Thanks to the murder, I'd decided against the graveyard scene I'd originally been thinking of for Halloween, and planned instead to create a whimsical cottage in the woods, with candy-corn shingles and licorice-string windows. I sketched candy pumpkins lining a licorice sidewalk and piles of autumn leaves made of crushed candy bits.

After a while, I stretched my legs out in front of me and touched Max's head tentatively. He must have been in a mood because he let out a growl, but there was no heat in his protest, so I left my hand where it was and watched a few minutes of Letterman. But tonight, even the monologue couldn't hold my interest.

When the show cut to commercial, Max stirred restlessly. I'd been working so long, I couldn't remember the last time I'd let him outside. Whenever it was, the sun had been up.

Definitely time for another walk.

I tugged on a jacket, but since I didn't plan to do more than walk to the end of the block, I didn't bother changing from slippers into shoes. After clipping the leash to Max's collar, I led him downstairs. He followed reluctantly, padding along the pavement and making little clicking noises with his claws as he walked.

How often did his nails need clipping? I wondered. How many times a year did he need to go to the vet? Do dogs need annual checkups? Visits to the doggie dentist? I had absolutely no idea.

I made a mental note to call Manny Garcia, the vet down the street, and bone up on doggie health. He might not be Max's regular vet, but it was a safe bet he'd know who was. With all the other changes in his life, Max didn't need a stranger prodding him.

It was a clear night, the kind you never see in the city. Stars littered patches of clear sky, and a nearly full moon hovered near the crest of Crescent Peak—a giant white orb in the midnight-blue sky. I could see the outlines of trees and the lighter belt of green where Devil's Playground, one of the area's more difficult ski runs, cut through the forest.

As I stood shivering, Max gave a planter box exquisite attention, and it occurred to me that owning a dog was a lot like having children. Not that children routinely sniff planter boxes. Or maybe they do. The point is, I wouldn't know, would I?

Simply put, it had been a long time since I'd felt so needed. Maybe I never had. Roger certainly hadn't needed me. He'd made that crystal clear early in our marriage. Even when the marriage ended, and I came back to assist Aunt Grace, I hadn't been necessary. Aunt Grace had been amazingly independent at her age.

Maybe having Max around wouldn't be such a bad thing.

At least not for me. I couldn't say how good the experience would be for Max.

Even though it was nearly eleven, the streets weren't entirely deserted. Light still burned inside O'Shucks on the corner. Music and laughter drifted outside each time the door opened to let someone in or out. For the first time in a week, I felt at peace, and I thought maybe I'd actually get a good night's sleep.

Max nosed around the planter boxes for a few more minutes, then sniffed his way toward the Dumpster as if it might contain something interesting. I had a fortune in dog food stacked in an upstairs closet, and he got excited over garbage. Go figure.

Without warning, he straightened, let out a whimper, and broke into a run. Pain shot up my arm, and the leash burned my hand as it slipped through my grip. Just before it flew out of my hand, I managed to grasp it tightly, but I nearly lost a slipper as the force jerked me forward.

"Hey, slow down!" I pulled backward on the leash, but Max plunged forward, hot on the trail of something only he knew. "Max!" I shouted. "Stop! Heel!"

He loped downhill, past a couple strolling hand-in-hand. I tried digging my heels in for traction, but slippers have no tread, and Max was too strong for me. He raced on, darting past a park bench, circling a lamppost, and finally dashing into the street only a few feet in front of a car.

My heart shot into my throat, but somehow I managed to get a bloodcurdling scream out around it. The driver slammed on his brakes, leaned out his window, and shouted after me. "Are you crazy? Why don't you control that mutt?"

Nice suggestion, buddy. Don't know why I didn't think of it.

This was the second time in a week I'd raced through town with pink fuzz on my feet, and I wished desperately that I'd taken the time to put on shoes. Lesson learned.

A low growl emanated from Max's throat and pulled my attention back to the race. We reached the opposite side of the street and he ran onto the sidewalk. Between Bighorn Real Estate and Beaver Creek Clothiers, Max made a sudden right turn and shot toward the steep wooden steps leading downhill. I don't know if it was my life I saw passing before my eyes, but something whizzed past, and I didn't think I'd survive the landing if Max decided to head that way.

To my immense relief, he veered back toward the street at the last second and barreled toward the corner. I'd never seen Max like this, but he was so focused, I was beginning to think this wasn't just a mood swing. He was after something. I just had no idea what it was.

We flew down another block, past Edelweiss Bakery, Once Upon A Crime, and Mondano. And then, as suddenly as it had started, Max ground to a halt, and the chase was over.

Chapter 17

Max stood, ears erect, nose working furiously. The growl gave way to the high-pitched whine I'd heard too much of already, and he turned to look at me as if I'd know what he wanted.

My chest heaved, and my lungs burned. My fingers tingled from the effort of hanging onto the leash. I dropped onto the edge of a planter box and tried to pull myself together. To my surprise, Max trotted over and sat beside me, just the way he used to with Brandon. While I concentrated on getting my breath back, he watched me, waiting for me to tell him what came next.

I had no idea what to tell him.

After a few minutes I was able to breathe well enough to smell the sweet, subtle scents of autumn-faded petunias and loamy soil. Max let out one last whine and sank onto the sidewalk with his head on his paws, depressed again.

Whatever he'd been chasing was gone now, and I still didn't know what we'd been after.

My tongue stuck to the roof of my dry mouth, and my chest felt as if someone had been herding elephants across it, but on the off-chance I could find what Max had been chasing, I dragged myself to my feet and led Max to the corner.

Cars lined the street, and a handful of people moved together in a group along the sidewalk, but Max showed no interest in any of it. I couldn't see anyone who made me uneasy.

Had it been a person? The only places still open were nightclubs, but I couldn't take Max inside to search. Maybe I could have tied him up outside while I went in, but an odd, uneasy feeling warned me not to leave him alone.

Confused and uncertain, I turned back toward home, but my mind raced with possibilities as we walked. I was pretty sure Max hadn't been running on a whim. Brandon had paid a fortune to have him trained. He might look like a killer, but he didn't attack people indiscriminately. So, if he'd been after someone, it was someone he considered a threat. I'd have bet everything I owned on it.

But who?

I think that's when the reality of Brandon's death finally hit me. There was a killer in Paradise, and it was probably someone I knew.

I wouldn't even seriously consider Wyatt as a suspect. Stella Farmer had motive—such as it was—but Chelsea had had opportunity. She could have slipped into Man About Town at any time without being noticed. Even if she'd been seen, nobody would have thought twice about her being there. They might not even remember seeing her.

She wasn't the only person who'd had access to the store, I reminded myself. Lucas Dumont's paychecks had bounced just as high as Chelsea's had.

Warnings to be cautious whispered in the back of my mind, but I ignored them. I'm not that good at taking advice from myself, either.

"Tell her she's crazy," Karen demanded the next morning. "Go on, tell her. She won't listen to me."

At one of the wrought-iron tables inside Divinity, Rachel Summers froze with a piece of fudge halfway to her mouth and split a look between my cousin and me. She wore a bright blue sweater with a matching pair of pants. A scarf in bold geometric patterns covered her neck, and earrings in the same color palette dangled from her ears.

I, on the other hand, looked sublime in a pair of jeans, a UCLA sweatshirt, and a pair of dirty sneakers. It didn't matter. Nobody was going to see me today, anyway. Some time during the night, a bone-chilling wind had blown into the valley, and this morning it tore through Paradise flinging leaves and bits of dirt around.

The streets were almost deserted this morning, and the weather was another sharp reminder that winter was just around the corner. I wouldn't be able to leave Max outside in the snow, but if a candy shop was going to have an inventory retrieval specialist, it probably shouldn't be one who licks himself . . . well, you know.

I didn't have the heart to leave Max outside, but leaving him in the small room upstairs had turned out to be a disaster after only a few minutes. He'd scratched the paint off the door frame, chewed holes in three chairs, and knocked three potted plants onto the floor before we heard the commotion. Leaving him in my apartment wasn't an option. That ratty old furniture might not be much, but it was all I had. That meant I either had to keep him in the kitchen or in a corner near the display cases. Either way, the Health Department was sure to get us.

I sighed, closed the glass display case, and poured myself a cup of coffee. "I'm telling you, Max knows something," I said to Karen and Rachel. "I don't know what he knows, but he knows *something*."

Rachel nodded agreeably. "They do say that dogs are incredibly smart."

She was the only agreeable person in the room. With a sour expression, Karen pulled the plastic cover off the thermostat and nudged up the heat a couple of degrees. "Not *that* smart. Honestly, Abby. You want us to get all excited because the dog went for a run last night? You're crazy!"

"No," I said as patiently as I could. "I want you to get excited because he *knows* something."

Karen rolled her eyes. "Great. So what do you think he knows?"

"I have no idea. Maybe he knows who killed Brandon.

Maybe last night he picked up the scent of someone he recognized."

"Or maybe he saw a squirrel," Rachel suggested.

I glared at her. "That wasn't it."

"You're sure about that?" Karen asked.

"I'm positive."

"And you came to the conclusion that he's in possession of this vital piece of information because he ran for a couple of blocks last night?"

She was trying my patience. I straightened a stack of one-pound assortments on a glass shelf and explained again. "It wasn't that he ran. It was the *way* he ran."

"Like he was chasing something," Rachel chirped.

"Exactly."

Karen wasn't having any of it. "He's a dog, Abby. His job description is 'chase things.'"

"Not that dog." I jerked my head toward the canine in question who lay on his stomach with his chin on his paws. That forlorn look had returned to his eyes, and his body language clearly said *despondent*. "Does that look like a dog that chases things for a living?"

"He's resting."

"He's depressed. He barely eats or drinks anything, and he spends all day just lying there, staring at the door, and waiting. The only sign of life he's shown at all was last night. I think he knows something about Brandon's murder."

Karen still hadn't roused herself to actually work since we opened the store, but now she sipped her coffee, set the cup aside, and crossed to the baskets we keep filled with old-fashioned penny candy. "Okay, so let's assume, for the sake of argument, that Max was chasing the murderer. That someone here in Paradise murdered Brandon, and Max knows about it. What are you going to do, line up everyone in town and let Max start sniffing?"

"The sarcasm isn't helping," I growled. "The point is that Max might just be able to identify the killer, and the next time he starts acting weird, I'm going to pay closer attention."

"You do that," Karen said, stuffing a few more grape sticks into the basket. "Do we have any idea what motive someone could have possibly had to kill Brandon in the first place?"

"That depends on who the murderer is, doesn't it?" Rachel asked.

"Absolutely."

Karen ran an absentminded glance across the root beer barrels. "And I suppose you have a theory about that, too?"

"Sort of." I still wasn't sure who to trust and who to suspect. Maybe I shouldn't voice my suspicions in front of Rachel, but in that moment she seemed like my staunchest ally. "I think it was Chelsea or somebody she knows. I think that's why she was so anxious to get rid of Max."

"But why would Chelsea murder Brandon?" Rachel asked. "If she had a thing for him, wouldn't she want to keep him around?"

"Maybe she was jealous. If all the gossip is true, Brandon wasn't exactly the faithful type."

Karen scooped peppermints into a container. "If Chelsea was that eager to get rid of the dog, why didn't she just take him to the pound?"

"She was going to until I stopped her."

"I thought you said she practically begged you to take him."

"Well, she did. Although 'begged' might be too strong a word. But it *was* her idea."

Rachel scooted her chair around so she could see us better. "If she was trying to get rid of Max because he can identify the killer, why would she suggest that you take him? It doesn't make any sense."

She had a point, but I defied anyone to tell me which parts of this case *did* make sense. "I never said I had all the details worked out," I admitted.

Karen blurted out a laugh. "You don't have *any* of the details worked out, and your source of information is a dog. You can't tell the police to arrest Chelsea because the dog decided to run."

Frustrated, I crossed to the window and looked outside. Gray clouds hugged the mountains and cast a depressing pall over the day. "Can't you just admit that maybe I'm right?" I asked Karen. "Maybe he knows something about the person

who murdered Brandon. Maybe Brandon knew that he was in
danger of some kind. Maybe *that's* why he sent Max home
with Chelsea."

Rachel tilted her head and regarded Max for a long moment. "Maybe Brandon didn't send him home with Chelsea.
Maybe she just wants everybody to think he did."

I nearly tripped myself turning around again. "Say that
again."

"Maybe Chelsea just took Max, you know? Maybe Brandon didn't have anything to do with it."

Karen laughed and grabbed the feather duster—a sure
sign that she was annoyed. "This is crazy, Abby. All this talk
of murder. This is Paradise. People don't commit murder
here."

"People commit murder everywhere," I said. "It doesn't
matter where you live. If Chelsea's not guilty, maybe Stella
Farmer is. I told you what she said."

Karen stopped working and turned to face me. "If you
don't mind me saying so, you have other things you should
be worrying about." She shook a finger at Rachel. "And you
stop encouraging her." She flicked dust from the top of the
cash register and turned her attention back to me. "You need
to return Maggie Sherwood's phone calls and get your car
fixed. Dana and Danielle are coming next weekend to help
you make candied apples. You need to get ready for that. Halloween's just around the corner, and Christmas is only a few
weeks away, and Janice Smalley called to order three butterscotch bouquets for day after tomorrow. Brandon's gone.
There's nothing you can do for him. But there are a hundred
things you can, and should, be worrying about."

Have I mentioned how much I love advice? Even knowing she had some valid points didn't seem to matter. "Yeah,
Brandon's gone, but Wyatt's not. I can't just pour lollipops
while the police haul him off to jail."

"They can't even find him. And what if you're *not* helping him? What if you're only making things worse?"

Suddenly angry, I jammed the lid on the lemon drops,
shoved them back into place, and yanked the jar of gumdrops
off the shelf. "Why would you say that?"

"Because, if you'll forgive me for saying so, you don't

know what you're doing. If you keep nosing around like this, you're only going to make the police mad. That's not going to help anybody."

"I don't care if I make the police mad, as long as they don't railroad Wyatt into prison for something he didn't do."

Rachel leaned forward eagerly. "So what are you going to do?"

"I don't know. Keep trying to find Wyatt. Maybe talk to Lucas Dumont and find out what he knows."

"You think Lucas knows something?"

"He worked with Brandon. He'll know stuff."

"You're delusional," Karen warned. "Lucas comes from one of the richest families in Paradise. You'll never get the contract for those gift baskets if you make enemies in the wrong places. You probably won't even be able to renew your business license."

Karen might be right, but Jawarski wasn't going to listen to me unless I could produce something he couldn't ignore. Besides, what harm could one or two little conversations do? If the tables had been turned, Wyatt would have done the same for me.

I was almost certain of it.

Chapter 18

The very next chance I got, Max and I cruised up Prospector Street, determined to talk to Lucas Dumont, no matter what Karen said. It had been a full week since I last saw Wyatt. If anyone else had been missing that long, I'd have been worried, but Wyatt knows how to handle himself, and he's resourceful. None of his buddies had come to me acting worried, and that told me he was safe.

Which was good. Because I wanted to hurt him.

I'd looked everywhere I could think of except for one place—but to get to it, I had to go through Charlie Stackhouse, Wyatt's oldest friend. I've known Charlie since I was a kid, but I haven't seen him in years. I know he and Wyatt are still friends because Wyatt's a creature of habit, and Charlie's notoriously loyal—and because I'd heard Wyatt say something about Charlie a few weeks ago.

The two of them had gone to school together, graduated the same year, and then married within a few months of each other. Two peas in a pod, they'd trotted down the road to Harrison Rifle Works and were hired on at the plant on the very same day. Wyatt still worked there today. He'd been moving steadily up the organizational chart to upper middle-management.

A few years back, after inheriting money from his grandfather, Charlie had traded in life at the factory for life on the river. He'd purchased a little land and opened Sage Fork Outfitters. Since then, his business had grown from a few fly-fishing trips in the summer months to guided tour service for every kind of hunting imaginable, scenic tours of the Rockies, and snowmobile excursions in the winter months. He'd even been talking about adding an annual fishing trip in the Bahamas to the lineup. I figured he'd probably pull that off like he did everything else.

Charlie keeps a handful of rustic cabins geared up and ready for clients who want a place to stay while they're in town. Jawarski had probably already checked there, but I was betting he didn't know about Grandpa Stackhouse's old cabin at the top of that mountain. They hadn't used it much in recent years, but when they were boys Wyatt and Charlie had practically lived there during the summer months.

With Charlie's help, Wyatt could probably hole up there for weeks—maybe even months.

I drove out of town on the old mine road and pulled into the parking lot at Sage Fork Outfitters twenty minutes later. I'd heard all about this new location when Charlie moved here, but I hadn't paid much attention at the time, and I hadn't been here since I came back to town. You can only process so much at one time.

After coaxing Max out of the Jetta, I looped his leash around the trunk of a nearby aspen and climbed the steps onto the long wooden porch that stretched from one end of the building to the other. It's a long, low building carefully constructed to look as if it's been around forever. A handful of chairs had been positioned in inviting conversational groupings, probably by Nora, Charlie's wife. Charlie wouldn't think of such a thing.

I could imagine Wyatt and his buddies swapping tales here after a successful hunt. Today, the porch was deserted.

The breeze set flyers tacked onto a large bulletin board near the door fluttering. I gave them a cursory glance, but the legislation of turkey decoys and the ongoing struggle of the hunter with the landowner don't really interest me.

Out of habit, I wiped my feet on the mat before letting

myself inside. The screen door banged shut behind me, and
Nora Stackhouse glanced up from behind the counter with a
big smile. I was glad to see her and, under the circumstances,
she looked surprisingly pleased to see me. That must mean
that Wyatt wasn't causing them too much grief.

Nora had gone through school a couple of years ahead of
me, but we only really knew each other because of the men
in our lives. She'd always been petite, but she seemed thin-
ner than I remembered. Her short, dark hair is beginning to
turn gray, and smile lines radiate out from her eyes, even
when she's not smiling. I guess the years get to all of us
eventually.

She pushed her work aside and leaned her arms on the
counter. It was a friendly gesture that relieved some of the
tension I'd been feeling. "Abby? Well, this is a surprise. I
was going to stop in and see *you* in a couple of days."

"Oh? Any special reason?"

"Christmas. Charlie and I always order the large confec-
tion assortment for special clients at the holidays. I hope
you're still planning on making them even though Grace is
gone."

"I'm not planning on making any changes at Divinity," I
assured her. "I'm still trying to find my feet and trying to figure out why Aunt Grace left the place to me instead of someone else."

"Don't be silly. Who else would she have left it to?"

"One of the other cousins. Karen, maybe. Or even Wyatt.
They both stayed close to home. Dwight has a degree in business. Mimi loved the store as much as I did when we were
kids . . ."

"Yes, but Mimi has dollar signs in her eyes. She's always
seen that store as the means to an end, and with that kind of
attitude the store wouldn't last long. Grace knew that. And
Dwight might have a degree in business, but he has no heart.
Not the kind that store needs." Nora shook her head firmly.
"He would have come in there with a bulldozer and changed
everything. No, Grace left the business to the right person.
You're the only one who'll treat it the way she would have."

"I appreciate the vote of confidence," I said. "I just hope
I can live up to it."

"Don't worry so much. Just let instinct guide you, and you'll be fine. So what brings you here, anyway?"

"This and that. Is Charlie around?"

She shook her head. "He took a group out the other day and won't be back until tomorrow. Is there something special you're after? Maybe I can help."

I wasn't sure how much to tell her. Not that I don't trust Nora, especially after what she'd just said, but letting family secrets out every time you open your mouth isn't always smart. Besides, I wasn't sure which side of the fence she'd come down on when it came to the war between Wyatt and Elizabeth.

But there was only one way to find out. "I'm looking for Wyatt, actually. Have you seen him?"

Her expression didn't change, and that surprised me. I knew she'd heard about the murder. Everyone had. It seemed odd that she wouldn't show some emotion. "I haven't seen him since last week. Why?"

"I just need to talk to him. I was hoping Charlie would know where he is."

"He probably would if he was around. Why don't you just wait and call Wyatt at home?"

I guess that answered my question about how close she was to Elizabeth, but I still wanted to be careful. Maybe Nora didn't know anything. And maybe she was just a damn good liar.

"I would," I said, "but he's not *at* home these days."

Her expression underwent an abrupt change as understanding raced across her face and escaped her lips on a sigh. "Elizabeth kicked him out?"

"That's what they tell me."

She raked the fingers of one hand through her hair. "I was afraid of that. How long ago?"

"Nearly a week. He told me that he'd be staying at the High Country Inn, but I haven't been able to find him there. I think he must be somewhere else."

"Maybe you've just missed him."

"I don't think so. His truck is never there, and I've left at least a dozen messages, but he hasn't called me back. If he was getting the messages, he'd call—if only to yell at me to back off."

Nora laughed softly. "You might be right, but he could just be ignoring you. You know Wyatt."

"Yeah, I do. I also know Charlie. I think Wyatt's up on the mountain."

Nora stiffened almost imperceptibly. "That's not possible. Charlie hasn't been around to let him in."

"He wouldn't need Charlie to let him in, would he?"

She nodded and dragged a stack of mail across the counter. "We started locking the gate across that road about ten years ago. Too many trespassers. Wyatt doesn't have a key."

That wouldn't stop my brother if the stakes were high enough.

"Besides," Nora went on, tossing an advertising circular into the trash, "I was up there just yesterday. I had to get the cabins ready for a group coming in on Friday. If he was up there, I'd have seen him."

"Not if he's at Grandpa Stackhouse's cabin."

Tilting her head so she could study me, Nora slid an envelope into a box on the counter. "You think he's up *there*?"

"Can you think of a better place? He knows that area like the back of his hand. At least let me drive up there and look."

"I could do that, but it would be a waste of your time. That old cabin burned down two years ago."

That took the wind out of my sails. "It burned down?"

"Lightning strike. It was gone before we even knew there was a fire up there."

I couldn't hide my disappointment. I'd been so *sure*. The coincidence of two fires felt a little spooky to me, but the West had been in a serious drought for the past six years, and a lot of forest land has been lost to dry thunderstorms in that time.

Nora stopped sorting and watched me chewing my lip. "You're worried, aren't you?"

"Wouldn't you be?"

"About Wyatt?" She laughed and turned a catalog over so she could check something on the back. "He's a big boy, Abby. He can take care of himself."

"Under normal circumstances I'd agree with you—"

"He's fine." She met my gaze and held it. "I'm sure of it."

I felt the hair on the back of my neck stand up. "If you know where he is—"

Her gaze dropped. "I don't."

"I just want to talk to him," I pressed. "He was in town the night of the fire, and I want to know why."

Nora laughed and crumpled the last envelope in her fist. "Really, Abby. What do you *think* Wyatt was doing in town that night?"

"I don't know."

"What do he and Charlie ever do when they get together?"

Unless the world had changed dramatically in the past few years, I knew the answer to that. "They were drinking? *Together?*"

"You know how they are."

"But that means that Wyatt has an alibi. Why didn't he just tell me that?"

"You're his little sister. He doesn't think he should have to answer to you."

"Has he told the police? Have *you* told the police?"

"We will if it's necessary. If he's innocent, he won't need one."

"In a perfect world, maybe. But that's not the world we're living in."

"You're going to have to trust, Abby. Wyatt knows what he's doing. So does Charlie. Things will work out fine, just you wait and see. Now, I'm sorry, but I can't tell you anything more. Wherever he is, I'm sure he'll be in touch when he's ready."

I wanted to scream. Maybe tear my hair out in frustration. "Wyatt has an alibi, but nobody wants to share that tidbit with the police? Why in the hell not?"

I could almost see the walls snapping up around her, and I knew I'd pushed far enough. "I'm sure Wyatt can explain it all . . . if he wants to."

"Yeah, and what are the chances of that?" Doing my best to swallow my disappointment, I pulled my keys from my pocket and turned toward the door. "If you hear from him—"

"I'll let you know."

Yep. I believed that. Just like she'd been so quick to tell me Wyatt had the damn alibi in the first place. I'd just have to keep trying to find answers, and hope that Wyatt would eventually come to his senses.

The trouble is, we're talking about my brother. Common sense isn't something Wyatt Shaw has in abundance. I just hoped it wouldn't be his downfall.

Chapter 19

I was halfway across the valley when it hit me. Wyatt didn't have an alibi at all. Charlie was just prepared to stand up in court and perjure himself to keep him from going to prison. Take what I said about Wyatt and common sense. Multiply it by ten. That's Charlie Stackhouse for you.

Don't get me wrong. I'm glad my brother has such a loyal friend. I don't think anybody would do something like that for me. But since Charlie could lose everything and *still* not save Wyatt's sorry hide, it didn't seem like the smartest move he could make.

Knowing that only made me more determined to find out what really happened at Man About Town.

Midway between Paradise and Aspen, in a broad valley gouged into the mountains by some long-ago glacier, lies the tiny community of Thomasville. For more than a hundred years, a group of hardy folks scraped a living from the soil.

Farmhouses still dot the landscape today, but few of the people who live there work the land. Some work at regular jobs. Some have been bitten by the tourist-trade bug. And developers are hungry for any piece of land in that area they can get their hands on. One by one, those old houses are being purchased and replaced.

The Dumonts just happen to be one of the area's oldest families and owners of just about all of the prime land in the center of the valley. According to local legend, the land where Devil's Playground sends skiers careening down the mountainside once belonged to the Dumonts.

Lucas's great grandpa, old Horace Dumont, lost it to a developer during a high-stakes poker game back in the 1940s. They say he was flying high on tequila at the time or he never would have let that land go.

Horace was pretty upset when he sobered up, but he was as good as his word, and signed over the deed as promised. Lucas's daddy, Nathan Dumont, frequently holds up old Horace as a shining example of good sportsmanship. What Nate neglects to mention is that Horace never recovered from the emotional shock and ended it all by driving his truck off the side of that same mountain a few years later.

Maybe he wasn't such a good sport after all.

Lucas is in his early twenties. He's worked for Brandon since shortly after high school, but he still lives with his parents. And why not? They have money, and he likes the stuff that comes with it.

To tell the truth, I'm not sure why he even bothered to work at Man About Town. His wages might have been competitive within the market, but I'm sure they were nothing to brag about—especially when the checks didn't clear the bank.

I like driving fast, and I was in the right mood to indulge myself. Within minutes, the town fell away behind me and the road curved through a mountain valley of lush, green grass and river willows. Sage-dappled hills rolled into granite cliffs on either side of me, and afternoon shadows stretched across the meadow. Even Max roused himself enough to take an experimental sniff or two of fresh air.

The turnoff to the Dumont property was impossible to miss. The ornate wrought-iron fence that spans the turnoff clearly marks it as leading to Something Significant.

Within a few feet, the lane turns to gravel, and I bounced along slowly, stirring up dust in my wake. Aspen trees surround the drive, and this evening their leaves shimmered golden in the fading sunlight. A dozen outbuildings had been sprinkled among the trees over the years, but I didn't see anyone stirring until I drove into the broad clearing at the end of the road.

There, a large modern cabin made of honey-colored logs and glass holds center stage. The setting sun reflected off its high, wide windows, turning everything around me—house, trees, and glass—into gold.

Fitting, I thought. Nate Dumont would love the illusion that he had the Midas Touch. If it were possible, he'd pay off Mother Nature to create a moment just like this.

Lucas was a bit too much like his daddy for my taste. Almost from the beginning, Brandon had run into trouble with his attitude. Lucas liked arriving for work late and leaving early, and his favorite part of the job was break time, which he exercised frequently and often extended beyond the usual fifteen minutes. I would have fired him a long time ago, but Brandon was either more patient or more of a pushover than I am.

A BMW, a Hummer, and a Denali were parked on the driveway when I pulled up. If these were the cars they left outside, I wondered what treasures they had locked away. I parked at the edge of the drive so I didn't block anyone's exit, and took a few seconds to get my bearings.

From somewhere nearby, music blasted into the silence, and I had a gut feeling that Lucas was responsible. Urging Max to come along, I followed the noise and found a set of long skinny legs that could only have been Lucas's poking out from beneath a restored Chevy pickup that looked older than I am.

A hand snaked out from under the truck and pulled something from an open tool box. When it disappeared again, a clang echoed across the clearing, and a few choice words I'd bet his mother didn't like followed.

Max trotted obediently at my heels as we approached the truck. He didn't seem unduly concerned or interested, so I reasoned that he hadn't been chasing Lucas through the streets of Paradise.

Lucas must have seen us standing there since he couldn't possibly have heard us over the stereo and the cursing. He rolled out from under the truck and stared up at us, shielding his eyes from the sun with one grease-stained hand.

He's rail thin, probably about six-two, with short-cropped dark hair and a chin covered with facial hair. Today, he wore a pair of coveralls that looked as if he'd picked them up at the Goodwill.

"Hey, Abby. What are you doing here?" I think that's what he said. I couldn't actually hear him.

"I'm looking for you," I shouted back. "Do you have a minute?"

He pushed a button on the stereo and a deafening silence fell over the old homestead. "Sure. What's up?"

"I'm trying to piece together what happened the day Brandon died, but there are a few things that just don't make sense to me. I wonder if you can help me."

He turned away to close the lid on his tool box. "I doubt it. Seems pretty simple to me. The store caught on fire, and Brandon died. What doesn't make sense about that?"

"Someone started the fire," I reminded him. "It wasn't caused by spontaneous combustion."

He leveled a glance at me. "I know that."

"Any ideas about who did it?"

With a smirk, Lucas reached for a rag and rubbed at the grease on his hands. "Is that a serious question? Everybody knows who did it."

"My brother is innocent."

Lucas shrugged and tossed the rag over his shoulder. "If you say so. But he was mad enough to kill *somebody* last time I saw him."

That wasn't exactly welcome news. "You saw him? When was that?"

"Last Monday. About five-thirty."

My stomach lurched. "Where?"

"At the store."

"You mean Man About Town?"

Lucas nodded. "He just about took the door off its hinges when he came inside, too."

I wasn't sure I wanted the answer to my next question, but I had to ask. "Do you know what he was upset about?"

"Do you really have to ask?"

"Do you know the answer?"

Lucas looked away and started gathering the tools he'd scattered across the lawn. "It was about his old lady, okay?"

"Elizabeth."

He looked up sharply. "What?"

"She's not his 'old lady,' she's his wife. Her name is Elizabeth."

"Yeah?" Lucas stared at me for a minute as if he was having trouble following. He scratched at the hair on his chin. "Okay. Whatever. All I know is that Wyatt was madder than hell."

"And what did Brandon do when Wyatt showed up at the store?"

"You knew Brandon. What do you think?"

Patience, I told myself. I wouldn't accomplish anything without it. "Why don't you just tell me?"

Lucas raked a glance at me. Shrugged. "Whatever. He didn't sound all that upset. He just kept saying it was all over. Everybody was going to know the truth."

"The truth? *What* truth?"

"Whatever your brother doesn't want people to know about."

Thank you, Captain Obvious! "Did you hear anything my brother said? Details would help."

"Just enough to know they were fighting over his old lady."

"Elizabeth," I said automatically.

This time Lucas shook his head. "That wasn't the name."

My next question froze on my lips. "It wasn't? Are you sure?"

"I was there."

"Well, if it wasn't Elizabeth, who was it?"

Lucas tossed off a shrug. "Don't remember."

"Well, *think.*"

He dragged another lazy glance across my face. "Look, all I know is they were fighting over money and some woman."

"Money?" I actually felt myself do a double take. "What money?" Wyatt doesn't have any money and, apparently, neither did Brandon.

Lucas wiped his forehead with the back of his sleeve. "I don't know. *The* money. That's all I could hear."

"You weren't in the room?"

He shook his head. "Me and Chelsea were unpacking a shipment in the back when your brother went after him. It got pretty ugly, though. Chelsea was bawling like a baby, and Max was going berserk. It was insane."

The more I learned, the more confused I became . . . and the more guilty Wyatt seemed. "I suppose you've told the police all of this."

"Sure. I have nothing to hide."

A breeze stirred the leaves in the trees, and the clearing was filled with the *hush hush* of dancing aspen leaves. There were things that didn't make sense. Parts of the story that didn't add up. Had I missed something?

"What time did you say this happened?"

"About five-thirty."

Before Elizabeth met Brandon. Before—according to her story anyway—Wyatt found out about the meeting. But if that were true, why had Wyatt gone to see Brandon? What money—what *woman*—were they fighting about?

"At what point did Brandon ask Chelsea to take Max?"

Lucas shook his head. "He didn't. She just did it."

"She just took him? Brandon didn't tell her to?"

"You have to know Chelsea. She was scared. Said she knew that's what Brandon would want her to do."

"And Brandon didn't mind?"

"Of course he minded. He was royally pissed when he found out. And you know what? If she hadn't done that, Brandon would probably still be alive, and your brother would have been in a dozen pieces. Max would have torn him apart if he could have."

"Why did she take him?"

"I just told you. Max would have taken your brother apart. Chelsea knew that if Max hurt somebody, there'd be a lawsuit. It wasn't something she worried about most of the time, but that day—"

It was hard to imagine Max, who lay at my feet with his head propped on his paws, worked up enough to take my brother apart, but I knew firsthand how strong the dog was.

Even Wyatt would be hard-pressed to hold his own against him.

"What happened then?"

"I picked up the phone to call the police, but your brother left before I could."

"He left? Just like that?"

"Yeah. I guess he didn't want trouble with the police. I mean, he threatened Brandon before he left, but that's about it."

"Was it a serious threat?"

"Obviously serious enough."

I was having trouble working the scenario out in my head. If Wyatt had been that angry, he wouldn't have turned tail and run off just because Lucas picked up the phone. "Did you think it was a serious threat at the time?"

Lucas's dark eyes clouded as he gave that some thought. "I guess not," he said after a while, "or I *would* have called the police."

That's what I thought. Wyatt might have wanted to make Brandon nervous, but he hadn't been trying to harm him. "Besides my brother, who else do you think might have wanted to hurt Brandon?"

Dropping the last of the tools into his toolbox, Lucas toed the lid shut. "Who knows?"

"Tell me about the bounced paychecks."

He laughed without humor. "Seems to me, you already know about 'em."

"I want to know how you felt when you didn't get paid. Were you angry?"

With a grin, Lucas leaned against the pickup truck. "I wasn't happy, but it wasn't that big a problem for me. Chelsea was mad as hell, though. She never has money when she *gets* paid. Missing a paycheck or two was big trouble for her."

"She was angry? I thought she understood."

Lucas laughed again. "Is that what she told you?"

I nodded. "But it's understandable if she and Brandon were engaged."

"Engaged?" Lucas's amusement shifted in front of my

eyes. "They weren't engaged. Brandon never even looked twice at her."

"But I thought—"

"I told you that you had to know her. She's crazy. Always talking about her 'special relationship' with Brandon. Acting like she owned the place. Every time she got pissed at me, out would come the 'Brandon' card. It was bogus."

"They didn't have a special relationship?"

"In her head."

"So then she wasn't understanding about the bounced checks."

"Not even close."

"Do you think she was angry enough to kill him?"

Lucas pushed away from the pickup with a sharp laugh. "If you think I'm going to answer that, *you're* crazy. I'd be careful if I were you. You can't go running around Paradise saying shit like that without causing trouble. Somebody might take you serious."

The way someone had with Brandon? I suppressed a shudder. "I wish somebody *would* take me seriously."

"Not that way, you don't."

I met his gaze and held it. His eyes were brown, flecked with bits of green, and they flickered nervously as he stared back at me.

"What do you know about Brandon's death?" I asked.

"Nothing. Look, Abby, I know you're wigged out about this, but don't do something stupid, okay?"

A shiver skittered up my spine. Was that a warning? Or a threat? "I've heard that Brandon was seen arguing with another man the night before the fire. Do you know anything about that?"

He turned away and started toward the house. "This is getting old," he said over his shoulder. "I'm done."

I couldn't tell if I'd spooked him or if he'd really just grown tired of all my questions. "Who was the guy? Do you know?"

He ignored me and ran up the stairs, leaving me with a lot more questions than I'd had when I arrived.

Chapter 20

On my way into town again, I stopped at Mc-Donald's and ordered a Big Mac and large fries for myself, a Quarter Pounder plain for Max. After they shoved the order at me through the drive-in window, I drove to the edge of the parking lot and invited Max into the front seat so I wouldn't have to eat alone.

He took an experimental lick or two, but even beef didn't lift him out of his lethargy. After a few minutes, he curled onto the seat and dropped his chin on my leg.

I munched for a while, running over the conversations I'd had over the past few days. Stella Farmer. Chelsea Jenkins. Lucas Dumont. Had one of them murdered Brandon? Or was someone else responsible?

The whole thing was giving me a giant headache. I couldn't make sense of anything I'd learned. Time lines confused me, and the stories were all twisted up together. Maybe I needed to stop trying so hard and think about something else for a while.

But that was easier said than done. I was tearing open a package of ketchup with my teeth when something broke through the fog in my head, and I realized that I was sitting directly across the street from Paradise Auto Body. Actually, it occurred to me that I should get an estimate on the damage to my car. It probably wouldn't hurt to call my insurance agent, too. She'd left half a dozen messages for me, and to get Karen off my back I'd finally left a couple in return, but we hadn't actually made contact yet.

Meanwhile, I was driving around with a missing taillight and a dangling bumper. I was lucky I hadn't earned a glove-box full of tickets, compliments of Detective Jawarski. When I finished eating, I tossed the trash and drove across the street. A few cars dotted the parking lot, but both work bays were empty. Only the strains of a country-western song blaring into the night gave any sign of life.

Someone must have been watching, though. Before I could get out of the car, a burly mechanic with too much body hair strolled into the light. He wore grease-crusted jeans and a shirt that might once have been blue on which someone had stitched "Orly" in dark thread.

He ran a glance across the front of the Jetta and strolled toward my open window. "Help you?"

Max looked up at him without much interest. The mechanic looked back without so much as a blink.

"Do you have time to give me an estimate? I had an accident a couple of days ago, and I guess I really should get the damage taken care of."

"Sure. Whatcha looking at?"

Dislodging myself from beneath Max's chin, I slipped outside and guided Orly toward the back bumper. "I'm missing a taillight, and the bumper needs help."

With a soft whistle, Orly shot a glance at me. "Sure does. How'd you manage this?"

"Don't ask."

"It's just strange, is all." He scratched his belly and hunkered down to inspect the bumper. "I had another car in here yesterday. Broken headlight. Smashed-up grill. Belonged to a cop." Orly grinned up at me, revealing a set of badly stained teeth. "Said some crazy lady backed into him."

"If I admit it was me, will it change the estimate?"

He stood again and shook his head. "No. Just curious. But I've gotta tell ya lady, there's smarter ways to smash up your car than backing into a cop."

"Next time I'm looking for a way to smash up my car, I'll remember that. How much do you think it will cost to fix it?"

"Hard to say." He strolled slowly along the back of the car, ran a hand along the fender, cocked an eyebrow at the door, and flicked something from one of his teeth with his tongue. "You the lady that runs that candy store in town?"

I wondered if I should admit it. Divinity's trendy location just might make him think I had money, but lying wouldn't get me anywhere. "I am," I said. "Are you a customer?"

"Me?" He laughed through his nose. "Not me. My sister loves that place, though. She's got the money to burn, I guess. Bought me a box of your stuff once for Christmas. Them caramel doohickeys with the cherries in 'em were damn good."

Fix my car for a reasonable price, and there's a whole box of Divinity's Damn Good Caramel Doohickeys with Cherries in 'Em for you. Worried that offering such a precious bribe might cause me future problems, I held back the offer and worked up what I hoped looked like a sincere smile. "I'm glad you liked them. They're an old family recipe."

"Well it's a good'un." He jerked his head toward the car again. "How soon you need 'er done?"

"That's negotiable, but I don't want to get a ticket for driving around without a taillight."

He curled a yellow-toothed grin at me. "Seems to me, a missing taillight might be the least of your worries."

"Not if Detective Jawarski is a vengeful man."

That seemed to tickle his funny bone. Laughing through his nose again, he turned back to the building. "I'll write you up a form, but if you want 'er fixed here, you'll have to call and make an appointment. Probably won't be able to get to 'er 'til next week sometime."

I trailed him into the small office, but when Max let out a mournful howl of protest I moved back into the doorway so he could see me. I hoped he'd get over his depression soon. Life might get a little confining around a dog with emotional issues. Then again, life with Max would be pretty confining even if he was in perfect emotional health.

Orly dug around for the appropriate form, scribbled something on it, and shoved it at me. "There you go. That's the best we can do."

I glanced at the figure and heard myself gasp. "Nine hundred and fifty-three dollars? Are you *kidding*?"

He held up both hands to indicate that it wasn't his fault. "Cars are expensive. You got a deductible, dontcha?"

"Yes, but nine hundred and fifty-three dollars?" My voice rose a little higher with each word, and Max lunged to his feet, obviously aware that I was upset.

For the first time, Orly seemed to become aware of him. He backed a little farther into the shop and clutched the door with one dirty hand. "You don't like my figures, take your car somewhere else. No skin off my nose."

"Right." I crumpled the estimate and stuffed it into my pocket, crossed the parking lot, and slid into the car to comfort my new best friend. I cranked the Jetta to life and shifted into reverse. "Idiot," I muttered under my breath.

Max growled softly. An agreeable sort of growl, and I found myself grinning as I sped out of the parking lot and back into traffic. It had been a while since anyone had championed me. For the moment, at least, I didn't even care that my knight in shining armor drank out of the toilet.

Fifteen minutes later, I rounded the corner onto Prospector, and my spirits sank again. A familiar-looking Blazer with a broken headlight sat on the street in front of Divinity. The hulking shadow inside told me the truck hadn't come alone.

Of all the things I didn't need right then, a visit from Jawarski ranked right up there near the top. I thought about driving past, but I couldn't get away without him seeing me. Swearing under my breath, I pulled into my parking spot and opened the door for Max just as Detective Jawarski rounded the corner. He was wearing jeans, a black polo shirt, and a pair of well-worn loafers. He looked almost human.

To my dismay, Max trotted toward him for a sniff.

Jawarski roughed up Max's head a little, as if being sniffed by a vicious attack dog was an everyday occurrence. I wondered how much it would cost to reprogram a dog, since mine couldn't even recognize a threat when he had his nose buried in the threat's crotch.

"Whatever it is," I said, "can it wait until morning? I've had a rough day."

Jawarski stuffed his hands into his pockets and kept coming. "I took my car in for an estimate."

"So I heard. If your quote is anything like mine, I might as well declare bankruptcy right now."

"I thought you had insurance."

"I do," I said, suddenly exhausted. "It was a joke."

He jerked his chin and pretended to smile. "I see. Well, it was a good one."

"Yeah. Really cracked you up." I held out my hand and gave my fingers an impatient wiggle. "Okay, so hand it over."

"It's with my insurance agent. I tried to give him your agent's information, but I couldn't read the name you gave me."

"I don't need a critique of my penmanship, Jawarski. Besides, it was perfectly legible."

"To you, maybe."

My muscles ached with weariness, and my patience began to fray. "My handwriting is fine. My agent's name is Maggie Sherwood, and her office is over on Silver King. Is that all, Detective Jawarski?"

He looked at me strangely, but I was too tired to care why. "That's all . . . unless you're ready to tell me where your brother is hiding."

"I have no idea. Believe me, I've looked."

"Okay. Have you found proof to back up your theory that he's innocent?"

See? This is why I dislike the man. It wasn't even what he said as much as the way he said it. The snarky smile on his face made me determined to take Max in for a refresher course. "As a matter of fact, I've found out several things you should know."

"Oh?"

"Oh. For instance, did you know that Chelsea Jenkins had some kind of weird obsession with Brandon? And that she's having money trouble? She's hanging on to her apartment by a thread, and when her payroll checks didn't clear the bank, that meant big trouble for her."

"Is that right?"

"And I don't know what you said to Stella Farmer, but she came in here the other day and threatened me."

He actually looked interested in that. "Exactly how did she threaten you?"

I tried to recall the actual words, but they lost something in the translation. He would have had to be here. "I don't remember exactly, but Lucas Dumont—"

He held up one of his huge paws in a signal for me to stop. "You've been conducting your own investigation?"

"No, I've been talking to neighbors about the untimely death of a friend. And don't tell me that's against the law, because I know it's not."

He leaned against my car and crossed one foot over the other. "I shouldn't need to tell you how important it is to make sure the investigative process isn't tainted."

I hated how comfortable he looked standing there while I was practically itching to get away from him. "Spare me the lecture, Detective. I told you, it's been a long day."

He turned down the wattage on his obnoxious smile. "You want to talk about it?"

"With you?" I shook my head, slipped my fingers through Max's collar, and started toward the stairs. "Maybe another time. Right now, all I want to do is curl up in bed with a good book and something warm to drink."

"Well, then, I won't stop you."

I could hear the scuff of his shoes on the pavement, so I assumed he was actually going to leave. Thank God. He was difficult enough to take on a good day.

"Abby?"

I'm not sure what surprised me most—the fact that he called after me again, or the fact that he used my first name. I turned back and found him watching me from beneath the street lamp. "I wouldn't get too attached to the dog if I were you. Brandon's next of kin showed up today to claim his personal effects."

I didn't know whether to feel relieved that they'd found

Brandon's family or disappointed at the thought of losing Max. I settled for something in between. "Really? Who?"

"A woman by the name of Charlene Mills. Brandon's wife."

I didn't make a conscious decision to sit, but I knew my knees were folding, and I could feel the cold seeping through my jeans. "His *wife?*"

"Apparently so." Jawarski came a few steps closer—close enough for me to see the concern in his eyes.

I hated seeing it there. It made me feel weak and vulnerable. "He was *married?*"

"Yep. Judging from your reaction, I guess it's safe to say he never mentioned that fact to you?"

"No, he never told me."

"That's not the worst of it, Abby. He was in business with a partner in Texas. When he ran out on his wife, he also embezzled close to a million dollars." Jawarski's voice gentled. "I'm sorry you have to find out about it this way. I just thought it might be easier . . . you know . . ."

He seemed as uncomfortable with the conversation as I was, and that's saying something. I couldn't keep looking at him. It was hard enough to hear the pity in his voice. I didn't want to see it on his face, too. "Don't worry about it," I said, making a heroic attempt to sound normal. "We weren't *that* close."

"Yeah, but—"

"Look." I scrambled back to my feet and turned away. "It's not that big a deal, okay? Thanks for letting me know, but it's not like I'm heartbroken or anything. We were friends, that's all."

Somehow, I reached the top of the stairs and even managed to get my key into the lock. From the corner of my eye, I could see Jawarski watching from the shadows, but I let myself inside and shut the door without a backward glance.

Chapter 21

Sitting alone in a darkened room sounded pretty inviting, but I didn't want Jawarski to think I was feeling sorry for myself—even though I was—so I turned on the lights and went into the kitchen for that warm drink. I poured milk and cocoa into a pan, dragged a container of toffee closer, and listened for the Dodge to drive away. When it finally did, I picked up the phone and dialed Karen's number.

She picked up on the third ring. Her voice sounded muffled and a little out of breath, which probably meant I'd interrupted her in the middle of laundry or something. The woman never stops working.

"How is it," I asked as soon as I heard her voice, "that you ended up with the *one* guy on the planet who isn't a lying piece of dog poop?"

"I'm just lucky, I guess. What happened?"

"Turns out Brandon was married."

"No!"

"Yes."

"And he never told you?"

"If he had, I wouldn't be calling you to tell you about it now. I don't think he told anybody. Apparently, he didn't think it was important." I filled Max's dish with dry food and gave him fresh water, then carried the phone and the toffee into the living room. I curled into a corner of the couch and loosened the floodgates on self-pity. "Or maybe he just forgot. Yeah, I'll bet that's it. It just slipped his mind."

"But why keep something like that a secret?"

"Think about it, Karen. Why would any man keep his wife a secret?"

"So he could have sex with other women?"

"That would be my guess."

"And you think he wanted to have sex with you?"

I crunched on a piece of toffee and felt a slight flicker of satisfaction over the creamy, buttery flavor. Nothing soothes my jangled nerves any better. "Don't sound so shocked," I protested. "It could have happened." Elizabeth's image flashed through my head, and I gave in to the sharp stab of jealousy that followed. "I think he just wanted to have sex with everybody. Sergio should be grateful. You could have been next on the list. Instead, I was there the night he died, primed and ready for an evening of hot monkey sex, Brandon style."

Karen caught back a laugh, but it was too late. I'd already heard it. That was all right. When I get angry, I become sarcastic. Or is it sardonic? Whatever, Karen understands me. Always has. That's what family is for. "Are those the words he used?"

"It's my own interpretation."

"Maybe you're wrong. Maybe he was planning a perfectly lovely, romantic evening."

"Oh. Oh, sure. That's different. Only— With me? Or with his wife or Elizabeth? Because that kind of matters, Karen."

"Yeah, I know. Abby, I'm sorry."

That made me feel marginally better. Nobody hands out sympathy when I really need it like my cousin. "You know what bugs me most? He knew about Roger. He knew how I felt about the affair. How *dare* he think I'd do that to some other woman?"

Covers rustled, and I heard a muffled whisper. Too late, I realized she wasn't alone. She wasn't folding laundry, either. "So are you hurt or pissed?" she asked.

"I'm both." Max clicked back into the room, let out one

of his depressed whines, and sank to the floor. I wasn't sure which of us was in worse shape. "The worst part of it is, there's nothing I can do."

"Tell her to take a pill and get some sleep," Sergio grumbled close to the phone. "We're a little busy here."

Usually, Sergio can make me smile when he jokes, but not tonight. Just now, the sound of his lightly accented English only saddened me. I ignored his suggestion. My own pity party was too satisfying. "You know what the worst part is? I can't even confront Brandon and ask for an explanation."

"You think he had one?"

"*Is* there such a thing for why you need to commit adultery?"

"Look, Abby," Karen sounded impatient. Sergio must have been urging her to hurry . . . in some way. "The point is, you didn't have sex with him—right? Or is there something you're not telling me?"

"And speaking of sex . . ." Sergio grumbled.

Karen's question shot holes in my righteous indignation, so I had to pump it up again. "No, I didn't, but—"

"So technically nothing happened."

"No, but . . ." I let my protest trail away and tried to figure out just what I was so angry about. Was I angry with Brandon for leaving out such a minor detail about himself, for his interest in Elizabeth, or was I angry with myself for making more of our relationship than he had? "Nothing happened," I said, "but it might have. If he'd shown up that night, I just might have gone to bed with him."

"And you're having a crisis over that?"

Was she *not* paying attention? "I suppose you think I'm overreacting."

"No . . ." she said in that tone that really means yes. I heard Sergio say something, and her muffled response that meant she'd covered the phone with her hand. "Look, Abby, this isn't about the possibility that you might have had sex with Brandon if he'd actually gotten around to asking you. There's something else chewing on you, so lighten up okay? Read something. Watch something mindless on TV. Have a couple of pieces of that toffee I know you're eating, but then give yourself a break. Maybe you'll figure out what's really bothering you."

She was gone before I could argue, but it wouldn't have done much good anyway. She was right. I hate when that happens.

I tossed the phone onto the cushion beside me, dragged the toffee onto my lap, and dug around the couch for the remote. So Brandon had a wife. Who was she, anyway? Why hadn't anyone ever seen her around here before? And why *hadn't* Brandon told me about her? Even with the evidence mounting, I had a hard time believing that he'd been that cold.

Another miserable whine floated across the room, and Max lifted his head. I picked up on the sound of footsteps going by outside, and I knew Max was hoping they belonged to Brandon.

With a sigh, I slid to the floor, taking my pillow and the emergency candy tin with me. I could almost feel the extra inches settling on my hips, but at that moment I didn't care.

If Aunt Grace had found herself in this predicament, she would have rushed to the candy kitchen and started cooking, but I just couldn't imagine finding solace in hot sugar syrup and flavor oils. Not tonight.

"Never again," I told Max solemnly. "I don't care who comes along. I'm through with men, present company excluded. I authorize you to remove body parts—theirs or mine—if you ever feel me weakening."

He yawned noisily and settled more comfortably in front of the door, and my heart constricted. Yeah, maybe it was pathetic, but I was getting used to having the dog around, and I didn't like the idea of some stranger breezing into town and taking him away. I just wasn't sure whether there was anything I could do to stop her.

I slept fitfully, disturbed by nightmares as Brandon and Roger marched through my subconscious. Somehow, Max got mixed up in there, too, darting in and out of my dreams, agitated and growling. So I didn't feel any more rested when

I climbed out of bed than I had when I'd finally tumbled into it a few hours earlier.

Rubbing eyes gritty with exhaustion, I stumbled down the hall and into the bathroom. In front of the toilet, my foot landed in something cold and wet where nothing cold and wet should have been. I pulled back sharply and stared in dismay at a puddle that didn't look—or smell—like rain water.

Muttering under my breath, I cleaned off my foot and mopped up the puddle, then went in search of the offender. He lay nose-to-door like always, an air of canine innocence about him.

Disgusted as I was, I couldn't really blame him. I'd been distracted last night and hadn't taken him outside for his before-bed walk. It was a little harder to overlook the pillow stuffing on the living room floor and the deep gouges in the doorframe. Obviously, Max needed attention.

I picked up a handful of stuffing and held it in front of his nose. "Max? What did you do?"

He let out a heavy dog sigh.

"And the bathroom. What happened in there?"

The poor dog looked so dejected, I had a hard time staying angry with him, but it seemed to me that his mental outlook was getting worse, not better. I couldn't ignore it, so I sat on the floor and lifted his head so I could look into his eyes. The sadness in them wiped away the last bit of irritation I'd been feeling. "It's okay, buddy. It's just one accident, and we're going to get you some help. But next time come and wake me up, okay? Chewing up my stuff is not the way to win my heart." Nor was lying to me about your marital status but, thankfully, Max and I didn't have to deal with particular issue.

Unfortunately, I didn't have time to think for long about either issue. Janice Smalley would be here in two hours to pick up her butterscotch bouquets and, much as I hated to admit it, Karen was right about one thing. I hadn't spent enough time thinking about the store and its future lately. Hell, I'd barely even thought about the present. If I really wanted to carry on Aunt Grace's legacy, I needed to pull my head out and focus.

The candy bouquets were my own idea, the first and only

thing I'd changed at Divinity since taking over. I can't even claim that the idea originated with me. I'd seen something similar once in Sacramento, but it seemed like an idea whose time had come.

Using craft wire and floral tape, I attached pieces of candy to a "stem" and arranged the bouquet in some kind of decorative container. People seemed to like the brass tins for the butterscotch bouquets, but I'd also used everything from cut glass with cinnamon "roses," to popcorn containers for flowers made of taffy.

Determined not to let anything sidetrack me, I made an appointment with Manny Garcia, the veterinarian, then trotted down the hall and slipped into sweats so I could take Max for a walk before I started working. By the time I stepped outside, the sun had already crested the mountains, spinning a dewy web of spun silk across the mountainside. The stormy weather had moved out again, and we were in for a glorious autumn day.

I led Max down the stairs and started toward the street, but as we passed the patch of flowers bordering our parking strip, he stopped walking so abruptly, I thought my arm would come out of its socket. Once again, the despondent dog was gone and Max the Protector was back.

Growling long and low, he followed the edge of the parking strip, searching for whatever scent had caught his attention. I gave him his way, partly because I knew it would be useless to fight him, partly because I wanted to see what had roused him out of the doldrums.

Halfway back to the apartment stairs, he stopped and lifted his head, staring off into the distance and breathing through both mouth and nose. I thought I remembered reading once that taste helps dogs to process what they smell, but I might have been making that up.

On the street, cars swished past as people started their morning, but Max paid no attention. He let out a whine and started sniffing again. This time he plowed through the flower bed and finally came to a stop near the bottom of the steps.

He looked back at me as if he expected something. I had

no idea what he wanted, but I stepped carefully into the flower bed beside him. "What is it, boy? What did you find?"

He whimpered again and buried his head in the flowers. He even seemed impatient with me for not understanding.

Far be it from me to irritate the dog. I squatted beside him and looked at the ground. Several of the flowers had been smashed, and two cigarette butts lay crushed in the middle of a large footprint. In fact, there were several large footprints in the mud.

"Is that it?" I asked Max. "The footprints?" It seemed like an odd place for them, but let's face it, people do strange things. And a town like Paradise is full of strange people doing strange things.

Thoroughly confused, I straightened again. As I did, I realized that whoever had been in the flower bed had been facing my apartment and a chill iced my spine.

Jawarski was my first thought. He'd been concerned about me last might. Maybe he'd stood there for a while. But I'd never seen him smoking, and I'd heard him driving away last night. Besides, these prints had been made by someone wearing a heavy boot. Even I could tell that from the waffle print on the sole. Jawarski had been wearing loafers last night.

I'm no expert in footprints, but unless I was mistaken, the prints hadn't been made by a woman, which meant Stella Farmer and Chelsea Jenkins were probably off the hook. But who could it have been? And why had he been there?

I didn't want to make too much of it, but I'll confess it left me a little shaky. I stood there for a few minutes contemplating my options. Just when I'd about decided I was overreacting, I heard a footstep on the pavement behind me. My heart slammed against my ribs, and I whipped around, eyes wild, to see who was there.

Holding up both hands to ward off an attack, Jawarski quick-stepped backward, out of my reach. "Whoa there, Ms. Shaw. Slow down."

Heat rushed into my cheeks, and I offered a sheepish smile. "Sorry. Two visits in two days. I know it's not because you like the pleasure of my company, but please don't tell me you have more good news."

He shrugged with his mouth and looked over my shoulder. He was wearing jeans again, this time with a pink polo shirt under a police-issue windbreaker. Roger always said it took a very secure man to wear pink, and Jawarski didn't disprove his theory. "You seem a little jumpy this morning. Something wrong?"

I shook my head. "Max found some footprints in the flowerbed. I was just looking at them."

"Footprints?"

"Yeah, but they're no big deal."

"Mind if I take a look?"

"Be my guest."

He did some looking, hunkered down and peered a little closer, then straightened again with a frown. "Is there somewhere we can talk?"

That question didn't fill me with warm fuzzies, but I nodded. I hadn't brought my shop keys, so my apartment was the only option. It always felt a little cramped, but it seemed downright minuscule with Jawarski standing smack-dab in the middle of it. He checked the door and the windows, and his scowl deepened. Finally, he stopped snooping around and plopped on one end of my couch.

I couldn't bring myself to sit on the couch beside him, so I sat with Max on the floor, winning the brief argument over my choice of seating, and settled back against the door with my arms wrapped around my bent knees.

Jawarski spied the candy dish and helped himself to a piece of toffee. He crunched happily for a minute, then held up the uneaten half and said, "Good. Did you make it?"

I had no idea why we were talking about candy, but I shook my head. "Aunt Grace did."

He popped the rest into his mouth and slipped another piece from the dish. "I should have known, I guess. This toffee of hers was one of my favorites."

"Mine, too," I admitted. "But I didn't realize you knew Grace."

"I thought everyone knew her," he said, and his smile was almost friendly. "I've been into Divinity a few times."

Why didn't I know that? I studied him closely, looking for something familiar. I came up blank, but he did have a strong chin. A firm mouth. Thick hair. All in all, he really wasn't bad-looking.

He kept talking as if he hadn't noticed me mentally cataloging his features. "Grace was a good lady, you know. A lot of people miss her."

I nodded slowly. "Yes, she was." He pulled a notebook from his shirt pocket and flipped to a new page, all set to interrogate me about something, but I wasn't ready to move on. Not just yet. "Jawarski?"

"Yeah?"

"Thanks."

He looked up in surprise. "For what?"

"For last night. For missing Aunt Grace."

His gaze met mine and locked on for a minute. "Sure."

Okay. Well. That was enough of that. I looked away and changed the mood. "So . . . you wanted to talk?"

He switched gears almost as quickly as I did. "Those footprints outside. How did you come across them?"

"Max found them. We were heading out for a walk, but he must have picked up on the man's scent."

"You didn't notice anyone hanging around out there?"

"Believe me, if I had, you'd have known about it."

One corner of his mouth lifted. He might even be pleasant-looking when he smiled. "Max didn't give any indication during the night that something was wrong?"

"He peed on my floor and chewed up a couple of pillows, but I don't really think that was a warning of danger." I thought about the dreams I'd had and wondered if they'd been more than dreams.

Jawarski made a note and took a third piece of toffee without even looking up. "If it was, it wasn't very effective. Any idea who it might have been?"

"Well, I don't think it was a woman. The feet are too big."

"Agreed."

"But I don't have any idea beyond that. I suppose it could have been Lucas Dumont, or maybe Duncan Farmer."

"Do either of them smoke?"

I shook my head slowly. "I don't think so, but I'm not sure. Maybe whoever it is only smokes when he's stalking people."

"I've heard of stranger things." He leaned forward, wiggling his fingers to lure Max. The big traitor scooted across the floor on his belly, and Jawarski commenced scratching behind his ears. "I'll have a couple of patrol officers talk with your neighbors to see if any of them noticed someone in that flower bed."

"I wouldn't count on it. I don't think the footprints were there last night when you came by. Max would have noticed them at the time if they were. Do you think they're something I should be worried about?"

He shook his head, but he didn't seem entirely convinced. "It wouldn't hurt you to get a little security around here, Ms. Shaw. You need a dead bolt at the very least, and some way to secure those windows. A five-year-old could break in here without any trouble at all."

I tried laughing, but the sound caught in my throat. "We're on the third floor."

"And you have a porch."

"You're making nervous, Jawarski. What's going on?"

Grim-faced, he tucked the notebook away. "We got the complete coroner's report back today. There was smoke in Brandon's lungs, so he was alive when the fire broke out. There was also a large contusion on the back of his skull. But the most interesting thing the coroner found was evidence that Brandon had been shot. Looks like someone put a bullet in him and then left him there, alive, when he started the blaze."

My stomach buckled, and my fingers went numb. "He was burned alive?"

"The smoke probably got him first, but it's pretty clear that we're not looking for a nice person who just stepped over the edge for a minute."

"Then you can't still believe my brother did this?"

Jawarski dipped his head slightly. "I still think it's a possibility."

But not a certainty. That was a step in the right direction. "Well, I know he didn't leave the footprints," I said. "Wyatt doesn't smoke, and his feet are a lot bigger than that. Besides, he wouldn't really need to hang around outside, would he?"

"Maybe not," Jawarski conceded, "but if your brother *is* innocent, we have another problem. Because whoever killed Brandon Mills may be watching you to see how much you know. All things considered, I think this might be a real good time for you to stop talking with neighbors about the untimely death of a friend, don't you?"

My empty stomach heaved. "But why would someone be watching *me?* I don't know anything."

"Not through any fault of yours. You've been doing everything you can to find out about the case. If the guy we're looking for did leave those footprints, maybe he's not too happy about that."

That pretty much ruled out the idea of a stranger riding into town, murdering Brandon, and then riding out again. Most of the people I'd spoken with were people I'd known forever and considered friends.

"Why don't you tell me who you've talked to in the past few days?" Jawarski urged. "That might help point us in the right direction."

I stared at him blindly—not because I didn't want to answer, but because the reality was hitting me for the first time, and I couldn't think. "What?"

"Tell me who you've talked to since Brandon died."

"I don't know . . ." I struggled to my feet and stared down at the street through the window. "Stella Farmer. Twice. Rachel Summers. She runs the candle shop just down the street." I rubbed my forehead and tried to get my brain working. "Iris Quinn. She has a bookstore around the corner."

I could see his reflection in the glass, and I watched until he finished making notes and looked up again. "That can't be all," he said. "You've been busier than that."

"I'm trying to remember. I talked to Nora Stackhouse out at Sage Fork Outfitters. Her husband is Wyatt's best friend. I talked to Lucas Dumont and Chelsea Jenkins. But there just doesn't seem to be anybody who hated Brandon enough to want him dead."

"Except your brother."

Filled with anger born of fear, I rounded on him. "I wouldn't have asked questions if you hadn't been so busy accusing Wyatt of something he didn't do."

"Good detective work means not rushing to judgment, Ms. Shaw. I have to explore every possibility. Shake the tree and see what falls out."

"Well, we know what fell out *now,* don't we? For the record, it wasn't *me* who gave Stella Farmer the impression that she was a murder suspect."

"I didn't mention your name."

"Apparently, you didn't need to."

"Apparently not. Look, Abby, it's probably nothing to worry about. We've probably all got our knickers in a twist over nothing. But don't take chances, all right? No more questions."

"That's fine with me as long as you do your job."

"I am doing my job, and it'll be a whole lot easier to keep doing it if you're not out there stirring up trouble."

Our disagreement disturbed Max. He lumbered to his feet, looked back and forth between us for a few seconds, then finally came to stand beside me. I felt as if I'd just won the lottery.

I shot a triumphant smile at Jawarski and decided to broach a subject I'd been avoiding. "Tell me something. Have you met Brandon's wife?"

"I have."

"Did she say anything about Max?"

"I asked what she wants to do about him. She's going to let me know."

I took a deep breath and let it out slowly, but I couldn't even breathe right. "And you'll let me know?"

"As soon as I hear anything."

"Okay, then. Thanks." It was hard to get that last word out, but I managed.

Jawarski actually smiled. An honest-to-God, turn up both corners of his mouth smile. To my chagrin, I discovered that I'd been right. He *was* reasonably pleasant to look at when he did that.

We stood there for a few seconds until Jawarski realized there was nothing left to say and turned away. But it didn't take long for me to decide that I didn't feel completely safe.

Completely? Hell, I didn't feel safe at all.

I mean, sure, I live at the top of the stairs, and since Aunt

Grace blocked off the inside staircase years ago, there's only one way in. But that means there's only one way out, too— if you don't count taking a dive out of the bedroom or kitchen windows. Anything could happen downstairs in Divinity without me knowing and, as Jawarski had pointed out, a child could get inside my apartment without even breaking a sweat.

For the first time in my adult life, I was afraid to be alone.

Chapter 22

Nothing on earth could have kept me hanging around that apartment after Jawarski left. Not even Janice Smalley and her butterscotch bouquets. At least not until I'd installed that added security he was talking about.

Even though Jawarski had sent a couple of uniforms through the building, I dragged Max on an inspection with me so I could be one-hundred-percent convinced that Karen wouldn't be in any danger if she showed up before I got back. To my immense relief, Max trotted obediently behind me and didn't show any interest in anything.

Fairly certain we were safe for the moment, I scribbled a hasty note for Karen, then loaded Max into the car and headed into traffic. I tried not to think about the footprints in the flower bed as I drove, but it was hard to think about anything else.

Traffic was light, so I made it to K-Mart in just a few minutes. It was a cool day, so I rolled down the windows a few inches for Max and hurried inside. Picking out dead bolts, window alarms, and a motion sensor took a little while, especially since I had to stop what I was doing every time someone passed me to look them over, make note of their choice in footwear, and sniff for the scent of stale tobacco.

Finally, I had everything I needed, and the total sale left me with renewed determination to make sure the store had a prosperous winter season.

I'd just finished paying when I noticed Urban Ross buying a half-case of cold beer at one of the self-pay machines. Even though I was trying not to think about the bombshell Jawarski dropped on me the night before, I couldn't make myself walk away. I had too many questions.

Since I didn't want to ask them inside where others could overhear, I left the store, tossed my bag into the car, and sat on the trunk to wait. I could see Urban's Harley from where I'd parked, so I killed time breathing clear, fresh air unlike anything I'd ever experienced in the city. A touch of autumn took the edge off the sun's warmth, and a slight breeze sent showers of leaves from the trees every few minutes.

Urban came outside toting a twelve-pack and wearing leather chaps over brown corduroys. His T-shirt bore a picture of a pirate advising people to "Abandon All Hope." Cute. Brandon would have loved it.

Halfway across the parking lot, Urban saw me sitting there, wedged a pair of sunglasses onto his face, and shifted direction so that he was walking toward me.

"Hey, Abby." He grinned and detoured to the back window and left the beer on the ground so he could scratch Max's nose. "Heard a rumor that you ended up with custody of the kid. How's it going?"

I shrugged. "Okay, I guess. He misses Brandon."

"Yeah. I'll bet he does. You're out early."

"So are you." I watched a solitary leaf float across the parking lot and considered telling him about my visitor last night. Urban was the one resident of Paradise I knew personally who both wore heavy-soled boots and smoked, but I couldn't figure out why I didn't suspect him. Gut instinct, I guess. Still, it might be a good idea to keep a few things to myself.

"I need to ask you a question," I said, "and I need you to be honest with me, okay?"

He cut a glance my way and straightened slowly. "Sure. What's up?"

"Did you know that Brandon was married?"

"Married?" He whooped a laugh, realized I wasn't joking, and stared at me, incredulous. "Married? Are you kidding me? Where'd you hear that?"

"From the police. Apparently, his wife has arrived to claim his personal effects."

"Holy sh—" Urban ran a hand over his face and shook his head. "You're serious?"

"Does that mean you didn't know?"

"Hell, no, I didn't know." He scratched at the tangle of curls on his head and laughed uneasily. "That's a hard one to believe. Just when you think you know a person, huh?"

"Yeah. Just when. Did you know that when he ran off and left his wife in Texas, he also absconded with close to a million dollars?"

Urban gaped at me, and I believed that his shock was real. It took a minute, but he finally got his head wagging back and forth. "Uh-uh. No. That I won't believe. Brandon did not have that kind of money."

"What makes you so sure?"

"Because he didn't. He was always scraping by, running through his books in his head. Trying figure out how to pry money out of one place so he could plug a hole in another. If he'd walked off with that kind of money, his life would have been a whole lot different."

"Maybe he didn't want people to suspect."

"Look," Urban said, a trifle impatiently. "Brandon wasn't stupid. He wouldn't have started living the high life or anything, but he would have filtered the money into his pockets slowly. A little here. A little there. He wouldn't have been talking about getting small business loans and worrying about getting through the next season."

In spite of everything, I wanted to believe him. Brandon hadn't been perfect, and I wouldn't have lasted a month in an actual relationship with him. But he had been a friend when I needed one.

Urban touched my shoulder with surprising gentleness. "Hey. You okay?"

"Yeah. Of course I'm okay. Why wouldn't I be?"

"Finding out . . . well, it had to be kind of a shock."

"It was a surprise," I said, hoping I sounded convincing.

"But I've learned a lot of things that have surprised me in the past week."

"Yeah, but the married thing. That's harsh."

"Brandon and I were friends," I said firmly. "We weren't a couple. You know that."

Urban rested one hand on the trunk of my car. Once again, I felt that strange sense of comfort I'd felt in his living room. "You were more than friends, Abby. Brandon dug the hell out of you."

I didn't want to believe that. Couldn't let myself believe it. "Brandon liked a lot of women. It was just my turn."

"Abby—"

"We had a mild flirtation, but that's all it was. If Brandon had lived, he'd probably already be moving on to the next woman on his life."

Urban nudged a fallen leaf with the toe of his army boot. "Look, I know Brandon had a reputation. Maybe now we know why, huh? But he did like you, Abby. A lot. You wouldn't have been just another weekend fling to him."

I still wasn't sure if that made me feel better or worse. "That's nice of you to say, but—"

"Hey, I'm serious." Urban held up both hands, as if proving he didn't have fingers crossed would convince me. "I don't know anything about a wife. I don't know what was going on with Chelsea or Elizabeth. But I do know how he felt about you."

I knew now. I felt worse. "I could have gone all day without you telling me that."

Urban laughed and chucked me under the chin, just the way Brandon used to, only his touch didn't make me weak in the knees. "It's going to be okay, Abby. All you need is time."

"I hope you're right."

"Being hurt isn't fatal. Trust me. Just be patient with yourself, okay?"

I nodded, and he walked over to his Harley. As I watched him ride away I realized that trusting other people wasn't the problem. What I really wondered was how long it would take me to trust myself again.

　　　　　•　　•　　•

Manny Garcia told me Max's behavior wasn't unusual. Urinating in the wrong place could be a symptom of the dog's anxiety. So could chewing things and scratching holes in walls. He gave me some suggestions for lifting Max's spirits, along with a prescription. Not a wonder drug, he warned me. I'd have to work with Max to help him through his separation anxiety.

I just hoped I'd get the chance. I also wished Manny had come up with another way to reach Max. I didn't want the apartment destroyed because the dog was having emotional issues, but if not for him, I wouldn't know someone had been watching my apartment. Did I really want to sedate him?

After a lengthy internal debate, I slipped the bottle into my purse and left it there. Just in case. Never say never.

I drove back across town and pulled into my parking space next to a shiny black Lexus I recognized from its vanity plates. Maggie Sherwood is between sixty and sixty-five with salt-and-pepper hair and a Tennessee accent so thick it curls vowels when she talks. She's not a skier, hates the cold, and complains from October to May every year, but her husband loves it here, and she, for reasons only she understands, has made the sacrifice. I'm not sure I could. Maybe I've just never loved anybody that much.

"I've been trying to reach you for a week," she said before I even got out of the car. "You can't plow into a police officer's car and then avoid my calls. That isn't smart."

"I wasn't avoiding your calls," I assured her. "I've been busy, that's all."

"Too busy to cover your ass?"

I stood and sent a little half-smile to see if I could coax her into a better mood. "I thought that's what the insurance was for."

"Don't be flip, Abby. Just tell me how this happened."

"You haven't seen the police report?"

"I have. I want to hear your version."

I gathered the goodies I'd picked up at K-Mart and started walking. "My version pretty much matches what it says in there. I was backing out of the driveway, and I didn't see him."

"In spite of the fact that he was parked directly behind you? Parked, Abby. Not pulling in. Not moving. Parked."

I chewed the side of my lip and tried to decide just how honest to be. I didn't need my insurance rates spiking on top of everything else, but I didn't know if a tiny white lie or two could prevent that or if I'd only make things worse. "I was upset," I admitted. "I didn't check as thoroughly as I should have."

Maggie's scowl deepened the lines around her mouth. "Sounds to me like you didn't look at all."

"I did." I flashed a look at her and added, "I think. I don't really remember."

Closing her eyes in dismay, Maggie let out a sigh that could have launched a hot-air balloon. "This isn't going to be good, Abby. You have to know that. You're going to lose your preferred driver discount for sure, and I don't know what all might be involved."

She followed me into the candy kitchen and snitched a couple of butterscotch buttons from the mound Karen had left on the counter for me. "It was an accident," I said, sounding all of about twelve. "I didn't mean to hit him."

"Well, thank God for that! I can't even imagine what kind of mess we'd have if you had. Have you even bothered to get an estimate on your car?"

"I have." And thankfully I had it in my bag. I dug it out, a little worse for the wear, and passed it over. "Can you believe that? It's the only one I've gotten, but I can get others . . ."

She waved away the offer. "This is one of the approved body shops we work with. You'll be all right taking it there." She smoothed both hands across the form and studied it for a minute, and for some reason that seemed to cut the edges off her anger. When she looked at me again, her eyes were filled with the same warmth that had made me choose her for my agent in the first place. "You weren't injured?"

"Just my pride."

She nodded toward Max who was trotting behind me like a perfect angel. "And your friend? When did you get him?"

I gave her the short explanation of when and how, ending with, "I don't know if I'll be keeping him, though. Brandon's wife is in town to pick up his effects. I'm assuming that includes Max."

"Really? Too bad. He seems to like you."

"Yeah." I noticed a few mug arrangements sitting near the window, sent up a silent prayer of thanks for Karen, and shoved one toward Maggie. Each mug had an autumn motif with brightly colored cellophane "leaves" creating a background for the wrapped caramels inside.

Maggie's mouth pursed into a little "O" of pleasure, and I felt myself relax a little. I scratched the top of Max's head, and he lifted his nose for more. "The dog hasn't been around long, but I've enjoyed the company. Gives me somebody to talk to at the end of the day."

Maggie unwrapped a caramel and slid it into her mouth. She's a woman after my own heart. "We all need somebody, don't we? Nobody makes it through this life alone."

I knew what she meant. Technically, I wasn't alone. I had friends. I had family. I just didn't have someone to curl up with at the end of the day. On the other hand, I hadn't had that when I was married, either.

In true Maggie fashion, her moment of softness was over almost before it began. Her head snapped up, and she whipped toward the door as if the world was about to come to an end somewhere else, and she had to get there first. "I'll have Marielle call you for a complete accident report. Meanwhile, get your car fixed. You'll feel better."

"Right," I called after her. Then, to myself, "The very minute I can afford the deductible."

I settled Max outside the back door with some food and water, thought again about giving him his medication, and decided against it. Maybe in a day or two after my nerves settled again. I was just coiling the hose behind a park bench when a new Trailblazer pulled up in front of the curb at Picture Perfect. It was either the color of sand or champagne, depending on the way you look at life, and I recognized Duncan Farmer behind the wheel.

Since Max was with me, it was the middle of the day, and cars were passing at a regular rate on the street, I decided to wait a minute and see how Max reacted to him. One growl, and I'd be on the phone to Jawarski.

Duncan heaved himself out of the SUV and squaddled toward us. He's a large man whose reddish-gray hair seems to shrink away from his face. Even when his clothes make it all the way around him, he seems to be overflowing them. He was big enough to have made the footprints outside of my apartment. But had he?

He didn't look happy to see me but, then, Duncan never looked happy to see me. He didn't look unhappy, either, so I took that as a positive sign. Puffing a little, he stepped onto the curb and glanced at Max. "Abby."

"Duncan."

If Max had any objection to Duncan's presence, he wasn't sharing it with me.

"You've got my Stella mighty upset. I guess you know that, don't you?"

"She mentioned it."

He pulled a handkerchief from his pocket and mopped his forehead. "It's not a good thing to go around accusing people of things. You can make enemies that way. That's one thing nobody needs."

"I never accused her of anything, Duncan. The detective asked me a question, and I answered it. If I hadn't, someone else would have."

He turned one of those "there, there" looks on me. "Now, Abby, you know Stella isn't capable of hurting another human being."

"I know she was angry with Brandon," I said, "and I know she has a temper."

"She's a passionate woman." Some of the syrup in Duncan's voice dried up. "She feels strongly about things, and she has a real dislike for people who take advantage. If that's a crime, this world is a sorry place."

"Look," I said, "I know Brandon wasn't perfect, but I still don't know what he did to upset her so much. From what everyone says, he wasn't in good shape financially, so it doesn't make sense for him to try putting you out of business."

"And yet he came up with that lame suggestion for expanding the Arts Festival."

"Not as a means of driving you out."

"You don't think so?" Duncan smirked as if he felt sorry

for me, and I battled the urge to wipe that smile right off his face. He mopped his forehead again and stuffed the handkerchief back into his pocket. "I guess we'll never know what he was up to, will we? I'm just glad the question of expanding that damn Arts Festival is finally out of our hair."

"There's been no vote yet."

"Well, sure, but without Brandon to spearhead it, the idea's pretty much dead in the water."

"Unless somebody else takes it up." Yeah, I know. It wasn't exactly smart to antagonize him, but I liked the idea, and not because Brandon had suggested it. Getting all those tourists walking around the downtown area for days at a time with money burning a hole in their pockets? Sounded like a great idea to me.

Duncan narrowed his beady little eyes at me. "You aren't getting any big ideas about that are you?"

I shook my head and flashed a reassuring smile. "Not me." I hadn't decided anything for sure, and I figured one little white lie wouldn't hurt.

The relief on his face was so thick it might have been laughable if we'd been talking about something else. "Well, that's good. That's real good. I'm not worried about many of the others. Stella and me, we can talk sense into the rest of 'em, no problem."

I knew all about Stella's brand of "talking sense," and I didn't like it. "I wouldn't be too sure," I said. "There are plenty of people who like the idea."

"Not anymore. Look what it got Brandon."

"You think someone killed him over the Arts Festival?"

"I wouldn't be surprised."

"But why? It's only four days out of a lifetime."

"Not to some people."

Was he serious? "Who?"

"Griff Banks, for one. He's spent the past ten years trying to put Paradise on the map with the film festival. Then along comes Brandon, and instead of joining forces the way Griff suggested, Brandon takes off with a whole different idea and steals the thunder for himself."

A disbelieving laugh escaped before I could stop it. "*What* thunder?"

"There's a lot of prestige attached to events like the Arts Festival, Abby. A *lot* of prestige. Griff's had his eye on the mayor's seat for the last few years. Building a name for himself is important."

I knew Griff, of course. I think everyone in town did. But he's also a regular customer at Divinity and a surprisingly gentle man. I just didn't see him as a serious murder suspect. "And he saw Brandon as a threat to that?"

Duncan arched an eyebrow at me. "He saw Brandon as a big threat. Ask anybody who was at the Gaslight last Monday night."

"What happened at the Gaslight?"

"The two of 'em got into quite a squabble, from what I hear."

"Brandon and Griff? At the Gaslight?" Talk about mental images that just won't form. I had trouble enough picturing Brandon there, but the Gaslight just isn't the kind of place a hopeful future mayoral candidate ought to hang out.

Duncan looked as if he might say more, but his cell phone let out a beep, and he moved away to answer it. I didn't know whether to wait or leave, but when he tossed a wave at me and headed toward Picture Perfect, still chatting away, I figured it out.

I wondered if Jawarski knew about Griff Banks, and even briefly considered telling him. But it also occurred to me that Duncan might have been blowing smoke to divert suspicion from himself. I still wasn't completely convinced that Stella wasn't dangerous.

So maybe I'd drive over to the Gaslight and see what I could learn there. There'd be plenty of time to tell Jawarski if I found out that Duncan was telling the truth.

Chapter 23

The Gaslight Lounge is one of the holdovers from Paradise's mining days. It squats on the edge of town near the turnoff to Sapphire Lake, a low gray building with only a few neon signs to relieve its sheer ugliness. I'd never been inside, and as I pulled into the parking lot I wondered if I was being foolish.

When I saw Wyatt's truck nosed right up next to the front door, I decided I didn't care. All the days of worry and sleepless nights came rushing back at me. The times I'd defended him, the accusations I'd defended him against. And here he was sucking down beer.

Furious, I wedged the Jetta into a parking space, tied Max's leash to the front bumper, and stormed inside. Unfortunately, my grand entrance was spoiled by the murky interior. It's hard to look like somebody capable of dropping a man on his ass when you can't see a thing.

Gradually, I was able to make out a long U-shaped bar across the room, a deserted dance floor right in front of me, and several tables, most of which were empty, scattered along the walls. The whole place had an air of sad neglect, from the mismatched chairs to the smell of mold that stale cigarette smoke can't quite disguise. You don't find that

musty smell much in the Rockies, where humidity has been
sucked out of the air by the altitude, but the Gaslight had it,
strong enough to make me crinkle my nose.

Only a couple of tables were occupied. One, by a stunning
brunette and her blond companion. The other by a couple of
guys who were already slobbering all over themselves. The
brunette watched me walk in, probably making the same
kinds of value judgments about me that I was making about
her.

The low hum of conversation gave way to an eerie silence. I heard a muffled curse and turned toward the sound of
my brother's voice. The long walk across the deserted dance
floor gave me plenty of time to work on what I wanted to say.

He was sitting, hunch-shouldered, at the end of the bar
looking like one sorry piece of humanity. His hair was sticking out in all the wrong places, and stubble darkened his
cheeks and chin. I hitched myself onto the stool beside his
and made eye contact, which wasn't easy considering how he
was sitting. "Where in the hell have you been?"

"Around."

"Do you have any idea how much trouble you're in?"

He blurted a laugh, and his bloodshot eyes voluntarily
lifted to meet mine. "Do I know how much trouble I'm in?
Hell, yeah. And you don't know the half of it, Abs."

I'd seen Wyatt drunk before, but I'd never seen him like
this, and I don't mind telling you that I was worried. I wondered when he'd changed clothes last, and I would have bet
the deed to Divinity that his last shower was nothing but a
dim memory. "What's going on," I demanded. "And don't
play games with me this time. You're in deep. The police
have been looking for you all week."

"'Cuz they think I did it."

"Yeah. Because they think you did it. I've been busting
my butt trying to prove that you're innocent, but you're not
making it easy for me." His shoulders sagged, but that only
made me angrier. I had a week's worth of complaining to do.
I hadn't even gotten a good start. "What in the hell were you
doing at Man About Town the night of the fire?"

"I wasn't there," he protested.

"I saw you."

"But I wasn't *there*." He held back a belch and sucked down about half of the beer in front of him. "I was just picking somebody up."

You've gotta say one thing for my brother. He knows how to deliver the unexpected. "You were picking somebody up? Who?"

"I don't want to say."

"How long were you with this person?"

"Most of the night."

"Well, then whoever it was can give you an alibi."

He snorted a laugh. "Yeah. Great. Trouble is, I don't want it."

"What?" I lunged off my stool and grabbed him. His head seemed a little loose on his neck, but his eyes stayed focused. "What do you mean you don't want it? How could you not want an alibi?"

He shrugged away from me. "Just what I said. I don't want it."

"But that's insane, Wyatt. An alibi could prove that you didn't murder Brandon."

"I'll get off."

"You know a miracle worker? Because I don't. You were there the night of the fire. You fought with him the day of the murder. Your wife was involved with him—maybe not sexually, but involved. You've been hiding for more than a week, and God only knows what *real* evidence Jawarski has on you. You'd better grab that alibi and hang onto it with both hands all the way to an attorney's office."

He shook his head again and stood. "Not gonna happen." He tossed a twenty onto the bar and walked away. Just like that.

I don't think I've ever been so angry with him in all my life. He wasn't making any sense. Why would an innocent person refuse an alibi? Because he was protecting someone else?

Still seething, I watched Wyatt shove through the door and into the parking lot. Nope, I didn't think he was protecting anyone. So then why was he being so obstinate? What other reason could there possibly be?

I knew the answer to that the instant the question formed, and I was off the stool and across the floor like a shot. He was already in his truck and backing out by the time I got outside. I climbed onto the fender and threw myself across the hood, trusting that he wasn't drunk enough to drive away with me on there.

"Dammit, Abby, get off." He jammed on the brakes and nearly sent me flying.

I grabbed the windshield wipers and held on—barely.

Swearing again, he ground the truck into gear, turned off the ignition, and came out of the cab after me. I scampered off before he could throw me off. "Who was she?"

His step faltered, only for a heartbeat, but long enough to let me know I was right. "Who *was* she?" I demanded again. "And don't even bother trying to lie because I can see the truth in your eyes. You were with another woman."

"Abby—"

That was the wrong thing to say. I launched myself at him like a crazy woman, pounding his chest when I could get close enough, swinging wildly when I couldn't. Tears filled my eyes and burned my throat. "You cheated on Elizabeth? With who? Who is she?"

Across the parking lot, Max shot to his feet and started barking. I couldn't worry about him, though. I could only think about releasing the frustration and disappointment burning inside of me.

Wyatt ducked and wove, dodging most of blows I aimed at him, but that was all right. I landed enough to satisfy me. I've never been able to win a fight with him, and this was no exception. He caught my wrists and held my arms apart.

I used my feet instead. "How could you do this?" I shouted, planting a well-placed kick to the shin. "How could you do this to Elizabeth? How could you do this to your kids?" I didn't ask, but my heart was screaming, *How could you do this to me?*

"Knock it off, Abby!" He shoved me against the truck and held me there. I thrashed as hard as I could, trying to get away, but I'm no match for him. "Stop. Okay?"

I hurt everywhere. I couldn't tell whether the pain was physical or emotional. It just hurt. But somehow Wyatt managed to make eye contact with me, and the misery I saw reflected there finally broke through. I stopped kicking.

My pulse pounded in my ears, my breath burned my lungs. I could hear Wyatt panting and, in the distance, Max's frantic barking. Dimly, I was aware of someone leaving the bar. Of murmured conversation and hurried footsteps. Some part of me still cared whether Wyatt went to prison, so I tried to look as if everything was hunky-dory.

"Let. Go. Of. Me," I said between gasps.

"Not if you're going to take after me again."

I shoved against him, but he didn't budge. "Wyatt. Move. I need to make sure the dog doesn't kill you."

He eyed me skeptically, but he slowly released me. I heard a car door closing. Then another, and I decided we were probably safe.

Rolling my wrists to restore the circulation, I started away. "Maybe I should let him do it," I called back over my shoulder. "Someone as stupid as you are doesn't deserve to live."

He trailed after me. "Look, I screwed up. I know that."

"Oh, but you had *such* a good reason, right?"

"Are you going to let me explain, or are you going to just assume you know everything the way you usually do?"

That brought me around on the balls of my feet, ready for another round. Wyatt has had a chip on his shoulder about that since the day I left for college. Only the sound of a car's engine starting up a few feet away kept me from lashing out at him again. "I don't think I know everything," I said, struggling to remain calm. "But I *do* know that cheating on your wife is *wrong*!"

"And you think I don't know that?"

"Apparently not." I couldn't bear to look at him, so I started walking again. With Wyatt only a step behind me, I rounded the last row of cars separating me from the Jetta. Half of the front bumper hung at an odd angle, and Max was working on tearing the other half from the car. He saw me, but instead of calming down, his barking grew louder and more frantic.

Maybe I should have given him that doggie sedative after all. I sure wasn't going to attempt it now. I waved Wyatt back, wanting him to get out of Max's sight. But Max knew he was there. He must have remembered the threat to Brandon.

Wyatt didn't stay out of sight long. "What's wrong with him?"

"You are." I had no idea how to calm Max down without losing a limb. Would he even let me get close to him? I wasn't brave enough to try.

Wyatt inched closer still, propped his hands on his hips, and rolled his eyes in exasperation. "Get off it, Abby. Dogs don't judge people."

"I don't mean that," I snapped. "I'm talking about you and Brandon. He must remember you." There might even have been a little protectiveness for me floating around inside Max's reaction.

Somewhere in the lot, a car's lights blinked, on and Max ripped another six inches of bumper from the Jetta. My poor car would never be the same. Frustrated, I backed closer to my lug of a brother. "You owe me a new bumper."

"Me? Why?"

"This is your fault. If you hadn't lost your senses, my car would be in one piece. So get out of here, wouldja?"

"And leave you here with that crazy mutt? Nothing doing."

"You're going to be a gentleman *now?*" Hoping nobody else had come outside, I shot a glance over my shoulder. People tend to freak out around dogs that seem vicious, and I didn't want anybody calling Animal Control. The coast was clear, so I let myself ask the burning question. "Why *did* you go after him?"

"After who?"

"Brandon." I had to shout to make myself heard. "Why did you go barging into Man About Town that day? What *truth* did he know about you that he was going to make public? Was it about your affair?"

Wyatt's brows knit in confusion. "What are you talking about?"

"The day of the fire. Lucas and Chelsea saw you there. They heard Brandon tell you the truth was going to come out."

"They couldn't have. I wasn't anywhere near that place until later that night."

I groaned in frustration. "Will you please just be honest with me. It's way past time to stop playing games."

"No games," Wyatt shouted, "I wasn't there."

How many times had he said that in the past week?

He seemed serious this time, but I didn't know who to believe. "Lucas told me he saw you."

"Then Lucas is lying." All at once, Max fell silent, and Wyatt's words echoed in the sudden stillness. He lowered his voice and went on. "I'm being straight with you, Abby. I wasn't there. I was out at Charlie's until after six."

"Then why—" Something whispered through the back of my mind, casting doubt. Still restless, the dog paced back and forth in front of the car, and the bumper groaned each time he reached the end of his tether.

I tried to remember exactly what Lucas had said about that day. He and Chelsea had been in the back room, unloading a shipment. He'd talked about what he heard, but had he actually *seen* Wyatt? I didn't remember him saying so.

"If you weren't there," I said uncertainly, "then who was?"

"I don't know."

I still didn't know what to think. Max sank onto his haunches and looked at me with that tell-me-what-comes-next look on his face, and I realized, slowly, that Wyatt was still here, and Max wasn't going berserk.

With my heart in my throat, I whipped back toward my brother. "Get a little closer," I said, jerking my head toward the dog.

"What?"

"Move a little closer. See what he does."

"Are you nuts?"

"No. Trust me. I don't think it's you he's worried about."

"And you want me to prove that by sticking my head in his mouth?"

"Just move a little closer, but not close enough for him to actually reach you. Just *see*, Wyatt."

He didn't look happy about it, but he did what I asked. Max's ear twitched, but that was the extent of his reaction. But if it wasn't Wyatt who'd set him off earlier, then who? "What kind of car was that?"

"What car?"

"The one that just left here. Did you see it?"

"I was a little busy."

"Me, too." And I could have kicked myself. "Did you notice who was in it?"

Wyatt shook his head. "I wasn't paying attention. I think it was small, though. And white. I think it was white."

That was almost no help. There were a million small white cars on the road. "Did you see anyone you know inside the bar earlier?"

Another shake of the head. "A few people who look familiar, maybe, but I don't know who they were."

Acting strictly on impulse, I untied Max's leash and loaded him into the Jetta. Locking the doors, I turned toward the bar, grabbing my brother's sleeve so I could drag him with me. "Come on," I said, hoping I knew what I was doing. "We're going to see who's not there anymore."

Chapter 24

It was hard to tell what had changed in the time we'd been outside. I'd been so focused on finding Wyatt, I hadn't paid that much attention to the crowd when I came in. Crowd's the wrong word to use, anyway. There were only a handful of people scattered around the cavernous room; you'd think I should be able to remember.

Wyatt walked in wearing a hangdog expression, probably embarrassed at having been chased down by his sister. He muttered something about needing the restroom and loped off toward the back of the building.

The bartender, a tall man in his thirties with jet-black hair and a thick face, eyeballed me as I approached the bar. A toothpick dangled from one corner of his mouth—such a stereotypical image I almost laughed.

"You need something?" he asked.

I thought about ordering drinks and trying to engage the man in small talk, but Wyatt didn't need more alcohol. "Did you see who just left here?"

"Besides you and Wyatt? Nope."

"There aren't that many people in here," I pointed out. "You didn't notice one of your customers getting up and walking out?"

Slowly moving the toothpick from one side of his mouth to the other, the bartender picked up a glass and wiped it clean. "Nope."

It was obviously a lie, and I felt my nerves twitching. "So you saw Wyatt and me leaving, but you didn't see anyone else?"

"That's right."

He was probably holding out for a bribe, but I didn't think he'd be interested in the handful of butterscotch buttons rubbing together in my pocket. "This is important," I said. "I *know* you saw whoever it was. You must have. And if you didn't, all you need to do is take a look around and tell me who's missing."

He gave me a long, slow once-over. Judged and found wanting by a loser. My night was complete. "And just why would I want to do that?"

"Because I think those people know something that might help my brother."

"Yeah? And who's your brother?"

I jerked a thumb in the direction of the restrooms. "Captain Courageous."

The bartender actually laughed at that. "You're Wyatt's sister? Well, I'll be damned." He held out a hand, shook mine once, and released. "The name's Scotty."

"Pleasure." So I lied to him. It just seemed like the thing to do. "So, Scotty, what do you remember?"

"Couple right over there left a few minutes ago," he said with a nod toward a table near the door.

"A couple?" I thought back and felt my blood rush. "She was a brunette, right? The guy with her was blond?"

"Yep."

"Do you know who they are? Have you ever seen them before?"

"No idea. But, yeah, I've seen 'em once or twice."

This was important. I just *knew* it was. "When? Do you remember?"

The more agitated I became, the calmer Scotty seemed. He leaned against the counter behind him and folded his arms. "They've been in a few times in the past week or so. Why?"

"I think they may have known a friend of mine," I said, finally remembering why I'd come to the Gaslight in the first place. "As a matter of fact, I think my friend might have been in here last week. Maybe you remember him."

"Lots of people's friends are in here all the time," Scotty said with a tired smile. "You'll have to give me more than that."

"His name was Brandon Mills. Tall. Dark—"

Scotty cut me off before I could finish. "Brandon? Sure, I knew Brandon. Damn shame about him dying that way."

His answer surprised me. "Did *he* come in here often?"

Scotty shrugged and came out from behind the bar. "He wasn't a regular, if that's what you're wondering." He walked toward the table the couple had vacated, talking over his shoulder. "But, yeah, he came in sometimes."

I followed behind him. "Do you remember the last time you saw *him*?"

"Sure." Scotty emptied an ashtray and gathered glasses from the table. "He was here the night before he died."

"Do you know why?"

"There's two reasons people come into a place like this, sis. One's to get a good drunk on. The other's to get a good drunk on where nobody's gonna see 'em."

"Which of those was Brandon after?"

"Which one do you think?"

It was a rhetorical question, so I didn't bother answering. "Did he meet anyone while he was here?"

"So what are you, a cop or something?"

"Just a friend."

"Why all the questions?"

"I'm trying to figure out what happened to him. He was supposed to meet me the night he died, but he never showed up. Now Wyatt's suspected of murdering him, and I'm suspected of being an accomplice. Not true, by the way. Anyway, someone told me that he was here on Sunday, and that he had an argument with someone while he was here. I thought maybe you'd know what he was doing."

Either Scotty felt sorry for me, or my story appealed to his sense of the dramatic. Bartenders enjoy a good story as much as the next person. "Yeah, he met somebody," he said. "And yeah, he had an argument."

"Do you know who the other man was?"

"I've seen him around. Don't know him by name. Short, maybe two-twenty. Dark hair."

That description could have fit Griff Banks, so maybe Duncan had been telling the truth. "Do you know what they argued about?"

He gave his shoulder another hitch. "I didn't pay attention."

I didn't believe that for a minute, but I decided not to argue with him and cut off the flow of information. "How angry were they?"

"You wanna know if I think the other man was angry enough to commit murder? No, I don't. They had words, but it wasn't anything to write home about."

"If you didn't hear what they said, how can you be sure?"

"I know people. I see arguments in here all the time. It's not hard to tell when somebody means business and when they're just blowing off steam. The other guy? He was blowing off steam."

I don't know what I'd expected, but I was disappointed anyway. "Well, that figures."

"Yeah, but that guy wasn't the only person pissed off at Brandon that night."

My head popped up as if somebody had pulled a string. "Oh?"

"Lady over there," he said with a nod toward the table.

"The brunette?" I tried to process that, but I could swear I actually felt the cogs in my brain freeze up. "The one who just left? She met Brandon here?"

"Came right in and walked over to his table like she knew where to find him."

"Who is she? Do you have any idea?"

"Nope."

"And I suppose you didn't hear any of her conversation with Brandon?"

"Not much."

"What part did you hear?"

"Just the part where he told her to save her breath. The truth was coming out whether she liked it or not."

I stared at him for a long moment while I shuffled that around in my head. That was the same thing Lucas had overheard at Man About Town, which meant that she and her blond companion were probably in this together. But *who were they*?

"He knew something about her she didn't want made public? Was he blackmailing her?"

"I wouldn't know that, but she was fit to be tied, I can tell you that."

"Do the police know about this?"

"Don't ask me."

"You haven't told them?"

Scotty treated me to a snaggletoothed smile. "What can I say? The cop wasn't as pretty as you."

Be still my heart. The people you meet when you don't have a gun . . .

To my relief, someone at the end of the bar ordered another beer, and Wyatt finally reappeared before Scotty came back. I herded my brother outside, relieved to see that he seemed a little more steady on his feet this time around.

"So what did you find out?" he asked as the door closed behind us.

"There was a couple here earlier," I said. "The woman has dark hair, the man's a blond. She met Brandon here the night before the fire, and they had an argument. I think the man with her is the one Lucas heard in the store that day."

Something flickered in Wyatt's eyes. Hope? Relief? Maybe a little of both. "So what now?"

For the first time in more than a week, someone had asked me a question I could answer. "Now I'm going to call the police."

"You think they'll believe you?"

"He'd better." I pulled out my cell phone, stalked around the parking lot for a while until I got a few bars of service, and punched in the number. While I did that, Wyatt managed to manhandle my fender off the ground far enough for me to drive home.

Jawarski wasn't in, so I left a message asking him to call

me as soon as possible and stressing that I had information about Brandon's murder. The fact that I'd called at all should get his attention.

I slipped my phone back into my pocket just as Wyatt got to his feet again. Deep lines of worry had etched into his face and, now that my own anger had faded, I could see in his eyes what a toll the past week had taken. I had the urge to put my arms around him and tell him everything would work out, but I refrained for two reasons. One, we've never had a huggy kind of relationship. Two, I wasn't sure things *would* work out between him and Elizabeth.

"So what happened, anyway?" I asked. "Why'd you do it?"

The lines in his face seemed to deepen right in front of my eyes. "Hell, I don't know. I was drunk." He shot a glance at me and tried to smile. It didn't work. "I was upset about Lizzie. We had all that trouble a couple of years ago, and I thought it was over. And then Nate called and said he saw her with Brandon outside the diner, and I flipped. I wasn't thinking straight. Otherwise, I never would have—"

"Does Elizabeth know?"

He nodded. "Why do you think I'm not living at home?"

"But I thought—"

"Yeah, well, she's a good woman. She doesn't want the kids to know until we decide what's going to happen between us."

"So she took the blame herself?"

"She told the truth. She just left out one minor detail."

"The one where you slept with somebody else."

He turned and took a couple of steps away, then whipped back to face me. "I didn't ask her to, Abby." His voice caught, and misery seemed to pour off him. "I didn't ask."

I was angry with him, but something inside me shifted. "Where have you been staying?"

"Charlie's cabins."

"Nora lied to me?"

He managed a thin smile. "She's a friend."

I hated to think of him alone in an isolated cabin, so I started up where we'd left off. "Come and stay with me. The couch folds down into a bed."

He shook his head, but his smile grew a little wider as he rubbed his chest with one hand. "Not on your life. You're stronger now that you're all grown up."

I laughed, but the sound came out sounding kind of choked. "You're sure?"

He nodded and turned toward his truck. "I'll be fine. Don't worry about me."

Yeah. Right. If only it were that easy.

Chapter 25

Everything was dark when I pulled into my parking spot next to Divinity. I hadn't been home since early morning, so I hadn't bothered to turn on the light outside my door. Clouds covered the stars and blocked the moon, and only a little light spilled into the parking strip from the street.

Yawning, I opened the back door to let Max out. He was calmer than he had been, but he was still agitated, so I held tightly to his leash. I didn't want any surprises. Just as I turned toward the door, I heard a whisper of sound behind me.

Heart pounding, I wheeled around to see who was back there, but the parking strip was empty, and I couldn't see anyone on the street. I laughed nervously and turned toward the stairs, but when Max stiffened at my side, I knew I wasn't imagining things. Someone was out there.

Words filled my mouth, but I bit them back. What person in their right mind expects an answer to, "Who's out there?" under circumstances like these? Instead, I clutched Max's leash tightly and tried to decide on my best move.

Before I could do anything, a murky figure moved out of the shadows in front of Picture Perfect and stepped into the light. Max growled again, and it felt as though my heart jumped into my mouth, wiping out any chance of coherent speech. I told myself to move, but I guess my feet weren't getting the signal.

"Here, Max." A woman's soft voice floated out of the gloom, followed by a soft whistle. "Come on, boy."

Max? She wanted *Max*? What in the—

The growling stopped, and he tilted his head from one side to the other. He'd practically torn my car apart at the Gaslight when he saw her. Now, with no one else around, he decided to be calm. The reason came to me with the very next breath I took. He knew her.

"Come on, boy. Come see Mommy."

Pieces clicked together all at once. I still couldn't get my feet to move, but somehow I found my voice. "You're Brandon's wife."

She looked at me strangely, almost as if she'd forgotten I was standing there. "Widow," she said, her voice soft and low. "He's gone, remember?"

Like I could forget. "Did you kill him?" Not a smart question, but my body was working on its own now. Nothing my brain came up with seemed to be getting through.

"Did *I*— Of course not. How could you even ask such a thing?"

"Then your friend. The blond guy I saw you with tonight at the Gaslight. Is he the one?"

The expression on her face changed abruptly. "I don't know what you're talking about. I only came to collect my late husband's effects. I believe that's my dog you're holding."

I could hardly breathe, but I knew I couldn't back down. My mind whirled, trying to figure out my next move and, at the same time, trying to remember her name. Jawarski had mentioned it, hadn't he? "If you want him, you'll have to go through the police."

"I'm through talking to the police. Give me the dog."

I inched sideways ever so slightly. I had no intention of turning my back on her, but her friend had to be somewhere, and I wasn't all that comfortable standing with my back to the stairs. Should I run upstairs? In the dark, would I be able to get the key into the lock before she caught me?

No. Once I got up there, I'd be stuck with no way out.

She was blocking my way to the street, which left the stairs to Bear Hollow. But could I make it up them with Max? Would he even follow me if I commanded him to?

It turned out to be a moot question.

While I ran through my options, Max's mood sheered off into the dangerous area again, and I knew that the blond man was somewhere nearby. I turned, fully intending to release Max and let him go after his prey, but I was too late. Before I could react, the man behind me lunged at Max, striking him in the head with some kind of club.

With a yelp, Max crumbled to the pavement beside me. I was dimly aware of myself screaming, "No!" but when the man pulled a gun from his waistband, the sound gurgled to a stop in my throat. I had no idea whether Max was still alive, but a deep and desperate need to preserve my own life over-shadowed everything else.

"Get rid of the dog," he ordered Brandon's widow. "I'll take care of her."

So this is what it came down to? Thirty-nine years of living all boiled into this one moment in a parking lot? It couldn't. I had too much to do. I had Aunt Grace's legacy to carry on and a brother who needed me. I had nieces and nephews to get close to, and a sister-in-law who deserved an apology.

Desperation drove me to bluff. "Killing me won't solve your problem," I said. "I'm not the only one who knows your secret."

"Secret?" The former Mrs. Mills laughed. "You think one of *us* killed Brandon? There's plenty of evidence to prove otherwise."

"I know one of you killed him, but that's not the secret I'm talking about." My voice came out sounding high and tight with fear, but I prayed that neither of them would know how terrified I was. I needed for them to believe that I knew whatever secret they'd killed to protect.

"She doesn't know anything," the man insisted.

"But what if she does, Jack? What if she's not lying? You know how Brandon was."

I filed his name away in my memory bank and kept digging for hers. "It's no bluff," I said, trying desperately not to show my terror. "I know the whole story. So do several other people. Killing me isn't going to protect you, Jack."

His eyes shot to mine for a split second. Just long enough to let me know that I'd connected. For all the good that did me. There were still two of them and one of me, and I wasn't the one with the gun.

His moment of uncertainty didn't last long, either. Gripping my arm, he pulled me off-balance and shoved me toward the Jetta. "Get in."

All the warnings I'd ever heard about not allowing myself to be moved to a second location kicked in, and I let out a bloodcurdling scream. At the same time, I let myself drop, weightless, to the ground. The force of my weight broke his grip, just like they'd promised it would in self-defense classes. Imagine that.

Still screaming my lungs out, I scrambled to the front of the Jetta and crouched down in front of my sagging fender. Maybe he'd kill me, but he'd have to do it right here. I wasn't going anywhere willingly.

The noise didn't seem to bother Jack, but it made the woman nervous. She shot a glance over her shoulder and sidled toward the street. "Come on, Jack. Let's get out of here. We'll leave. We'll go somewhere else. We have enough money to start over."

"She's bluffing. Brandon didn't tell her anything. He didn't *know* anything."

"He could have made some phone calls. You don't know what he did after you left the store."

Teeth bared, Jack backhanded her across the mouth. "Shut the hell up, Charlene. I'm not leaving here with loose ends." He moved closer to where I crouched, his voice low and menacing. "Come on out, Abby. You and I are going to take a little drive."

Fear shot through my veins, and I tried to remember something else I'd learned in self-defense classes, but I'd already used my entire arsenal. I glanced around, searching for an escape route, but Charlene stood between me and the street, and Jack blocked my way to the stairs. Getting past Charlene might not be hard, but could I do it before Jack got a shot off?

I inched toward Charlene, but Jack was smarter than I'd hoped. He leveled the gun at me. "Stop right there. If you think I'll have trouble shooting you, think again. You've been a pain in my ass since the very first day."

Since the very first day? How had I—

All at once, a wisp of memory came back to me. That very first day after the fire, while I'd been arguing with Jawarski, a blond man had bumped into me in his hurry to avoid the camera crew. I hadn't gotten a good look at him then, but the solid build was about right. He'd been there, on the street that morning, surveying his handiwork, making sure nothing went wrong.

Bile rose in my throat at the sheer ugliness of it, but I couldn't let myself stop to think. I had to find a way to escape this lunatic before I ended up with Brandon in the next world.

"Get out here," he ordered. "Now. This is already taking too long."

Fighting to keep my head clear, I felt around for something I could use as a weapon. My fingers encountered a crushed soda can, two or three small rocks, and various other pieces of trash, but none of those would be of any use against a gun.

"Come on, Abby." He moved into the shadows. I couldn't see him anymore, but I could hear him coming for me.

I thought frantically, trying to remember if I'd seen him drop the club he'd used on Max. If I could find that, I might stand a chance. But I was hunkered down near the front of my car, and Max was lying inert near the trunk. I'd never make it that far alive.

Unless I could disable him somehow.

His footsteps moved relentlessly closer, and fear made every second feel like an hour. I wasn't even sure my heart was still beating. I tugged feverishly at the fender, hoping I could pry it loose, but I was no match for Max's strength. Growing more desperate by the second, I seized on the only weapon I could think of and closed my fingers around a fistful of soil from the flower bed.

He moved again, and when the clouds parted I could see him standing over me with his gun drawn. "Get up."

I did as I was told.

"Get in the damn car."

That I wouldn't do. Taking the one chance I had, I lunged toward him, flinging the soil into his eyes and ducking as I did. Using every muscle I had, I threw myself into his legs, hoping I could at least make him lose his balance. He let out a roar, and grabbed for me, but I dodged his grasp and hurled myself toward the other end of the car.

Scrambling on hands and knees, I felt around for the club. *Please*, I prayed. *Please*. I could hear Jack behind me, and I was aware on some level of Charlene shouting something, but there was no time to think.

I found Max, and a few feet away, the club. Somewhere, I found enough strength to scream as I lurched to my feet and swung the club with all my might. I connected with something, and Jack bellowed in pain. I heard the gun clatter to the ground and skitter away, and that was all I needed.

Knowing I couldn't let him go after it, I swung again. This time, I hit his shoulder. I lowered my aim, connected with his legs, and he dropped like a sack of potatoes. I lunged after the gun and found it, miraculously. Shaking like a leaf, I lifted the barrel and aimed it straight at the man who'd killed my friend. "Move one inch," I ground out, "and I'll shoot."

I dug my cell phone from my pocket and punched 9-1-1. A few minutes later, as the thundering of my heartbeat slowly receded, I heard the wail of sirens in the distance.

Chapter 26

I didn't see Jawarski for nearly a week after that night. He'd come rushing to my rescue, along with probably every officer on duty that night. Between them, Jack and Charlene had finally revealed the whole story, or at least enough of it to put them both away for a very long time. I was sure the district attorney would have a heyday digging up the rest.

It was an age-old story, really. One that's mirrored every day in every town across the world. Only this one had a twist. Brandon had learned about the affair his wife was having with his business partner, but instead of confronting the pair, he'd left town. Jack had seen his disappearance as a golden opportunity, so he'd embezzled money from their partnership and laid the blame at Brandon's door.

It had worked perfectly, until someone who knew Brandon came to Paradise. When Brandon learned that he'd been accused of embezzling funds, he called Jack and demanded that Jack do whatever it took to clear his name. That was his first big mistake.

Admitting that Brandon was innocent would mean admitting that he was guilty, and Jack wasn't about to do that. With an unsuspecting Charlene in tow, Jack came to Paradise, claiming only that he wanted to reason with Brandon. But Jack never had any intention of risking the life he'd created for himself, and he knew that Brandon was too honest to go along with the lie.

Brandon may have had his faults, but he had a few good qualities, too. I guess that made him human.

It was late in the day when Jawarski showed up at Divinity, just a few minutes before closing time. I was a little surprised to see him since I was pretty sure I'd taken care of all the paperwork down at the station. But he'd been almost nice since the arrest, so I decided to follow suit.

He paused on the threshold to pet Max, who'd come through surgery with flying colors but hated the bandages he was still forced to wear.

"Hey, Jawarski," I said as the door swished shut behind him. "Here for a toffee fix? I made some fresh this morning."

He nodded and came toward the counter. "Sure. Wrap me up a pound."

There was something different about him tonight. Something I couldn't quite put my finger on. Whatever it was, he looked . . . good. Black leather jacket. Pale blue shirt to match his eyes. Clean Levi's. "You're all dolled up," I said as I started measuring the candy. "Hot date?"

He shrugged and leaned against the counter to watch me. "I don't know yet."

"You don't know? You haven't called her?" I laughed and checked the weight on the scale. "Let me tell you something about women, Jawarski. This last-minute stuff just doesn't cut it. Women—*most* women—like to know you care enough to ask in advance. Otherwise, we're always kind of wondering if we were a stand-in for someone else."

He lifted a small piece of toffee from the scale and slipped it into his mouth. "Is that right?"

"I'm afraid so."

"I didn't know that." He chewed for a minute. Swallowed. "So how far in advance are we talking? A day? Two?"

"More than that if you can do it. If she means anything at all to you, don't just assume she's sitting around with nothing to do. That's insulting."

"I didn't know that, either. So we're talking what? A week?"

"A week. Five days." I added a little extra toffee to the scale and nudged it up over a pound. I didn't want him to think I was giving him special treatment, so I scooped the candy away before he could see the numbers on the scale and stuffed it into a one-pound box. "If you want a date on Friday, at least call by Monday."

"That's good to know." He pulled out a twenty and waited for me to ring up his sale. "Thanks for the advice. I wouldn't want to get off on the wrong foot or anything."

"Any time." I handed him his change and the box, a little surprised that I found that spark of uncertainty kind of endearing. I didn't let myself analyze the other emotions that plucked at me. I'd given up on men, remember?

He made it all the way to the door before he turned back and caught me watching him. "Abby?"

"Yeah?"

"It's Tuesday right? So you wanna grab some dinner with me on Saturday?"

My mouth fell open. I could feel it, but I couldn't stop it. "Me?"

"Well, seeing as how tonight's out and all."

"Me?"

"I was thinking, maybe, Mondano. But if you'd rather go someplace else . . ."

I managed, with effort, to close the gaping hole in my face. Somehow, I even got my head moving up and down. "Okay."

"Seven o'clock?"

"Yeah. Fine." Other words zinged around inside my head, but it took me a while to get some of them out of my mouth. "That's perfect."

He smiled, and my heart did a little tap dance. Jawarski. And *me*? I wouldn't have believed it if I hadn't been standing right here.

Nodding with satisfaction, he turned away and opened the door, but I couldn't let him leave without asking one question. "Hey, Jawarski . . ."

"Yeah?"

"You got a first name?"

"Sure do," he said with a grin. "It's Pine."

Pine. Tall, strong, and solid. I guess that fit him perfectly.

"Okay. Pine. See you Saturday."

"It's a date." He let himself out into the night and shut the door behind him.

This time, I stopped everything and watched him walk away.

Candy Recipes

Divine Almond Toffee

2 cups packed brown sugar
1 cup butter
1/4 cup water
1 tablespoon vanilla extract
1/2 teaspoon baking soda
12 ounces chocolate chips
1-1/2 cup sliced toasted almonds, coarsely chopped

Lightly grease a 10 x 15-inch baking sheet and set it aside. In a large heavy saucepan, combine the brown sugar, butter, and water and bring slowly to the boil, stirring occasionally to prevent burning.

Insert a candy thermometer and cook until the mixture reaches 285° F (soft-crack stage).

Remove from heat and quickly stir in the vanilla and baking soda.

Immediately pour the hot mixture onto the greased baking sheet.

Sprinkle the chocolate chips over the hot toffee. Let the whole thing sit for 5 minutes, then spread the chocolate evenly over the surface of the toffee with a spatula. Sprinkle the nuts evenly over the top.

Cool completely. Break the hardened toffee into pieces and store in an airtight container.

Makes about 1-1/2 pounds

Divinity's Cream Cheese Mints

2 ounces cream cheese, room temperature.
(Keep the cream cheese refrigerated until one hour before
serving to prevent bacteria from forming.)
1/4 teaspoon oil of peppermint
food coloring
1-2/3 cup confectioner's sugar

Mash cheese well. Add the oil of peppermint flavoring and coloring as desired, and mix in the sugar. Knead the mix with your hands until you have a texture like pie dough.

Shape into balls, one at a time, press one side ONLY, into granulated sugar.

Press sugar side into rubber mold of your choice. Unmold at once.

Makes 30 pieces

Divinity's Caramel-Dipped Apples

Making the caramel requires the use of a clip-on candy thermometer, which should be tested for accuracy before starting. Attach it to the side of a medium saucepan of water, and boil the water for three minutes. The thermometer should register 212°F. If it doesn't, take the difference into account when reading the temperature.

1 pound dark brown sugar
1 cup (2 sticks) unsalted butter, room temperature
1 14-ounce can sweetened condensed milk
2/3 cup dark corn syrup
1/3 cup pure maple syrup
1/2 teaspoon vanilla extract
1 teaspoon robust-flavored (dark) molasses
1/4 teaspoon salt
12 chopsticks or Popsicle sticks
12 medium Granny Smith apples

Assorted decorations such as chopped nuts, dried apricots and dried cranberries, toffee bits, mini M&M's, and candy sprinkles
Melted dark, milk, and/or white chocolate

Combine first 8 ingredients in heavy 2-1/2-quart saucepan (about 3 inches deep). Stir with wooden spatula or spoon over medium-low heat until sugar dissolves (no crystals are felt when caramel is rubbed between fingers). Occasionally brush down sides of pan with wet pastry brush. Takes about 15 minutes.

Attach clip-on candy thermometer to side of pan. Increase heat to medium-high; cook caramel at rolling boil until thermometer registers 236°F, stirring constantly but slowly with clean wooden spatula and occasionally brushing down sides of pan with wet pastry brush. Takes about 12 minutes.

Pour caramel into metal bowl (do not scrape pan). Submerge thermometer bulb in caramel; cool, without stirring, to 200°F. Takes about 20 minutes.

While caramel cools, line 2 baking sheets with foil; butter foil. Push 1 chopstick/popsicle stick into stem end of each apple. Set up decorations and melted chocolates.

Holding by the stick, dip 1 apple into 200°F caramel, submerging all but very top of apple. Lift apple out, allowing excess caramel to drip back into bowl. Turn apple caramel side up and hold for several seconds to help set caramel around apple.

Place coated apple on prepared foil. Repeat with remaining apples and caramel, spacing apples apart (caramel will pool on foil). If caramel becomes too thick to dip into, add 1 to 2 tablespoons whipping cream and briefly whisk caramel in bowl over low heat to thin.

Chill apples on sheets until caramel is partially set, about 15 minutes. Lift 1 apple from foil. Using hand, press pooled caramel around apple; return to foil. Repeat with remaining apples.

Firmly press decorations into caramel; return each apple to foil. Or dip caramel-coated apples into melted chocolate, allowing excess to drip off, then roll in nuts or candy. Or drizzle melted chocolate over caramel-coated apples and sprinkle with decorations.

Makes 12

Hard Rocky Mountain Candy

This recipe is for spicy, cinnamon-flavored hard candy. During the holidays, wrapping pieces in decorative bags makes it perfect as a stocking stuffer.

You can vary the flavor by substituting lemon, orange, anise, or other oils. (Flavored oils can be found in candymaking supply or craft stores, and sometimes drugstores.)

1 cup confectioner's sugar
3-3/4 cups white sugar
1-1/2 cups light corn syrup
1 cup water
2 teaspoons cinnamon oil
1 teaspoon red food coloring

Roll up the edges of two 16-inch square pieces of heavy-duty aluminum foil to form a tray. Sprinkle the foil very generously with confectioners' sugar.

In a large heavy saucepan, combine the white sugar, corn syrup, and water. Heat over medium-high heat, stirring constantly until the sugar dissolves.

Stop stirring, and boil until a candy thermometer reads 300° to 310° F (149° to 154° C).

Remove from heat.

Stir in the cinnamon oil (or other flavor) and the food coloring. (If your flavored oil is more than six months old, you may need to use a little extra.)

Pour onto the prepared foil and allow to cool and harden.

Crack into pieces and store in an airtight container.

Prep Time: approximately 15 minutes.
Cook Time: approximately 45 minutes.
Makes 48 servings (approximately 3 pounds)

Turn the page for a chapter of the
next novel featuring Abby Shaw

Chocolate
Dipped Death

by Sammi Carter

Coming from Berkley Prime Crime
in March 2006

"I can't *believe* she had the nerve to show up." Without taking her eyes off the woman in question, my cousin Karen shoved an empty tray in my general direction. It teetered precariously on the edge of the table and would have fallen if I hadn't snatched it away from her. "What is she doing here, anyway?"

With an irritated roll of my eyes, I slid the tray out of sight beneath the flowing white tablecloth that hid extra containers of candy, score sheets, programs, and other necessary but unattractive supplies needed for running a three-day cooking competition.

Wishing I had some Advil, I rubbed the back of my neck in a vain attempt to get rid of the nervous knots of tension. I'd been running behind all day as I put the finishing touches on Divinity's Tenth Annual Confectionary Competition.

It might have been the tenth annual event for the candy store I'd inherited a few months earlier, but it was the first ever for me. I was nervous as a cat and desperate for the weekend to go well, and I didn't need Karen—my only help and the one person providing continuity and history for the contest—to be distracted.

When I realized that she was waiting for me to say something, I followed the direction of her gaze. "Who are you talking about?"

"Savannah Horne, who else?"

I'd gone to high school with Savannah and I'll admit she's never been my favorite person, but I didn't want to encourage Karen, so I shrugged casually. "She's here to compete, like everyone else."

Karen snorted a laugh and narrowed her eyes. "Savannah doesn't compete, she just takes whatever she wants. She's up to no good, Abby. Mark my words."

Trying to ignore Karen's dour warning, I concentrated instead on the colorful swaths of flowing fabric that draped the walls and the crisp white cloths covering the tables in the judging and staging areas. After the day we'd had, I was tempted to believe her. Somehow, in spite of the never-ending setbacks, we'd managed to transform the bare second-floor meeting room at Divinity into a thing of beauty—as long as no one looked too closely. To my relief, most of the silver candy trays we'd placed around the room were still reasonably full, and the candy bouquets I'd settled in strategic spots, hoping to convince people that they were an acceptable alternative to traditional flowers on special occasions, seemed to be generating some interest.

So far, so good. I didn't want to upset the delicate balance. "Maybe Savannah was like that in school," I conceded, "but that was twenty years ago. People change."

Karen ran a judgmental glance across Savannah's tall, willowy figure and scooped a peppermint crunch from the candy dish at her side. "No they don't. Especially not people like her."

"You don't know that. You haven't even seen her in how long?"

"Five years. Maybe six."

"And you told me yourself that you didn't even speak to her last time she was in town."

Karen's brows knit in a deep scowl. "So what's your point?"

"That maybe she's doing exactly what she told us she's doing. Maybe she's here to see Delta and she wants a diversion while she's in town."

"I don't believe it," Karen said with a curl of her lip. "What could Savannah Horne possibly want from this competition?"

"How about recognition?"

"As the best candymaker in Paradise? Be serious." Karen watched as Savannah swept past Evie Rice on her way to the judging table. If Karen disliked Savannah, Evie positively loathed her. Neither of us missed the venomous look on Evie's face as Savannah placed her dish in front of the judging panel. "Evie agrees with me," Karen whispered. "If looks could kill, none of us would have to worry about Savannah."

"That's not funny," I whispered back. "I have enough to worry about this weekend without borrowing trouble. If Savannah wants something besides a plaque at the end of the competition, I don't want to know about it."

"You only say that because you don't have a husband," Karen muttered. "If Roger was here with you, you'd be worried."

So that was it? Karen thought Savannah was still interested in Sergio after all these years? Thank goodness it was nothing more serious than that.

There's no tactful way to tell a woman that her husband isn't the stud he used to be, so I didn't even try. Instead, I filled a tray with chocolate peanut clusters and shoved it toward my cousin. "I'm sure I would be worried if Roger were here. He wasn't exactly the faithful type, remember? That's why we're divorced." She started to speak, but I cut her off. "Look, I know you have reasons to dislike Savannah. I'm sure a lot of people do. But that all happened eons ago. It has nothing to do with today. So please, just let it go for now, okay? Help me get through this weekend, and you can go back to hating her on Monday morning."

Karen's lips curved into a grudging smile. "By then, it might be too late."

I pressed the tray into her hands and locked eyes with her. "Sergio loves you, Karen. He may have wandered that one time before you were even dating seriously, but you have nothing to worry about now." I paused to let that sink in, then tried to draw her attention to what really mattered. "Would you mind checking on the judges to make sure there's nothing they need? They'll be announcing tonight's finalists in a few minutes, and I want to make sure everything goes smoothly."

Still scowling, Karen actually looked as if she might refuse, but before we could launch into *that* argument, a shrill cry went up from the other side of the room. The buzz of excited voices rose and folks standing nearby surged toward the sound. I met Karen's shocked gaze a split second before we both sprang into action.

Praying that no one had been hurt, I slipped out from behind the serving table just as Rachel Summers, owner of the candle shop a few doors away, burst through the crowd and waved for Karen and me to join her. "You'd better get in there," she warned as I closed the distance between us. "I swear one of those women is going to kill the other."

"Who is it?" Karen asked. "Savannah and Evie?"

"Of course." Rachel's round face clouded. "I knew there'd be trouble the minute I saw Savannah walk through that door. You never should have let her register, Abby. She's going to ruin everything."

She might be right, but how could I have known? Most people don't drag childhood rivalries with them into middle age. At least, I don't think they do. Savannah and Evie had been opponents in almost everything since junior high, maybe even earlier than that. I distinctly remember them going nose-to-nose over which one got to do their seventh-grade research paper on France, and who could ever forget the war over first violin position in eighth-grade orchestra? Apparently, their rivalry was still going strong and Divinity was about to become just another in a long line of battlegrounds.

Determined to regain control, I pasted on a smile and crossed the room toward the rabble-rousers. Savannah is tall, full-bosomed, and curvaceous in a way that appeals to men. She's probably a few pounds heavier than she was back in high school, but the extra inches haven't dulled her appeal. She still wears her dark hair long and loose, and her blouses low and tight. Even in the middle of January, she was showing an ample amount of cleavage. You had only to look at the sparkle in the eyes of the men around her to know that she hadn't lost her touch.

I didn't want to admit it aloud, but I've always considered Savannah more trouble than she's worth. The fact that she'd driven all the way from Gunnison to compete for a prize she couldn't possibly want was typical of her. I didn't blame Evie for challenging her. I just wished that she'd found somewhere else to do it.

Evie stood in front of the judge's table, red-faced, breathing heavily, and waving a pink scoring sheet under the judges' noses. She stands barely five feet tall, her blond hair hasn't begun to show even a hint of gray, and she's maintained her teenage cheerleader figure by religious use of a membership at the Paradise Health Club, but she's always been a more wholesome type than Savannah. Evie's the kind of girl boys took home to meet their mothers. Savannah's the kind they hid in the back seats of their cars.

"Something has to be done about this," Evie pronounced when she saw me. "It's a travesty."

"You're making a fool out of yourself," Savannah grumbled. "Why can't you just accept the fact that the judges prefer my entry to yours?"

All three judges sat stone still behind the judging table. Beverly Lembeck, the judge whose round face was currently being threatened by the scorecard, rose to her feet when she realized that help had arrived—a move that finally put her out of Evie's reach. Under the watchful gaze of his wife, Henry Stokes tried not to even look at Savannah while Marshall Ames, the third judge, couldn't tear his eyes away.

"I certainly hope you don't condone this kind of behavior from your contestants," Beverly said. "All decisions of the judges are supposed to be final."

"And they are," I assured her. I ignored the I-told-you-so look on Karen's face and put a little more warmth into my smile. "What seems to be the problem, Evie?"

Whipping around so fast I worried she might fall off the soles of her platform sandals, Evie shoved the score sheet in front of my face—too close to let my almost forty-year-old eyes focus. "Have you seen this?"

"No, and I can't see it now, either." I tried without success to nudge her hand away. "I take it you have a complaint?"

"She wants to know if you'll rearrange the scores from tonight's competition to suit her," Savannah said. "Apparently, she's having trouble believing that I scored higher than she did."

Years of pent-up fury flashed in Evie's violet eyes. "Only because *you* forgot the requirement to use an original recipe." She turned back to me impatiently. "She downloaded her recipe from the Good Cooks Network website, Abby. She should be disqualified. And this isn't the first time she's done something like this, either."

"I'd be careful if I were you," Savannah warned. "An accusation like that could get you in trouble."

Evie squared her shoulders and straightened to her full height, which put her roughly even with Savannah's chest. "I'm not worried. It will be easy enough to prove. I warned you that your nasty little habits would come back to bite you one of these days."

I could feel the crowd closing in around us, angling to get a better view of the altercation. So much for holding a dignified, professional contest. If I didn't do something fast, the whole weekend would be in danger.

Trying to look bored, Savannah flicked a wrist, but I

don't think anybody missed the sudden flush of color that suffused her cheeks. "You're accusing me of cheating?"

"I'm saying straight out that you've cheated—again. But this is the last time, Savannah. I swear to God, this time I'm going to stop you." Evie wheeled back toward me and shoved the score sheet under my nose again. "Do something, Abby. I'm counting on you to make this right."

I backed a step away, wanting to put some distance between myself and her anger and hoping to prevent anyone else from thinking that I was taking sides. "Evie," I said quietly, "I don't—"

"You don't what? Don't believe me?"

"I didn't say that, I just think it might be best to discuss this somewhere else." I glanced over my shoulder at the rapidly gathering crowd. "Privately?"

"Why? Everyone here knows what Savannah's like. If she's not sleeping with somebody's boyfriend or husband, she's finding some other way to take what's yours. There's probably not a soul in this room she hasn't hurt."

"Why don't we try to stay focused on tonight's contest," I said, still struggling to remain neutral.

Tall, blond, and surprisingly handsome considering what a nerd he'd been in high school, Marshall Ames pushed away from the judge's table and came to stand beside Savannah. "Don't you think you're being unnecessarily harsh, Evie?"

Funny. I didn't remember him being a friend of Savannah's back in high school. Maybe she'd been more interested in the chess club than any of us realized.

Evie leveled Marshall with a look of disdain. "Why don't you let her fight her own battles, Marshall? I told you, I can prove what I'm saying."

"Prove that I cheated?" Savannah said with a laugh. "Impossible. *If* there's a recipe for Kentucky Colonels on some website, I certainly didn't copy it. This recipe has been in my family for generations."

I doubted that, but maybe that's just because Savannah had never seemed all that interested in her family. Though she claimed to be in town to visit her older sister, I had it on good authority that she'd barely spoken to Delta in years. According to Karen, she hadn't even come home for her mother's funeral the previous spring. Then again, maybe she *had* had a sudden spurt of familial feeling. Bourbon-filled chocolates have that effect on some people. Who was I to say?

The nervous ball of energy in my stomach grew stronger and I tried again to take the argument away from the public eye. "Why don't both of you come downstairs with me so we can get to the bottom of this in private?"

Savannah blurted a laugh. "Don't be ridiculous, Abby. There's nothing to get to the bottom of. Tonight's scores were fair, and I, for one, refuse to give in to Evie's raging paranoia." She straightened majestically and cast a royal glance around the crowd. "One of you take the poor thing out for a drink and make it all better. I'll see you tomorrow night."

She turned away, hitching her purse strap onto her shoulder and dismissing Evie's protests at the same time.

Maybe I should have stopped her, but I just wanted the argument to be over. At least this gave me a chance to look into Evie's allegations without the whole world looking over my shoulder. If I was lucky, I could clear the whole mess up before tomorrow night's segment of the competition.

I should have known better. Just take a look at the way my life's been going lately and you'll realize that luck and I aren't on speaking terms. I couldn't know it as I watched Savannah disappear from view, but things were about to get a whole lot worse.

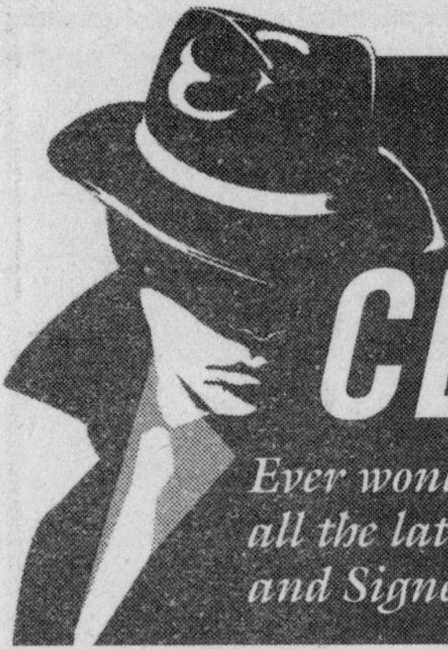

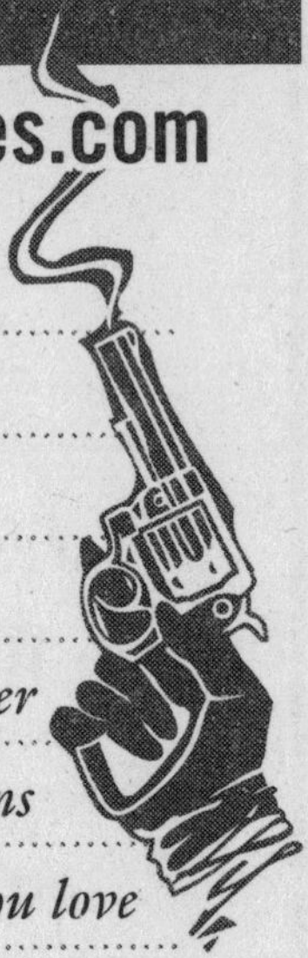